Tourist in the  Dead

He moved forward. When he was fifty yards from the reflecting objects, he knew they were humans, and dead.

Six of them lay scattered in a line near the east wall of the tunnel: four adults and two children. They wore the glossy clothing Pierce had seen in some of the pictures retrieved from Ulro. Their skins were yellow-brown, drawn tautly over their bones: they had been mummified here. Strewn for yards around them were bags of leathery material, now crumbled away and revealing more clothing, some plastic containers, a piece of burst metal that might once have held water. In the shirt pocket of one corpse, a flickreader nestled.

The bodies seemed to be screaming.

By Crawford Kilian
Published by Ballantine Books :

The Chronoplane Wars

THE EMPIRE OF TIME
THE FALL OF THE REPUBLIC

The Fall of the Republic

A Novel of the Chronoplane Wars

Crawford Kilian

A Del Rey Book

BALLANTINE BOOKS • NEW YORK

A Del Rey Book
Published by Ballantine Books

Copyright © 1987 by Crawford Kilian

All rights reserved under International and Pan-American Copyright Conventions. Published in the United States of America by Ballantine Books, a division of Random House, Inc., New York, and simultaneously in Canada by Random House of Canada Limited, Toronto.

Library of Congress Catalog Card Number: 87-91227

ISBN 0-345-34273-9

Manufactured in the United States of America

First Edition: September 1987

Cover Art by Stephen Hickman

This one is for the mentors:
Hugo and Jean Butler,
Dalton and Cleo Trumbo,
Stanley and Jeanne Ellin

One:

When his working day began at midnight, he did not yet know that he would kill a man before dawn.

Rain was falling steadily. In his small apartment near the headquarters building at Mountain Home Air Force Base, T-Colonel Jerry Pierce sat down at the computer in the living room. It was one of the new Polymath machines, voice-actuated, with more artificial intelligence than any other microcomputer yet built.

"Boot, Polly."

The monitor turned deep blue, and a small female figure appeared in the lower right corner of the screen. It was the image of a little girl wearing a frilly dress. Her blue eyes gleamed as she smiled.

"Booted, Jerry." Her voice was chirpy and friendly.

"Give me a survey of the day's disruptive incidents."

"Sure will, Jerry."

Apart from the corner in which the girl's image stood, the screen began to flash page after page of dense text, at a rate of sixteen pages per second. Pierce watched without expression.

The afternoon and evening had produced the usual events: assaults on police officers in Coeur d'Alene, gas-station robberies in Boise, the firebombing in

Nampa of a food dispensary (idiots: how did they expect to go on eating?). A survivalist colony had fired on a National Guard patrol a few miles north of Ketchum; no casualties, but the colony would have to be interdicted.

The twenty-seventh page flashed at him and he said: "Stop."

"Sure, Jerry."

It was a police report from here in Mountain Home. The body of Maxine Schultz, age seventeen, no fixed address, had been found in Room 204 of the Big Country Motel at 22:30 hours this evening, September 2, 1998. Manager had looked in after a complaint from another tenant about noise, and had found the subject. Cause of death, to be confirmed by autopsy, reported to be strangulation. Subject had rented the room at 16:20 this afternoon. Manager had not seen her after that, alone or with anyone else. Homicide would be on the scene after investigating an earlier murder in a West 4th liquor store.

"Damn!"

Polly said nothing.

"Damn." Jerry Pierce stood up and walked across the living room, hands jammed in the back pockets of his Levi's. He was tall, over six feet, with the build of a racing-shell oarsman. His hair was close-cropped, dark brown like his eyes. His straight mouth turned down at the corners now, and his jaw was harder than usual. His biceps bulged in a dark-blue golfing shirt.

The room was a typical one for officers' housing, with a blue shag rug and walls painted a flat white. Pierce had changed it only by installing the Polymath. At the far end was the dining area, and beyond it the kitchen. Pierce walked in, opened the refrigerator, and took out a cold Budweiser. Popping the can, he walked back to the computer.

"Polly, give me the file on Social Security number 095-566-3122."

"Glad to, Jerry."

The screen gave him the seventeen sad years of Maxine Shultz's life, from her birth certificate (father unknown) through the prescriptions for her childhood ailments to her social workers' reports to her more recent criminal record. Her charges included prostitution, drug possession, weapons possession (firearm), weapons possession (knife), possession of forged ration stamps. Polly's high-resolution monitor showed him Maxine's mug shots, starting with one in Missoula at age thirteen and ending with another here in Mountain Home just a month ago: a pouting, acne-scarred blonde with intelligent eyes that grew steadily more cynical over the four years. Convictions: none since last spring, just before Pierce had arrived to take charge of the 23rd Military Emergency District. She had been one of Pierce's most reliable sources; thanks to her, he had put away a whole ring of stamp counterfeiters, a cocaine distributor, and too many outside black marketers to count.

Now someone had killed her, made her the third murder victim of the week in Mountain Home. Her parents might mourn her; more likely, when they got the news they would only feel sorry for themselves. Three or four other young hookers would feel bad about it, until they'd zonked themselves enough to forget her. No one else would care, except T-Colonel Jerry Pierce.

"She was mine, Polly."

"I know, Jerry."

"I don't like it when one of my people gets killed. I'm here to see that it doesn't happen, right?"

"Gee, sure, Jerry."

"Call Homicide. Right now."

The computer's loudspeaker hummed softly, then clicked as the desk sergeant downtown picked up the phone.

"Sergeant Anderson."

"It's Pierce."

"Yes, Colonel." Anderson was a solid cop, a professional: some of them revealed their dislike and distrust of Trainables, but not Anderson.

"Where's Bert Klemper? Still on West 4th?"

"No, sir, he should be at the motel killing by now."

"Good. I'll call him directly."

"Yes, sir."

He told Polly to call the motel room. After one ring, Klemper answered.

"Pierce."

"Yes, sir."

"Update me on this homicide."

"The manager found her on the bed, Colonel. No clothes. Facial abrasions. Severe bruising on the throat. Looks like she'd been doing business with somebody who couldn't get affectionate without getting rough."

"Any prints?"

"Not yet, sir. We're still working on it. I've talked to two other tenants. They didn't see anybody or hear anything until she started yelling about 10:20."

"Give this one top priority," said Pierce.

"Well, Colonel, the West 4th homicide was a law-abiding citizen, and this is just a hooker—"

"Top priority."

"Yes, sir."

"I want reports every two hours until morning. Sooner if anything urgent turns up."

"Yes, sir."

"Thank you."

The loudspeaker clucked as Klemper put down the phone. Pierce finished the beer and tossed the can across the room into a wastebasket. Then he sat down again.

"Okay, Polly. We've got work to do."

"Shoot, Jerry!"

From the file on Maxine Shultz he branched out into scores of cross-references: her associates, their associates, her johns, their families. In the next fifteen minutes he reviewed hundreds of files.

He took a short break, mulling over what he'd learned, pondering associations. Then he went into the files on unsolved homicides throughout the western United States and Canada in the last five years, flagging those of young female prostitutes in particular. The files were very long, especially in the last couple of years. Social and economic breakdown always brought out murderous misogynists.

At one o'clock he paused and rubbed his eyes. The computer hummed, announcing an incoming call. "Answer."

"Colonel, it's Bert Klemper."

"Yes."

"We've got a nice semen smear. Should be able to get a fine DNA print."

"Get it to the lab at once. Wake the techs if you have to. I want the print filed as soon as possible."

Klemper's voice suggested that he was catching Pierce's hunger. "I'm on my way with it, sir."

Pierce slumped onto the cheap Naugahyde couch and put his feet on the coffee table. His subconscious was working on the data, correlating, comparing, eliminating. He was pretty sure that in those hundreds of files he had found the killer of Maxine Shultz, but it would take time and more data to confirm it.

The room was quiet. Somewhere down the road, a Scout guard vehicle groaned on its rounds. Pierce studied the prints on the walls, anonymous motel-art renditions of squirrels and kingfishers. In the silence of the night, it was easy to forget that the whole country was coming apart, that across the republic thousands were dying every night in street fighting, food riots, holdups. Without people like himself, thousands more would die and the breakdown would come all the sooner.

Five years ago, Training had been a half-understood new technique; now, Trainables were keeping the country, the world, from violent collapse. Five years ago he had been a kid in Taos, expecting to be drafted into the army as soon as he graduated from high school. But he had volunteered for Testing, and had been identified as one of the Trainable minority, the twelve percent or so of adolescents whose learning speed could be accelerated to computerlike rates.

So he had gone into the army, all right, but as an officer candidate. His basic training at Fort Ord had lasted six hours; graduate work had consumed the next week, and he had been commissioned as a T-Major. After four months working in central and northern California, he had made Colonel. For the last six months he had been the de facto ruler of Idaho and eastern Oregon, subordinate only to the district's Military Administrator, an unTrainable general who kept out of Pierce's way.

At a little after 2:00 A.M., Pierce made himself a couple of corned beef sandwiches, with a plastic cup of coleslaw from the officers' mess. While rain hissed on the yellow autumn grass outside, he sat eating at the dining-area table, looking at the glowing, empty screen of the Polymath.

"I've got two possibilities, Polly."

"Yes, Jerry?"

"This is a guy who just likes to kill hookers. That's one. Or this is a guy who kills hookers who talk to the authorities. That's two."

The little girl on the monitor didn't move for a couple of seconds. When she did, the computer speaker said: "Oh, I see. You mean the person who killed Maxine Shultz."

"I should have made myself clearer."

"I'm sorry. I'm kind of slow on the uptake sometimes."

"I lean to the first possibility. Maxine was pretty careful about seeing me. She didn't want a reputation as a snitch. And she wasn't the kind of kid who talks just to impress people."

"Which possibility would be easier for you?"

"The second. Then it'd be a matter of finding someone in the local underworld who doesn't approve of government interference. But I think it's the first. Someone who likes to kill hookers just for fun."

"I'm afraid so," Polly answered with a sigh.

"Okay, please correlate just the prostitute murders in District 23 over the last five years, solved and unsolved. Flag the ones involving strangulation."

The murders totaled eighteen. Four had been solved as the work of a single person, a soldier who was now in Fort Leavenworth. Three others had been traced to pimps or johns. The other cases were still open. This was the first one in Mountain Home in over a year; the others had been all over the district, with a cluster of six in Pocatello, ending about three years ago.

Interesting. "Give me all males arrested in Pocatello for violent offenses in the last five years." And the monitor began to flash twice a second, with mug shots and arrest sheets and disposition forms. Two hundred and sixty-two altogether; he began to eliminate them rapidly. In two minutes he had just eight men left. All but two lived in the Pocatello area. One of the others lived in Twin Falls, and the last in Mountain Home.

That man had a conviction for assault against a prostitute in Pocatello (plea-bargained down from attempted murder, by strangulation). He'd spent two years in the new state penitentiary at Burley and was now out on parole in Mountain Home. Donald Dwayne White.

"Give me his DNA print."

Ordinarily, Polly would have shaken her little finger at him and said, "That's a no-no, Jerry!" But he had circumvented that inhibition; any medical record in the district was his for the asking.

"Glad to, Jerry."

He studied the print sequence for a long time.

"Now give me his psychiatric file from Burley."

The file was brief but to the point. A fairly typical sociopathic profile, predisposed to violence against women. The transcripts of White's interviews with the psychiatrist were a tedious stew of lies, threats, sexual boasting, recollections of victorious brawls, and contempt for women in general and his mother in particular.

Pierce had read this file before; early on in this job, he had reviewed the records of virtually every convicted criminal still alive in the district. White's name had come intuitively to mind, but he had waited to test his intuition against the database.

Klemper called and transmitted the DNA print from the motel. The match with White's was anti-climactically perfect. Pierce said nothing about it to Klemper.

"Okay, Bert. You've done good work. What's next on your list?"

"That's it, Colonel. Want me to run some comparisons, see if I can find this turkey right away?"

"No, leave that for the day shift. Have to get a warrant for a DNA comparison anyway. You get back to the West 4th homicide and clean that up."

Klemper sounded a little surprised. "Yes, sir. Want me to get back to you about that one, too?"

"Yes, but I'm going out for a while. Just leave your messages with Polly."

"Will do, sir."

Pierce smiled. Klemper would be perplexed. First the motel killing had had top priority; now it could wait for morning. Well, Trainables were supposed to be temperamental, and tonight would provide Klemper with anecdotal evidence for that belief.

Pierce sat and thought for a few minutes. Then he pulled on a turtleneck sweater and a rain jacket and went outside. The rain had tapered off to a drizzle. At the curb was his car, a government-issue Plymouth. He got in and started the engine; the radio blared into life with an ancient Hank Williams tune. The country was coming apart in big chunks, and everyone was very nostalgic these days. The past was safe and comforting, knowable. The present was a series of insults, disappointments, and frights. The future could only be disaster.

"Well," said the disc jockey with soft-spoken intimacy, "it's 3:00 A.M. in KMVR country, time for a quick news roundup. Still no change in that hostage-taking in Denver. The People's Action Front is demanding one hundred million dollars for the release of over three hundred and fifty high school students being held at Reagan High. The PAF says they'll blow the school up at 8:00 A.M. if their demands aren't met."

Pierce headed for the main gate, past darkened barracks. He knew the T-Colonel in charge of Denver, down in District 25. She wouldn't get much sleep tonight.

"The Senate is debating a bill to make Testing mandatory for everyone at age fifteen. Senator Rolland Johnson of Illinois says the bill will only create an elitist group responsible to no one. Senator Diane Cooledge of California, one of the sponsors of the bill, says Trainable young people are a priceless resource. The bill isn't expected to pass."

Of course not, thought Pierce. UnTrainables were scared silly of people who could process information in a fraction of the time ordinary people needed and who could remember everything they learned. Trainables had answers before most people knew the question had been asked.

"Good news for meat eaters! The Secretary of Agriculture says we could see an end to meat rationing within a year if farmers continue to build up their herds as they have been."

That was a laugh, thought Pierce. The buildup was mostly on paper, ranchers and farmers cooking the books for the sake of federal subsidies and the government letting them do it because the alternative was an outright revolt and worse food shortages than ever.

Most livestock were too toxic for safe human consumption anyway. A year from now, rationing would be tighter than ever. Assuming a government still existed that was capable of enforcing the rationing.

The newscast went on through two or three more items—a riot in Pittsburgh, brownouts through the Southwest, someone taking a shot at the mayor of Atlanta. The newscasts during the day rarely mentioned such events; the stories then were always about disasters overseas, like the current riots in Hong Kong or the civil war in India. You mentioned your own bad news when no one was listening, and then you were balanced. A media fog, they called it. The Soviets had made it an art form long ago, but it was too good an idea to be neglected by the West.

He was out the main gate now, waving in response to the sentries' snapped salutes. Highway 67 went straight into town past abandoned strip development: deserted McDonalds and Burger Kings, carpet stores with their windows knocked out, a supermarket guarded by two young recruits with M-21s concealed under their ponchos. They looked cold and miserable.

Pierce drove through downtown, silent and deserted, and out Jackson Road to the eastern residential neighborhoods. On a side street he parked and locked the car, then walked quickly and quietly three blocks north. This was a neighborhood of small, shabby frame houses set back from the street behind waist-high cyclone fencing. The yards behind the fences were muddy and littered, with only here and there the remains of a summer garden. This was a working-class neighborhood in a time and town when no one had work. For years, neighborhoods like these had steadily rotted. People lived on unemployment, then welfare, bought lottery tickets (so dumb they'd even pay for their own fantasies of escape), did a little drugs, dealt a little drugs, scraped along. Sometimes they got busted and did a little time. It made a change.

He found the house he was seeking, saw that the car he was seeking was parked in front, and went on around the corner to cut back through the alley behind it. It was a drab little house like all others, with an overgrown backyard where a rusted pickup truck sat low on flat tires. Three people, all men, were supposed to live there; they could well have girlfriends and buddies as well. No lights showed.

The kitchen door opened easily. Pierce stepped inside, the hood of his jacket low over his forehead, the collar of his turtleneck pulled up to cover his mouth. The floor squeaked under his shoes, but he ignored the noise. A straightforward footstep in the dark would cause less alarm than a surreptitious one. A penlight gave him enough light to guide him into the living room, stinking of hashish and unwashed bodies. Someone was asleep under a blanket on the couch: a young man with a beard, his mouth agape. Pierce moved on down a short hall, past a small bathroom to a single large bedroom.

Two mattresses had been dropped on the floor. Another young man snored on one of them. He was Donald Dwayne White, right down to the scar on his chin and the Marine globe and anchor tattooed on his upper right arm. Not that the son of a bitch had ever been a Marine. He was alone. On the floor beside the mattresses was a pink scarf: Maxine's. A trophy hunter.

Bingo, thought Pierce.

He stepped into the room and drew a Mallory .15

from the inside pocket of his rain jacket. It was light and comfortable, almost all plastic. Using the penlight to help him aim, Pierce thumbed off the safety, set impact to maximum, and fired six flechettes into the sleeping man. They struck as silently as blown kisses, shoving Donald Dwayne White down into the mattress and bouncing him up again. The man made a coughing noise as air was forced from his lungs.

Pierce stepped forward carefully and studied the body. He was dead, all right. No need to look for a pulse. The mattress was already soaked red, and the man's eyes were rolled up. The room smelled of suddenly released urine and feces.

Walking back through the dark house, Pierce felt a mildly pleasant buzz. He had never killed anyone before, and it had been much easier than he'd expected. He'd thought he might have to shoot everyone in the house.

It was also much more satisfying than he had ever imagined, and he had imagined it very often over the years of his childhood and youth. He would be writing to his mother later in the day, and he wished he could mention it to her.

Three days later, in New York City, a young Trainable named Eric Wigner sat at his own Polymath.

"Serendipity," he murmured, pushing a little tobacco into the bowl of his pipe. In a simple survey of statistics on violent crime, he had run across the death of Maxine Shultz and the subsequent death of her presumed killer by a person or persons unknown. The detective in charge of investigating the two deaths surmised that some unknown enemy of Donald

Dwayne White had killed him, by coincidence, within hours of the prostitute's death. The case was still open.

Wigner took ten seconds to review all the documents, looking for some fact he might have missed. Nothing. So the conclusion remained: Wigner had serendipitously spotted a Trainable killer. He felt immensely cheered by the discovery.

Two:

In camouflage fatigues, Pierce went on patrol every morning during that cold, wet autumn. Usually he took a helicopter to another part of the district; on this particular morning, the patrol was through Mountain Home. He sat in the back of his Plymouth, being driven by an army Spec-5. Occasionally Pierce glanced at the laptop beside him, but he kept most of his attention on the outside. Reality was slower than a flickerscreen, but often revealed much more.

This morning, reality in downtown Mountain Home was a lineup in front of the federal food dispensary: over one hundred people, each of them known to Pierce in more detail than they could have imagined. Reality was a dozen men and women (he knew them all, knew how long they had been jobless) leaning against the front of a decaying English-style pub, waiting for it to open so they could spend their alcohol stamps. Reality was a row of empty stores: drugs, men's wear, insurance, video, coffee shop. Reality was a gas station that would not open until noon, but that had to have two bored young GIs guarding it to prevent fuel theft or even arson.

The Plymouth moved on through the rainy streets; a mile down the road, the Spec-5 turned into the parking lot of Hometown Mall. The lot was empty except for a cluster of camper trucks and RVs parked near the main entrance. Traders liked to live close to their work, especially with fuel so expensive these days.

Pierce saw the two new RVs at once and read their Utah license plates to the laptop. It silently flashed its answer back to him. Trouble. He'd known that already. The only people who drove gas-guzzling RVs from out of state were people who could afford to. If they could afford to and they weren't officials, they were crooks, confident ones.

"Stop here," Pierce told the driver. He ran a few more files and crosschecks through the laptop and then put it aside.

The mall was busy. Around the entrance, farmers had rigged stalls with orange plastic tarpaulins to keep the rain off their apples and potatoes. Usually they waved and nodded to him, but today they ignored the Plymouth. Pierce could see why: four or five young strangers in denim jackets with JACK MORMONS SLC embroidered across the backs. The strangers did nothing except to wander idly among the stalls; their faces were unreadable behind sunglasses.

Aware of the newcomers' casual interest in his official car, Pierce considered his choices. This was a case of illegal interstate travel by persons with criminal records. Technically, therefore, it was a matter for the police; under emergency regulations, the Military Administration was not to intervene directly in routine criminal matters. In practice, of course, it intervened all the time, as Pierce had in the Maxine Shultz killing a week before. The police didn't mind; it got them off the hook when the Military Administration decided to take unpopular steps.

If he handed this job to the police, however, he suspected the Jack Mormons would find a legal pretext to stall. Or they would simply buy off the police. Then

Pierce would have to discipline the officers, which would have political repercussions.

If he made this a MilAd matter, he would have to delegate it to the Air Police out at the base. Their senior officer would want fifty forms filled out and twice as many legal opinions from the Adjutant General. Meanwhile the Jack Mormons would be entrenching themselves, extorting money and goods from Pierce's people, beating up a few to ensure the rest kept silent. All Pierce wanted was to get them out of the district, as fast as possible, so his own people could get on with trying to make a living.

Logic dictated that he would have to deal with the matter personally. Politics dictated that he would have to deal with it publicly. He composed himself for a moment, then straightened his cap and picked up his swagger stick before leaving the car and walking into the mall.

Much of the mall was built around a domed plaza that had become a center of trade and commerce since the Emergency. At the benches and tables under the dome, gamblers played poker or shot craps. Around the curving rim of the plaza, various hustlers had moved into the abandoned shops: craftspersons, recyclers, labor brokers. Home brewers had moved into one boutique, and now traded their beer and berry wine for lumps of pork, FDA-certified minimum toxic and highjacked off federal trucks. Pierce didn't care as long as the trucks had been outside his jurisdiction.

He enjoyed the mall; it was surely livelier than it had ever been before the Emergency. He had no intention of dampening that liveliness. Under a regime as harsh as the Emergency, people needed a certain latitude. They had to feel they could beat the system in some small, meaningful way. Rob them of the joy of beating the system, Pierce believed, and they'd turn violent. Corruption was the great social stabilizer, the consolation prize for accepting a life of boredom, sickness, and hunger.

He knew whom he was looking for, and found them quickly. Another ten or twelve Jack Mormons sat in folding aluminum beach chairs in a former jewelry store, drinking beer and smoking dope. They looked at him with blank faces.

"I want Joe Bauer," Pierce said quietly.

"Go away, asshole," one of the young women said. "Now."

"Dinchu hear the lady?" said a young man. His words came out in smoky puffs. "Jack Mormons don't listen to no asshole in a crazy quilt uniform. We're minding our own business. Maybe you oughta do that, too. Asshole."

Pierce looked at the young man. "Your name is John Tyler Moore, age twenty-two, height six feet, weight one hundred eighty pounds. Your business is befuddlers and extortion. You have six arrests for drug trafficking, and four convictions." The laptop had told him all that, and more. Now for some creative use of John Tyler Moore's anxieties, as recorded by several Utah Corrections Service psychiatrists. "You're a bisexual—"

"Just a goddam minute!" The young man erupted out of his chair while his companions hooted and laughed. "I ain't no goddam bisexual, you son of—" He lunged at Pierce.

Pierce seemed to be leaning back, as if recoiling from the rush of the young man. That was to balance his right foot, which swept up in a graceful arc that intersected Moore's face. Pierce seemed to lose interest even before Moore dropped backward and thudded onto the dirty carpeting.

"I want Joe Bauer," Pierce said again. The young woman got up, shrugged elaborately, and slouched to the back of the store. A pale man, older than the others, stepped out of a doorway and approached Pierce.

"Yeah." Bauer looked at his friend, who was lying on the floor with his hands to his face. "Well, shit. Nobody does that to my people, buster. We take care of our own, and we take care of assholes like you."

"You have six hours to get out of District 23."

"No way. We like it here. We're patriotic Americans and we got a right to live where we want. You don't like us, you can move. While you still can."

"That just cost you an hour. If you and your RVs aren't out of the district by 3:00 P.M., you'll never get out of it at all."

"You don't get outa my face, boy, we'll ship you straight to Arlington in an orange crate."

Pierce was aware of scores of people watching them: his people, the people he was responsible for, and other Jack Mormons moving in to surround him. He read faces as he would read a flickerscreen. They told him the gang was about to attack. He would have to unbalance them.

He smiled at Bauer. "I know what happened to Judy Parkinson," he said loudly. "You pumped her full of Parydine and left her in that motel to die." Pierce's eyes snapped to another gang member. "Your sister, right, Brad? Did you know that your hero friend here poisoned your sister and tried to blame it on Maceo?"

"What a goddam joke!" Bauer snarled. Pierce read hesitation in the gang member's faces, but not in their leader's. Bauer was preparing to move.

"They've got all the evidence they need down in Salt Lake, and that's why you decided to move up here. You just got tired of her, Joe, didn't you?"

Brad, the brother, looked uneasy. "How's he know about Maceo?"

"Because your hero here is John Tyler's boyfriend, and John Tyler is a snitch for the Salt Lake cops. But none of you is *my* snitch, and now I want you out of my district by one o'clock."

He turned and walked away, listening to the sudden swearing and shouting behind him. At the doors to the parking lot, Pierce stopped and waited.

Joe Bauer was striding across the plaza toward him, gripping a baseball bat. His face had turned from pale to pink.

"You goddam liar, calling me a fag. Nobody says that to me, not even a fake soldier boy like you."

Pierce's swagger stick was a steel rod sheathed in leather and tipped at both ends with lead. He took it from under his arm, raised it, and flung it, whirling end over end, into Bauer's face.

Bauer staggered back, one hand going to his broken cheekbone, as Pierce moved quickly up to him and gave him a gentle shove. Unbalanced, Bauer fell heavily. Pierce took the baseball bat from him and threw it across the plaza at the clustered gang members. They ducked away; it clattered across the tile floor.

"You now have until 12:30 to clear the district," Pierce called to them in a voice that carried well. "Get going."

The Jack Mormons marched across the plaza, two of them carrying John Tyler Moore. Two others picked up Joe Bauer and gripped him at wrists and triceps. They passed Pierce without a glance and headed for the RVs.

"Way to go, Colonel!" someone yelled, and a ragged patter of applause ran around the plaza. Pierce did not respond to it, but stood at the door until the two RVs pulled away and headed for the road.

One of the farmers hurried over from his stall to shake Pierce's hand.

"Thank you, Colonel Pierce. Man, those guys turned up this morning and it looked like we had us some real trouble. But I knew you'd fix things up."

"That's what we're here for, Herb. Take it easy, now."

Back in the car, the Spec-5 asked Pierce what he'd told the Jack Mormons.

"Told 'em they didn't have a business license."

"Izzat right." The Spec-5 chuckled. "Way to go, sir."

Pierce looked out through the rain-speckled window at the decaying buildings. He felt a mild adrenalin buzz, not as strong as it had been last week with Donald Dwayne White, but agreeable. He'd bought his people another day or two of relative peace. They liked him a little more than they had, trusted him a little more. In the short term, that was good. In the long term, when he could no longer protect them, the goodwill and trust would turn to bitter hatred. At some stage, within the next year or two or three, what was left of the economy would break down completely and the ragged survivors would go looking for someone to blame. Trainables would be at the top of the list. Sure, you saved us last year and last month and last week, but what have you done for us lately?

Pierce slumped into the back seat of the Plymouth. "Let's go home," he muttered.

What we have done, he thought, is hold things together for you just a little longer. A few score thousand adolescents who were lucky enough to be Trainable and luckier still to be Tested and Trained before the latent talent could evaporate. You were illiterates who'd built a library and now you were wrecking it until we came along. We learned what you couldn't or wouldn't learn, and we applied it in your interest, and all the thanks we get is your pigheaded willingness to go on the same way you always did. We know we have no escape as long as you go on poisoning the air and water, parasitizing the land and anyone too weak to parasitize you. You have all the foresight of a cancer cell. You have enormous strength, and we have nothing except our knowledge. We ought to let you choke in your own filth, except that you'd drag us down with you.

Besides, he thought, looking through the rain-streaked window at two children splashing in a gutter, we love you. We care about you more than you care about yourselves. If we don't look after you, who will?

Back in his apartment, Pierce called Polly to attention and invoked a scrambler circuit. Once he was effectively sealed off from any kind of electronic monitoring, he patched into a network known only to district-level Trainables. It was an electronic bulletin board and wailing wall, where over a hundred young men and women exchanged the horror stories and bitter jokes that filled their lives.

Pierce watched the screen flash with hundreds of thousands of words, the chronicle of one more day in the Emergency, and felt depression settle more heavily still. After a time he shrugged it off and began to add his own contributions: a good-natured insult to the T-Colonel in Salt Lake who'd let the Jack Mormons slip unnoticed out of his territory, some police estimates on ration-stamp forgeries, a report from a medical committee in Pocatello on toxic effluent in the local drinking water. All of it was technically top secret. The MilAd could throw them all into stockades and brigs for such a major breach of security, except that MilAd couldn't have functioned without them.

After a few minutes, Pierce told Polly to put on some music. She did: Glenn Gould playing Bach. Nostalgia, Trainable style. He sprawled on the couch for a while, listening, and when the piece was over, he thanked Polly and went to bed.

In New York, Eric Wigner puffed his pipe and studied what Pierce had put on the bulletin board.

Pierce drove a dirty pickup truck two miles up a gravel road that ran off Highway 20 north of Mountain Home. Light rain fell through mist onto aspens and scrubby pines. Night had fallen.

As Pierce slowed for a curve, a tall man swung open the right-hand door and climbed in. He wore dark pants and anorak, and had taken pains not to appear in Pierce's headlights. Inside the cab, the man pulled back the hood of his anorak. His prematurely white hair gleamed faintly in the dashboard lights.

"Thanks for coming, Colonel." His name was Wes McCullough. He built log cabins, or had until the Emergency. Now he lived on basic ration stamps and a small retainer from Pierce.

"Glad to. How's Edith? And the kids?"

"All right, thanks. Listen, Colonel, I think you got some trouble ahead of you. From us."

"Serious?"

"Yeah, serious." Wes was an involuntary member of the Wabbies, the White American Brotherhood. They were the latest version of radical hick, an alliance of ranchers, loggers, miners, and survivalists. They blamed the Emergency on a conspiracy of Trainables, Blacks, and Zionist-Communists. For over a year the Wabbies had been building up arms caches and recruiting new members. So far they had been a rural nuisance but little more.

"There's going to be a protest march in town next Tuesday. To demand elections." Except that no elections had been held since the Emergency.

Pierce nodded. "A blow for democracy."

"Something like that, I guess. They're planning to start fights with the police, get some martyrs for the cause. Some of 'em are bringing in automatic weapons." Wes shook his head. "They're absolutely crazy, and they're my neighbors."

Pierce asked a few more questions about the time and leadership of the protest, and then turned the truck back toward the highway.

"Are you going to be there?" he asked.

"We'd better be. Even the kids. They say they'll take direct action against anyone who isn't."

"All right. You and Edith and the kids work out a hiding place somewhere in town, along the march route. Someplace you can duck into before the march gets to the Federal Building. We'll miss some of the marchers when we break it up, and we'll miss you. Then you get yourself back home and start calling around, see what kind of organization you can help put together once the leadership's out of action."

"You're going to arrest them?"

"Of course."

The Wabbies could certainly put on a show, Pierce thought. It was early afternoon, and the marchers had been driving into town since the night before. He would have wondered where they'd obtained the gasoline, except that he knew and would be taking appropriate steps.

They were tough-looking men, slouching around their muster point in down-filled vests and checked shirts. Many carried shotguns or rifles on their shoulders, or packed pistols on their belts. Their eyes were shaded from the watery autumn sun by baseball caps with the gold Playboy rabbit insignia of the Brotherhood.

If their women objected to that symbol, they gave no sign. They busied themselves with looking after children, making sandwiches on the tailgates of pickups, and gossiping with one another. They dressed like their men, and looked even tougher. As the wives of farmers and ranchers who had survived the last decade, they deserved to look tough, Pierce thought.

He studied them through binoculars from a third-floor window in the Federal Building, several blocks from the park where the Wabbies were gathering. This building would be their destination; obviously they didn't intend to tire themselves out with a long parade, when all the action would come when they got here.

Colonel Richard Howell, commanding officer of the base Air Police, stood beside him.

"You're sure you don't want to ban the march and disperse them, sir?"

"No," said Pierce. "They'd be all over town, making trouble in a dozen places instead of just one. Let 'em march, let 'em hear a speaker or two. The minute they try to break in, we grab their leaders and gas the rest. Then they're marched back up to the park and sent home. Anyone coming back into town in the next six weeks will be arrested."

"Okay, Colonel." Howell talked quietly into a telephone. "Everybody's set."

The march began with a band playing military songs as the Wabbies formed into a column in the park. With a dozen American flags at their head, the marchers stepped out smartly and headed down the street.

"McVey and Williams and Krebbs are right behind the flags," said Howell.

"They'll put themselves at the top of the steps, right at the main entrance," Pierce predicted. "They're armed, so don't mess around with them. As soon as they try to get in, tackle them, get their guns, and get them inside while everyone's still wondering what's going on."

"Right, sir."

All told, the Wabbies had brought in over five hundred people. Half were kids, but half the kids had guns like their dads. Even so, Pierce felt disgust at people who would knowingly bring their children into danger. They marched in step, with squad leaders counting cadence. The sidewalks were crowded with local people who had nothing better to do. Placards and banners flashed in the sunshine: End the Emergency, Give Me Liberty or Give Me Death, We Demand the Right to Vote, Right to Keep & Bear Arms, Free the Phoenix Six, Trainables are Kremlin Agents, For a Free White America.

The marchers crossed the square in good order and fanned out across the sidewalk and lower steps in front of the Federal Building as their band played themes from classic films like *Star Wars* and *Rocky*. Higher up, technicians had set up a podium and public-address system. Half a dozen Wabbie leaders, each carrying at least one gun, were clumped behind the podium amid a forest of flagpoles.

"Okay, let's go downstairs," Pierce said.

"It could get hairy, sir," said Howell. "I'd rather you stayed up here."

Pierce looked coolly at the colonel and shook his head.

The Air Police in the elevator with him were tense and eager. They licked their lips behind the clear plastic faceplates of their gas masks. Pierce said nothing and rubbed the tip of his swagger stick in the palm of his hand. He hoped he had chosen the right strategy.

The main floor lobby of the building was dark; the doors were locked and shaded, but the echoing snarl of Wabbie oratory penetrated and reverberated.

"The Communist Jewish bankers' conspiracy has succeeded... taken away our right to vote... Blacks are running our great cities into stinking slums... the real Americans are fed up and fighting back..."

Checking the seal on his gas mask, Pierce fidgeted. When were they going to make their move? After a long time and several speakers, someone (it sounded like Krebbs) announced that he was going to enter the building and demand the right to cast his ballot.

"An' God help the poor sucker who tells me I cain't!"

A fist thumped three times on the metal frame of the glass door, and then a rifle butt cracked it. Pierce pointed to an AP sergeant, who stepped out and unlocked the door. It swung inward, revealing Krebbs— a potbellied young man with long sideburns and a surprised expression on his face. The sergeant and another AP took the man's arms and drew him inside, into the dimness and out of sight of the crowd. The sergeant brought his nightstick down on Krebb's head; Krebbs dropped his rifle and sagged in the men's arms as they hauled him across the lobby.

"LeRoy?" Another Wabbie was standing in the doorway, peering into the dimness.

"Get in here," an AP ordered, and the Wabbie obeyed. Someone took his arm in a half-nelson and marched him away. In seconds, he and Krebbs were handcuffed together.

"Somebody's in there!" yelled a man on the steps. "It's a trap!"

"Let's have the gas," Pierce said quietly into his microphone. An AP promptly tossed two gas grenades out the door. They vented with a shrill, flatulent sound.

Pierce resisted the urge to check his Mallory's impact setting as he ran out the door onto the terrace at the top of the steps. It had been set low, so that the flechettes would barely penetrate and the drug they contained would do most of the work. He saw Williams, the number two man in the Wabbies, coughing in the tear gas and trying to bring his shotgun to bear. Pierce shot him twice, once in the arm and once in the chest, and Williams dropped the shotgun. Pierce grabbed Williams's beard and drew him inside. An AP took over and Pierce went back out.

The rally was breaking up nicely. The APs who had been hiding in the storefronts across the street had put several more gas grenades amid the demonstrators. No guns had gone off, but several Wabbies were down: nightsticks and Mallorys had taken them out. Children screamed; many of the demonstrators were already running back toward the park. APs and soldiers burst from other storefronts, clubbing the runners.

Standing behind the podium, Pierce felt the sting of tear gas on the skin of his neck and hands. Two APs flanked him, watching the remnants of the crowd stagger down the steps. Pierce pointed to one big, bearded man who was trying to aim his Armalite rifle at them despite the tears and snot running down his face.

"Shoot that man," said Pierce.

The AP on his right lifted his Mallory and fired. The bearded man's baseball cap flew off in a red spray; the Armalite clattered on the steps. The man kicked out with one booted foot and fell sideways.

"Shit," said Pierce. "You weren't supposed to kill him. Get him out of sight as fast as you can."

While the APs lugged the body up the stairs and into the lobby, Pierce watched the white mist of the tear gas dissipate. Perhaps twenty people were still on the steps or on the street, unconscious or paralyzed by flechettes. The bystanders who had been watching the demonstration were long gone. The Wabbies who had run the gamut back to the park had lost several dozen more to the APs and soldiers. The rest were frantically clambering into their trucks and cars and driving out. No one hindered them.

Stragglers were being clubbed. Pierce saw Wes McCullough knocked down, with his wife and children around him. A little closer, a soldier was shoving a young woman along the sidewalk. Pierce saw long, dark braids and recognized her.

"Private Ruiz," he said into his microphone, "apologize at once to the young lady, and then escort her up here to me."

"Yessir!"

The woman looked suspiciously at the soldier, then glanced in the direction he was pointing, toward Pierce. Pierce raised a hand. She began to walk up the street, coughing and wiping her eyes. The soldier left her at the bottom of the steps, and she walked up to face Pierce, who had removed his face mask.

"My name is Jerry Pierce. And you're Doria Killarney. I'm sorry you were involved in this mess."

"So am I. I was just on my way home from school when these kooks went wild."

"My kooks or their kooks?"

She smiled wryly. "Is there a difference?"

"I like to think so. Were any of your pupils caught in this?"

"They're too smart. The first tear gas grenade, and they were gone. I stayed around to see the Wabbies get their asses kicked. Didn't think I looked like Wabbie, too." She blew her nose. "I guess if you know my name you know all about me."

"I know some things."

"You Trainables give me the willies. I'm sorry if that sounds rude, but tear gas does that to me."

"Not at all. Can we do anything for you? Give you a lift home?"

"I wish you could give me a lift back about forty years. And let me take my kids with me, so they don't have to deal with any more of this crap."

"I wish I could do that, and go with you." He put out his hand. "Again, I'm sorry. Call me if I can do anything for you and your school."

She shook his hand briefly and firmly, and walked back down to the street: a small woman, very erect in a baggy sweater and patched slacks. Pierce smiled faintly as he watched her go. Very attractive, even if she was unTrainable. He turned his attention to other matters.

The American flags around the podium had all toppled; they lay scattered on the granite amid the dropped weapons and bloodstains.

Do they all end like this? wondered Pierce. All the countries that start with heroes, do they end up with empty symbols and psychopathic halfwits who think they're patriots?

He shivered. Once again he had bought his people a few more weeks, or days, or hours. The price was getting higher every time. The end was close, and he could see no escape.

That evening in New York, Eric Wigner pushed his chair back from his Polymath and smiled broadly.

"Jerry Pierce," he murmured, "I'm going to start your first fan club."

Three:

The Research Services Division of the Central Intelligence Agency maintained its New York offices on a floor of an anonymous building on East 52nd Street. Eric Wigner's cubicle was windowless, barely large enough for his desk and filing cabinet and a few houseplants. He didn't mind. The computer on his desk gave him, as he liked to say with a faint smile, "a window on the world."

The machine, like Pierce's, was a Polymath. Unlike commercial models, however, this one had no Polly. For security, it was not voice-actuated. But it had more power and intelligence than any commercial computer. Wigner had adjusted the screen to flicker at twelve pages per second, twice the normal rate for an Alpha-10 Trainable like himself. That was too fast for full conscious retention, but he had learned to trust his subconscious to alert him to useful information patterns.

As a result, he believed he possessed the best grasp of any individual in the CIA of current events in the United States. The knowledge had depressed him at first, when he had begun four years before as a raw seventeen-year-old domestic intelligence analyst. With time, however, he had developed the shell of most CIA Trainables. Those who didn't ended up taking their vacations in Dr. Franklin's clinic in Woodstock. If

Dr. Franklin's conditioning didn't take, the Trainable was rusticated to Records Division in Langley. Wigner had no intention of ending up there.

"The trick is to avoid living on a paper planet," he remarked to Jasmin Jones one day over coffee. She had nodded, understanding: their superiors, all Trainables, tended to believe only what was printed out and to deal with information as isolated bits. They seemed unable to grasp the messages encoded in the overall flow.

"Be grateful some people do," she replied.

"Oh, I am."

That was an increasingly typical Trainable conversation. Wigner thought as he returned to his cubicle: brief, elliptical, rich in nonverbal content. Talking, especially to unTrainables, took so long that it inevitably acquired an ironic quality. Jaz had told him that she was aware of the way he was manipulating Divisional Director Jonathan Clement; she had also conveyed neutrality on the issue, which was a little disappointing. One expected Trainables to ally themselves naturally against their plodding elders, but Jaz seemed almost fond of Clement.

She did not seem fond at all of Wigner, which he thought a pity because she was a dramatically good-looking woman, and which he thought a nuisance because it meant being circumspect with her when he would rather share his thoughts. Jaz was smart as well as Trainable, and the two qualities did not always go together. He would have enjoyed testing some of his ideas against her intellect and recruiting her into his own project.

That project was still vague, but the discovery of Jerry Pierce out in Idaho had helped to give it shape. Wigner was annoyed with himself: for too long he had simply daydreamed about what he would do when the Agency, and the government, came crashing down. Now he had a potential asset and must make up for lost time.

Wigner thought hard for most of the afternoon while data flashed steadily from the screen. At last he hooked into the office's local area network and paged Clement. The screen seemed to freeze.

STATE REQUEST.

THREE DAYS' PERSONAL LEAVE, EFFECTIVE MIDNIGHT TONIGHT.

PURPOSE?

REST & REHAB HERE IN NEW YORK.

A tedious pause, as if the request demanded serious thought. Clement knew perfectly well that Wigner had taken no leave in months. GRANTED. ENJOY YOURSELF.

THANK YOU. Wigner switched out of the LAN and returned his computer to shielded condition so that no one could monitor him. Then he used it to order a MATS flight to Mountain Home Air Force Base, leaving at 12:30 next morning.

Most RSD personnel lived within two blocks of the office, and Wigner was no exception. At the end of the day he shut down, locked his cubicle, and took the elevator to street level. Jaz Jones rode with him.

"I'm taking a couple of days off."

"Great. Going anywhere?"

"And leave show business?"

She smiled. Wigner promised himself to sound her out again, when events had worsened and his project was more advanced. She would see the reasoning. Good heavens, the Agency itself had supplanted plenty of unviable regimes when circumstances demanded. This would be no different.

The problem, he told himself as he walked down 52nd to Lexington, was that his project had no great life expectancy either. Have to work on that.

The apartment was one of the best perks the RSD could offer: large, airy, secure, with reliable water and electricity. Wigner had rejoiced in its bookshelves, and had filled them with an eclectic assortment of titles and houseplants. He kept the place spotless and tidy.

After a quick snack from the microwave, he showered and dressed for the flight. A shoulder bag took a change of clothes and his shaving kit, plus a newfangled gadget called a flickreader. It looked like thick, opaque spectacles made of brown plastic. A narrow slot on the rim of the right "lens" could receive a strip of microfiche holding up to three hundred pages, and the flickreader could move through it either automatically or selectively.

With the flickreader Wigner packed a handful of microfiches, reports he had not got around to yet; the flight west would be a convenient time for them. Then he activated the apartment's defenses and left.

He was taking a chance, he knew. He had lied directly to Clement about where he intended to spend his three days' R&R, on the generally safe assumption that RSD had better things to do than to monitor the holiday whereabouts of one of its analysts. But if Clement did find out that he'd left town, he would wonder what in Mountain Home, Idaho, could interest a young easterner. Wigner proposed to beg the question by ensuring that Clement remained ignorant.

A cab took him downtown, and he enjoyed a fine meal just off Washington Square. Half an hour of seemingly aimless wandering through the Village enabled him to shake off any possible tails; the streets were crowded, since the Village was still reasonably secure, so he could lose himself readily. On Houston Street he took a cab to Brooklyn, where he rented an old Buick at an agency on Bedford Avenue. The cost was outrageous, $400 plus gas and mileage for three days, but Wigner paid without a murmur.

"It's the insurance," said the rental agent. "It's killing us. Leave a car like this out and it's stripped in ten minutes. That's why you gotta promise to leave it only in locked, secure parking areas, unnastan?"

"Unnastan," said Wigner. He signed a false name to the contract, displayed adequate identification, and drove circuitously through the night to Old La Guardia.

Nowadays, of course, the airfield handled mostly military flights. A sentry with an M-21 slung over his shoulder inspected Wigner's false ID (not what he had shown the rental agent) and ticket before waving him on. Wigner parked in an almost empty garage and took an elevator upstairs to the main floor of the terminal building. At least in the military the elevators still worked.

The Military Air Transport Service counter was six deep in soldiers, sailors, and marines; hundreds more sat or slept on the benches. Wigner did not feel out of place. His ID said he was William Coules, a logistics consultant with the Defense Department, and therefore part of the family. He patiently took his turn, got his boarding pass, and went off to find a seat in the waiting room.

It turned out to be next to a young Black sergeant with infantry insignia on the lapels of his uniform and three Venezuela ribbons on his chest.

"You've seen some action," Wigner said.

"Some."

"Where you headed for now?"

"California."

"Good duty."

"Shit. Kickin' ass in L.A., keepin' the brothers from rippin' off food for their babies. Shit duty."

"Things'd be worse without you."

The young sergeant looked cynically at him. "Things'd be worse for *you,* my man." He picked up a discarded newspaper and began to read.

So the troops were indeed restless. Anecdotal evidence, but still of some value. He looked around the terminal and saw more evidence: a marine obviously high on cocaine, jabbering cheerfully with a woman clerk who ignored him; a master sergeant with a thousand-yard stare and a cigarette burning slowly toward his lips; two air force officers glaring around the waiting room and muttering angrily together.

Getting dicey, thought Wigner. When the military figures the civilians can't hack it any more, it's dicey. They'll try a coup in a few more months. Beat 'em or join 'em?

At last his flight was called. Over two hundred people straggled to the departure lounge and then to the aging 747. Wigner found a seat near the tail, and when the plane was in the air and most of the passengers were asleep, he sat in darkness and went through the reports with his flickreader.

The plane skipped across the country from one military airfield to another. After a while, Wigner finished his work and went to sleep. It was well past dawn when he got up and stepped out onto the rain-wet tarmac of Mountain Home.

Pierce was in the kitchen fixing himself lunch: a corned beef sandwich on caraway rye with hot mustard, sauerkraut, a green salad. The doorbell rang. He went to answer it and found a stocky young man standing there. The man stood with an easy erectness that reminded Pierce of someone he'd seen in old movies—Gene Kelly, that was it. Otherwise, though, the stranger was far from striking. Brown hair and eyes, a moustache no doubt intended to make him look older but that only made him look young. Unmemorable, unless you looked in his eyes and recognized the humor and intelligence in them.

"Good morning, Colonel Pierce. May I come in?"

"Of course." Annoying that the man should know his name. "You can join me for lunch."

"At 8:30 in the morning?"

"Middle of the day for me. Make you breakfast if you prefer."

They were in the kitchen now, the stranger casually dropping his raincoat and shoulder bag over the back of a chair and then settling into it like a roommate back from an all-night party. He was wearing brown wool slacks, a white shirt, and a beige cardigan. He was not merely stocky, Pierce saw: the man had the shoulders of a weightlifter as well as a dancer's poise.

"Actually, it's closer to lunch than breakfast for me. That sandwich looks good."

Pierce nodded and made another one. He popped a couple of beer cans and they sat down companionably.

"My name is Eric Wigner. Hi." They shook hands. "I'm a fan of yours, Colonel Pierce."

"My goodness," said Pierce dryly.

"I work for the CIA in New York. Research Services Division."

"I'm not aware of it."

"I'd be crushed if you were. We do most of the Agency's domestic surveillance. I ran across you in the files a few days ago."

"Indeed."

Pierce kept his face calm, interested, a little amused. Wigner reflectively bit into his sandwich, chewed, and sighed.

"You know, I rehearsed what I was going to say, but now I'm not so sure. I need to get on frank terms with you, and I need us to trust one another. So, I'll tell you right off that I think you killed Donald Dwayne White."

Pierce looked at him and smiled. He had a good smile, cheerful and infectious, and Wigner smiled back in response.

"You're Trainable, of course?"

"Alpha-10. Not as good as you. I don't think there are more than fifty Alpha-18s in North America."

"Assume that I had killed White. Why would you care?"

"Because it tells me that you're serious about what you're doing here, and you're prepared to do what needs to be done."

"What I'm doing here, as you must know, is a holding action. Most Trainables I know give us two years, maybe three."

"Back east we're even more pesssimistic. A coup by next spring, then a civil war and mass starvation. Just like Mexico."

"All the more reason to wonder why you're interested in one death in Idaho."

"The death is only part of what I'm interested in. I'm looking for Trainables with guts and brains. You got rid of a bad guy by killing him yourself. Guts. You got rid of the Jack Mormons by understanding their weaknessses and thinking fast. Brains. You broke up the Wabbies by good intelligence and planning. Guts *and* brains."

"Shucks," said Pierce.

"You still have to learn how to take compliments."

"I still have to learn a lot about you."

"Check me out." Wigner pulled a laminated plastic card from his wallet.

"Finish your sandwich."

They carried their beers into the living room and Pierce put the card in the Polymath. "Boot, Polly."

"Sure, Jerry."

"Test the input for authenticity."

"Authenticity is confirmed. For security reasons, Jerry, I can't vocalize or copy any data from this input, and you'll have to confirm that only authorized persons are present when I display data from this input."

"Confirm, Polly. Run from Frame 1."

Frame 1 was a marriage license issued almost thirty years earlier to Woodrow Wilson Wigner and Olivia Thompson. The screen flicked through Wigner's documentation: birth certificate, medical records, school report cards, personal correspondence, Agency dossiers, passport, Training transcripts. Several photographs portrayed Wigner at various ages and in various settings: summer camp in the Catskills, a wedding reception in Georgetown, on the baseball team at Lawrenceville, at a freshman beer blast at Yale. Three Agency psychological profiles asserted his emotional stability, dedication to duty, self-confidence, and willingness to take risks.

"Thanks, Polly," Pierce said. He took the card from the computer and returned it to Wigner.

"Stable and dedicated CIA personnel don't go off making friends with suspected killers."

"I wouldn't have the nerve to if I weren't stable and dedicated."

"You're at a disadvantage with me, Eric."

"I know."

"You think you have a use for me. I have no use for you."

"Oh, well—a friend in the Agency is always of *some* use, but you're right. I need someone like you who's capable of killing when necessary. And knowing when killing isn't necessary. You need only to protect your people."

"Fair enough."

"You know you can't protect them much longer. You *know* it. So what I can offer you is a chance—just a chance—to protect them when all other protection is gone."

"How?"

"I'm setting up a network of people around the country, people who can take charge before we go right down into civil war. Most of them have to be military or government. They all have to be Trainables. When the breakup comes, they'll be ready. They'll have the supplies, the support, enough to keep things going in their own bailiwicks. They'll succeed at first when everyone else is failing, so they'll go on succeeding."

"A shadow government."

"Nice phrase."

"Of Trainable kids. With no experience."

"What's experience got to do with anything? Experience just gives us anecdotal evidence for our personal prejudices. Trainables operate on a wider database."

"Fair enough. It still sounds like sedition."

"No. The system is wearing out, breaking down. I can't give my loyalties to a dead abstraction, not when live people need me. I serve the state only because it serves the people. When the state can't serve any longer, I have to find another way to. So do you."

"What odds do you give your network?"

"Very poor ones. But better than sitting back and letting things fall apart."

"How big is your network?"

Wigner grinned. "When you join, it doubles in size."

Pierce laughed in spite of himself. "Finish your beer," he said. "You can come on patrol with me this morning."

They spent the next two days talking, drinking, traveling around the district. Wigner sat in anonymously on an interrogation of LeRoy Krebbs, one of the Wabbies. Like the others arrested at the march, Krebbs had said almost nothing. In fifteen minutes, however, Wigner got Krebbs to identify two major figures in the Wabbies' national organization. Pierce put the word out on them and they were picked up within two hours by the FBI in Montana and Texas.

"You're wasted in front of a computer," Pierce told him.

"So are you. Do you want something better than this?"

"Not until you've got something better to offer."

"I'll work on it."

Pierce paused for a moment. "You need more people for your network. I can give you some."

"Who?"

Pierce showed him the bulletin board, identified the major contributors.

"I don't know how many meet your needs. But it's a start."

Wigner, sitting on the Naugahyde couch, looked at

the flashing screen of the Polymath. "Jerry—I understand what this means to you. You don't betray your people. Neither do I. I'll recruit the ones we need and leave the rest alone. No one's going to suffer because of this. No one."

"Good," said Pierce. He looked into Wigner's eyes and saw the friend he had needed for a long time.

Unseasonably early snow was coming down in little halos around the street lights. Pierce, in sweater and jeans, parked the Plymouth and walked around the corner. The neighborhood was only half a mile from Donald Dwayne White's house, but these houses were in better repair, their yards neater. Huge willows shadowed the sidewalks.

Enjoying the stings of the snowflakes on his face, Pierce strode up the walk to an old frame house behind a pair of aspens. She rented the main floor of the two-storey house, he knew, and no one lived upstairs at the moment. He knocked.

"Who is it?" a woman asked behind the door.

"Jerry Pierce. Is that Doria Killarney?"

After three locks turned, the door opened. She was wearing the same sweater she'd had on during the Wabbie protest, but her hair hung loose across her shoulders.

"What are *you* doing here?"

"Visiting, if it's not a bad time. I'm sorry I didn't call first."

"Come on in."

Doria led him into a small, curtained living room, sparsely furnished and lined with board-and-brick bookcases. A book lay open on the arm of an easy chair: Stephen Jay Gould's classic *The Mismeasure of Man*.

"Please sit down, Colonel. I'm just making tea."

Pierce settled in a rattan chair, skimming the titles of the books. Good taste, if a little too much nineteenth-century European fiction for his preference. A stereo sat silent in a corner. She didn't use it as Muzak. The tapes and CDs were nineteenth-century European also.

She came back in, carrying a teapot and mugs on a wooden tray. "What do you like in it?"

"Nothing. Thanks." He took a mug and held it, enjoying its heat.

"Well." She sank into the easy chair, put the book aside, and looked at him with a civil but careful smile. "What brings you here?"

"Inquisitiveness. I'm curious to know what the mood's like in your school. Among the teachers, the parents, the kids."

"Why don't you just phone my principal? Or the superintendent, and you can find out about every school in town."

"I'm not interested in official versions. I want to know what things look like to you."

Doria studied him levelly for a long moment. "I don't know if I want to tell you anything, Colonel. The minute you learn something, you start throwing tear gas or kicking people in the face. And I don't like being asked to be an army stool pigeon."

"Would you be happier with the Wabbies? Or the People's Action Front?"

"That's the fallacy of the false dilemma. Look, I know you mean well, but if I cooperated with you I don't really think we'd have the Bill of Rights back any sooner."

"We're not going to have the Bill of Rights back. Ever. And I'm not trying to put you in a false dilemma. The question now is how many people we can get through this mess into something better. Not something good. Just better than what we've got now."

"Fine. But why do you need me to help?"

"Because you're smart and perceptive—"

"—and susceptible to flattery?"

"I don't have time for flattery. You're smart. You're in touch with people on a level of intimacy that I can't reach. They tell you things, you notice things, that never get into the databases. I could get along without your help, but I'd get along better with it. You could get along better, too."

"Ah. What's in it for me?"

"Not much. But I can get your school a little more electricity, more supplies, some vitamin supplements."

"You bastard." She said it without venom. "You know just where to push, didn't you?"

"I wasn't going to offer you a Cadillac and a fur coat."

She thought for a long time before speaking. Pierce didn't mind. She was nice to look at. "I have to warn you. Nothing you supply is linked with me, and my school doesn't get special treatment. If we get vitamins, every school in town gets vitamins."

"Good."

"Okay, Colonel, let's talk."

"Call me Jerry."

The talk went on late into the night. They drank more tea; she made cookies. While they cooled, she took him for a walk around the neighborhood.

"I wish to God I could do this more often," she murmured as their shoes squeaked in the snow. "It's really demoralizing to have to barricade yourself in your own house when the sun goes down."

"You're pretty brave to be living alone."

"Nope, just unlucky. Turned out the family upstairs were illegals. They got shipped back to Mexico."

"I know."

"Of course. I forgot, sorry."

"Please—I wasn't criticizing or being snotty. I hadn't thought about the Galindezes since I read about them in September. Why didn't you move somewhere safer?"

"Oh—you get tired of moving after a while. I couldn't face boxing up all my books again, so I stayed put. Maybe somebody will move in upstairs, or not. I don't care."

"I can find you someplace a little safer."

"Uh-uh." They walked in silence for a block, past houses whose curtained windows revealed no sign of life. "D'you like being a Trainable?"

"Sure." Her question had surprised him.

"I guess it's a lot of responsibility."

"I don't mind that. I have the feeling I can make a difference."

"Can you?"

"Sometimes. Not often enough, but sometimes."

"That's how I feel about being a teacher. I look at my class every morning and I think: You poor little buggers, maybe I can give a couple of you enough of a break to help you hang on."

"My feelings exactly."

"'My feelings exactly,'" she mocked him. "Do you have room for feelings, when your brain's so packed full of data?"

"I wouldn't be here if I didn't have feelings, Doria."

"You keep them all bottled up, then?"

"Until I run into someone who understands them."

The snow was heavier now, and the street lights had gone out. The sky was a dark gray. Doria held his arm to steady herself, and then let go a little slowly. He took her hand.

"Let's go have those cookies and another cup of tea," he said. "I have to be back at the base by midnight."

He came to her house often after that—not every night, but three or four times a week, always after dark. Before long she took him into her bed and he found surprising consolation there: surprising because he had hoped only for the energy and grace of her body, and instead received an unexpected understanding. She did not mother him, nor did she dissolve into clinging anxiety; she was a partner, responding to his moods with laughter and intensity, anger and delight.

One night in mid-November, he left her house around 11:30. The Plymouth, parked as always around the corner, was beeping quietly when he unlocked it. He picked up the cellular phone and identified himself.

"You got a message scrambled on your Polymath, sir," said the comm technician. "It's eyes only, so I can't patch you through."

"Doesn't matter. I'm on my way home."

Pierce drove quickly back to the base and his apartment. He ordered Polly to boot before the door had even swung shut.

"Scrambled message, Jerry. For your eyes only."

"Very good. Run it."

The letters appeared on the screen for no more than a tenth of a second, but that was longer than Pierce needed: URGENT YOU BE AT FERMILAB BATAVIA ILLINOIS BY 0500 HOURS CST 12 NOV.

MATS WILL ARRIVE MHAFB BY 1230 HOURS
MST TO PICK YOU UP. WILL MEET YOU AT
O'HARE. ERIC.

Pierce spoke. "Polly, get me Base Air Traffic Control."

Four:

A helicopter took Pierce and Wigner from a remote corner of O'Hare to Fermilab, twenty-five miles west. From just under the early morning overcast, they could look down and see the burned-out neighborhoods, the ruins of last summer's riots. Strange, thought Pierce, that advanced scientific research could still go on under these conditions.

Wigner had said nothing about the purpose of the journey, but the spark in his eyes and the quickness of his step suggested his excitement. Pierce shoved his hands deeper in the pockets of his overcoat. The helicopter was cold and noisy. Wigner seemed not to care.

Fermilab looked superficially normal, but Pierce soon spotted the army posts scattered along the perimeter of the huge site. Roadblocks were up as well. Whatever was happening here, the military wasn't being very discreet about it.

The helicopter settled onto a parking lot beside a drab concrete building, evidently built long after the lab's glory days as an architectural showplace. Pierce and Wigner walked quickly to a side entrance to the building, a glass door guarded by a squad of riflemen and four dogs. A Green Beret captain, no less, inspected their passes and IDs before saluting and allowing them inside.

"What's up, Eric?" Pierce demanded quietly as they walked down a corridor past locked office doors.

"Maybe the best news we've ever had. And certainly the strangest. I just know the outlines. My boss sent me to pick up some details, and I thought you ought to be in on it, too."

The corridor opened into a foyer outside a lecture hall. Across the foyer was the building's main entrance, its glass doors now painted over with whitewash. Six Green Berets in combat gear stood at each of the two entrances to the lecture hall; they watched the two hundred men and women in the foyer with dispassion. No doubt, Pierce thought, more soldiers patrolled the outside.

The people in the foyer drank coffee and ate pastries; Wigner lighted his pipe, though few others smoked. A hum of conversation filled the room: the noise made by alert and intelligent people under stress. Too many people laughed.

The foyer lights blinked, as if this were some theatrical performance about to begin. The audience filed in past the Green Berets. Pierce recognized most of the faces: major scientists, mostly in physics, some electronics engineers, a few senior military officers with their T-Colonels beside them, and some of the most important people in the Civil Emergency Administration. Maybe half the people were Trainables, and some of those were part of the wailing-wall network. A few glanced at Pierce with curious smiles: What are *we* doing here?

Pierce and Wigner sat near the back of the lecture hall. The audience took up fewer than half the seats, creating an odd air of anticlimax—as if, thought Pierce, an important new play was a failure on opening night.

The stage at the end of the steeply tilted room was bare except for a couple of chairs and a lectern off to one side. A projection screen hung at the back of the stage. Without ceremony, a rumpled-looking man in a green cardigan stepped out of the wings and spoke into the lectern microphone.

"Good morning, ladies and gentlemen. My name is Hans Neumann, and I am the director of this facility. I welcome you to Fermilab, and I have been asked to remind you all that this briefing has been classified Top Secret." He glanced at a card in his hand. "Discussion of this briefing with unauthorized individuals will result in severe penalties under Section III of the Civil Emergency Act.

"Having said that, I must now be frank with you. We appear to have stumbled upon an absolutely new phenomenon here, a phenomenon that will have enormous impact on our understanding of the universe."

Pierce's eyebrows rose. Neumann did not have a reputation for that kind of language.

"The first part of this morning's conference will be a briefing by the discoverer of the phenomenon," the director went on. "After that we will discuss the implications, and you are invited to take an active part. Here is Mr. Richard Ishizawa."

A patter of applause rose from the audience as a young man came onto the stage and shook Neumann's hand. The young man wore an undistinguished gray suit and maroon tie, and carried a folder of notes under his arm. He looked a little nervous as he settled his notes on the lectern and adjusted the microphone.

"Thank you, Dr. Neumann. Good morning. I should explain that I am a doctoral student doing research here. We have been working on ways to isolate quarks more readily, but I will not go into the details of my project, especially since it seems beside the point now."

Pierce found himself mildly disappointed. Ishizawa's age meant he was unTrainable, or at least unTrained, and had, therefore, been toiling away on a single degree while people like Pierce and Wigner had already accumulated several. One had to avoid patronizing people like Ishizawa; they were bright and able enough, but inevitably handicapped.

Ishizawa explained how he had set up a hypermagnetic field in Cave 9 of the Superconducting Supercollider, and showed a couple of slides of the apparatus. Pierce could make out only a jumble of cables and magnets in a small concrete room. The generator of the hypermagnetic field was a shiny metal ring perhaps two meters in diameter and ten centimeters thick.

"On October 22," Ishizawa said, "we activated the field for the first time. The beam was to be diverted into Cave 9 and focused through the field to the target. Instead, the experiment was aborted. Next slide, please."

The concrete room was full of flying dust and dark scraps, and the light seemed different. Pierce saw that the circular arch of the field generator was now the frame of an irregular sequence of light and dark verticals.

"The vacuum in the cave was implosively breached by air at normal pressure," said Ishizawa. "We were lucky that the equipment wasn't damaged more seriously than it was. I saw what happened on the monitors and shut down the experiment at once. We went to the cave to see what had happened, and found it heavily contaminated by biological materials—chiefly soil, tree branches, and vegetation.

"I looked at the photographs that had been taken at

the moment of activation, and I saw these." Ishizawa took a couple of steps toward the projection screen and used a pointer to tap within the circle of the field generator. "I realized that they must be trees."

Pierce caught his breath, furious with himself for not having noticed it before.

"Well, we looked at all this stuff on the floor of the cave—dirt, leaves, bits of bark and stuff—and we realized something else. It was summer vegetation. And it was fresh. It couldn't have been some practical joke or hoax. Something had happened when we turned on the field."

He took a sip of water. Pierce saw that he was not just nervous. Another emotion held Ishizawa: exaltation.

"We decided to turn on the field again, without evacuating the cave, just to see what would happen. I had a Polaroid with me, and I took some pictures. Next slide, please."

Within the circle of the generator stood a dense grove of trees. Sunlight was filtering through them, turning leaves into patches of gold. Several trees showed freshly broken branches, and the nearest had patches of bark missing.

Ishizawa called for three more slides; each was of the same scene, from slightly closer than the shot before. The last showed a human hand gripping the stump of one of the severed branches.

"We kept the field on for about forty seconds," said Ishizawa. "At the end I took that last picture of my own hand holding a branch on the other side of the field. Then we started running out of power, and I closed down."

The screen went dark and attention returned to Ishizawa.

"We weren't sure what we'd discovered," he said. "First, we called it a topological singularity, since it certainly didn't seem to be part of the local topology. Then we decided it was a phase of reality that's out of step somehow with ordinary reality, but just as real. A kind of temporal incongruity. When I looked at the pictures I'd taken, and I thought about what we'd seen when the field was on, I thought it was one of the most beautiful places I'd ever seen, and it deserved a beautiful name. So, I called it Beulah."

Ishizawa looked at his listeners' blank faces and patiently spelled the word. "It's a name from the Bible, but I got it from the poetry of William Blake."

Pierce was annoyed. Poetry was a minor part of most people's Training, including his, and he knew Blake only as a name and a set of dates and titles. Yet this unTrainable knew Blake well enough to quote him.

"Well," said Ishizawa, "I took my Polaroids to Dr. Neumann, and my team and I explained what they meant. I'm grateful that he didn't kick us out of his office." Laughter rippled around the theater. "Instead, he authorized us to pursue the phenomenon with all the resources he could give us. We moved the field generator into a lab and did a lot of planning. Then we conducted our first serious probe of Beulah."

The screen now showed a holotape. The camera had been mounted, Ishizawa explained, on a robot tank borrowed from the Chicago SWAT team. The activation of the field was shown in sharp and dizzying detail. The cement-block wall of the lab, painted off-white, stood a couple of feet beyond the generator. Suddenly the wall vanished; within the circle of the generator, colors shimmered like the film of a soap bubble. Then they, too, were gone. The light in the lab changed. Inside the circle was a view of trees again, their branches swaying as air pressure equalized, but they were illuminated only by the lights in the lab: it was night on Beulah. A ramp had been built up from the floor of the lab to the lower rim of the field generator; whether by luck or calculation, the ramp met the Beulan surface almost perfectly. When the field was fully stabilized, the tank turned on its lights and rolled forward.

"The next part's kind of boring," Ishizawa apologized, but the audience sat uncomplaining through fifteen minutes of floodlit trees and underbrush slowly moving past the camera.

"The tank was on its own. We kept the field on for just a few seconds. The tank was programmed to seek out any clear space it could find, and then to return."

The clear space turned out to be a recently burned-out patch of woods: a few blackened trunks stood amid grass and wildflowers. A porcupine stared at the tank for a moment, then turned and scuttled away. The camera panned through a full circle, then tilted upward and scanned the sky. Computer enhancement was evident here: the stars were unnaturally bright and numerous despite the half moon. Pierce saw the Big Dipper at once, although enhancement cluttered it with stars normally not visible.

"We were hoping to get a shot like this," Ishizawa said. "The terrain and vegetation looked like temperate zone, probably North American, but we couldn't fix the location until we got a look at the night sky. Then it looked crazy. We seemed to be right on this latitude, except that some of the stars were out of position. Finally, we gave it to the computer and asked it to make sense of it."

He paused, evidently looking forward to what was

coming next. "The computer said it was looking at the night sky over Batavia, Illinois, at 3:45 A.M. on July 6, 1787."

Wigner evidently knew this much already; he grinned at Pierce, looking for a response. Pierce ignored him. Like most of the audience, he concentrated on the speaker.

"So, Beulah is like our own world, but over two centuries younger," Ishizawa went on. He would have gone on, but a broad-shouldered old man stood up in one of the front rows. "Yes, Dr. Johnson."

The Nobel laureate ran a hand over his bald scalp. "Richard, you seem to be telling us you've built a time machine and traveled into the past."

"No, sir, not exactly." Pierce admired Ishizawa's coolness; Johnson was a famous scientific cross-examiner. "I said Beulah is *like* our world, the way two beads on a string are like each other. But going to Beulah isn't really traveling in time, because it doesn't affect our own past. If I went to Beulah and found one of my ancestors and shot him, I wouldn't disappear or anything. I'd still be here—or there. But when Beulah's timeline reached the late twentieth century, two hundred years from now, no one named Richard Ishizawa would exist."

"So you're suggesting that a complete universe, over two centuries behind us, exists on the other side of this field of yours. With everything just as it was when our world was back in 1787."

"Pretty much so. We've kicked around the implications a little, and it seems likely that Beulah isn't exactly the same as our universe. The uncertainty principle might occasionally cause subatomic events to go in a slightly different direction on Beulah, but in most cases we'd never notice. Maybe one of those trees had a slightly different genetic makeup than its equivalent on Earth. We'd have to do a lot of research to find that kind of difference."

"But you could get a cascade effect, couldn't you?"

"Yes, sir. If enough subatomic events went a different way, you might end up with a whole new individual here and there, and that could change the course of Beulah's history. So far we haven't found any examples of such a change. Of course, we've been aware of this phenomenon for just a few weeks."

Johnson was still standing. "We've been using hypermagnetic fields for a couple of years now, and no one else has obtained your results. Why not?"

"Our generator is defective." More laughter, slightly nervous, erupted from the listeners. "We looked it over very carefully and found a failure in one of the microcircuits. A lot seems to depend on precise field intensities as well. By sheer luck, the generator was calibrated to the exact intensity signature of Beulah. Otherwise, we probably would have had nothing but a failed experiment."

"What else have you done besides send a tank through?" someone called out.

"I've gone myself, with my colleague Dave Emerson." He pointed to another young man in the front row, who stood smiling to receive a round of applause that began tentatively—the audience was still absorbing the implications of Ishizawa's answer—and ended with a roar.

The next holotape showed the two men, in hiking gear, stepping through the field into a sunny morning. Emerson carried a holocam and used it well. The sounds of Beulah were perfectly clear: a birdsong, the men's laconic comments, the splash of a brook over stones, boots scuffing through underbrush. They passed through the clearing where the tank had stopped, and continued for several minutes until the woods ended on the bank of a slow-flowing creek. On the opposite bank trees were sparser, and open meadows gleamed in the morning sun.

"It's even more beautiful than it looks," said Ishizawa. "Clean, peaceful, green. We didn't want to come back."

When the tape ended, silence fell for a moment. Ishizawa cleared his throat. "Actually, we've sent people through to Beulah four—no, five times, now. Dave spent three days there on one trip. We can give you the details if you want them, but it's pretty much the same as what you've already seen. No one's gone far enough to make contact with people, but Dave's seen smoke from their campfires. And he found a deserted camp with some broken pottery. Made in Birmingham, England, and definitely made in the 1760s."

A short, plump man raised his hand. Pierce recognized him as a senior bureaucrat in the Civil Emergency Administration.

"So, there's a whole new world, clean and empty, just waiting."

"It's clean, but it's not empty. The natives include people like Benjamin Franklin and Thomas Jefferson. George Washington will be elected president in two years."

"Don't misunderstand me, Mr. Ishizawa. Compared to today's population levels, your Beulah is virtually deserted. We could put millions of people into it without even disturbing the natives. We could grow crops in land that hasn't been poisoned, drill for oil and hit it every time because we'd know where it was. If the natives objected, I think we could negotiate mutually satisfactory agreements. Good heavens, we can cure most of their diseases, offer them advanced technology. They'd be fools not to agree."

Pierce saw the men and women in the lecture hall begin to stir uneasily. The bureaucrat had said what they had already realized, but to hear it spoken made them uncomfortable. In less than two hours, they had gone from ignorance to astonishment to rapid calculation of how to exploit this windfall. Yet they did so also knowing how the empires of the past, struggling to sustain themselves on a path of mindless growth, had destroyed simpler societies. Ishizawa had said one could not go back and murder one's ancestors, but in a sense one could. The infant American republic on Beulah was strong and would eventually grow into an empire mighty even in decay, but contact with the future would kill the republic almost instantly. How could Washington, Jefferson, Hamilton function, knowing what their fates would have been, knowing the verdict of history? How could Beulan social institutions survive the onslaught of advanced technology and newcomers determined to impose their own values?

Pierce shared the uneasiness of the others. No doubt the unTrainables were feeling the political equivalents of filial piety and parricide; for himself and his Trainable colleagues, that was not the issue. Patriotism was a fool's religion, a crude social bonding device that defeated itself by inciting violence and inviting reprisal. If Beulah could give Pierce a chance to save his people, he would seize that chance and let the Beulan Americans cope as best they could. What made Pierce uneasy was the quickness with which he had come to that conclusion.

"I understand your feelings," Ishizawa said quietly to the bureaucrat. "It may be a little premature to see

Beulah as an escape hatch. First of all, we could fill it with people to our present population levels in a very short time, and then we'd be back where we started. What's more, Beulah may have some unexpected hazards. You mentioned supplying the Beulans with cures for disease. I'll bet we lack immunity to many common diseases there, diseases that are brand new as far as our immune systems are concerned because we only have to deal with the evolved versions of them. We could spread those diseases awfully quickly and give the Beulans our diseases as well.

"I have another reason to leave Beulah alone for a while. I don't think it's the only world we can reach."

The lecture hall exploded in noise. They had sat in respectful silence through one revelation, but this one was too much. People shouted at one another and at Ishizawa, got up, and hurriedly gathered in urgent conferences. Finally they quieted and Ishizawa continued.

"We don't have much theory yet to explain what we've discovered. But it seems likely that other worlds exist at different points on the timeline, and we may be able to reach them. Some of them could be at remote points in the past, even before humanity has evolved, so we wouldn't face the same ethical problems about settling on them. Others could be in the future, and they may well have real answers to our problems."

"Wait a minute!" someone shouted. "If there are future worlds, they must have this time-travel device also, and they should have discovered us. Where are they?"

"That's what Enrico Fermi used to say about extra-terrestrial intelligence," Hans Neumann answered. "The only answer we can give you is that we don't know. Maybe we're the first bead on the string. Maybe future worlds have missed this discovery somehow. We don't know. But we propose to find out all we can. The Civil Emergency Administration has authorized Fermilab to suspend all other programs and to pursue research into hypermagnetic fields. You've been invited here to become aware of this project and to begin planning for whatever applications seem appropriate."

The bureaucrat leaped to his feet. "It seems obvious to me that this discovery must remain a secret as long as possible. It we can keep the Russians and Arabs and Japanese in the dark, we can develop an unbeatable lead in exploiting this invention. Otherwise, it'll be the arms race all over again."

More shouting broke out. Two scientists shook their fists in the bureaucrat's face, while others loudly applauded him.

Wigner took advantage of the uproar to murmur to Pierce: "The secret will be out before lunchtime. Then it'll be every country for itself. We've got to get our own field generator and stake out some territory ourselves."

"I want to go through," Pierce answered.

"You will."

The shouting died down: Johnson, the Nobel laureate, gained the floor.

"You're not going to keep this secret very long," he said. "Once a few other governments believe it, they'll want to know how to build their own fields. If we don't tell them, they may just make life uncomfortable for us in a lot of different ways. If we do tell them, they'll all be heading off for Beulah and anyplace else that Ishizawa discovers, and it'll look like the wildest nightmare of imperialism. We've got to reveal the secret, and we've got to make sure it's used wisely and humanely, for the benefit of everyone. Some kind of international control is going to be essential, and I for one intend to work to set up such a control. This is a chance to make up for all our mistakes since the Manhattan Project, people, and I don't want to throw it away."

Most of the listeners applauded; Wigner muttered: "International control my foot. No one's going to give up any sovereignty over this issue."

"Trainables don't care about sovereignty."

"Trainables have to live in the real world."

The first part of the meeting was adjourned; the second, Pierce suspected, would accomplish little but talk, and he was right. Well before the end of the day, Ishizawa and his colleagues had quietly left the lecture hall. Others, mostly Trainables, also slipped out.

"Smart," said Wigner. "These people are getting nowhere. Let's go; I've got to talk to a few people about this."

Wet snow was falling as the helicopter took them back to O'Hare through a twilit afternoon. It landed near Pierce's plane, but before he embarked Wigner took him on a short stroll across the tarmac.

"I want to get you out of Idaho and into the Agency. Is that acceptable?"

"They're my people out there, Eric."

"You'll be doing them more good than you could in your present job. We've got to be ready to move fast, and I'm going to need you."

"All right."

"It'll take a few weeks, but we should have you in place not long after the new year." Wigner looked up at the dull sky and the fluffy, clumped snowflakes drifting out of it. "'Now God be thanked who has matched us with His hour.' What an hour it is."

He clapped Pierce's shoulder and waved him off to the plane.

The next few days turned into weeks of laughter and astonishment. Each night that he visited Doria, he brought news: the first contact with the American government on Beulah, through a field generated in the basement of an Agency safe house on West 45th Street in Manhattan. (Only now the field was called an I-Screen in Ishizawa's honor.) Two new worlds discovered in a single day at Fermilab, and soon a third opened up by an I-Screen in California: following Ishizawa's lead, they too, received names from Blake's mythology. Eden was at the year A.D. 1166, and Ahania at A.D. 91. Los was at 981 B.C. More worlds were anticipated, scattered through time at points now called chronoplanes.

"Once you asked me to move you and your students out of this time," he reminded Doria. "Now you can have your pick."

Pierce lay comfortably in her bed, enjoying the scent of her skin and the softness of her hair as they talked in the darkness about what would happen next: the wonder of meeting the giants of history, the care they would take not to repeat all the ancient follies, the havens they would build in the paradises of the past.

"You pick."

"First, I want to look them all over. Then I'll pick the best one for us—for you and me, my mother, your parents."

She held him fiercely. "I can't wait."

* * *

His Polymath switched itself on, and Polly's little-girl voice called urgently: "Jerry! Jerry! Emergency message!"

It came through the wailing-wall network, and soon was confirmed by Wigner. Ishizawa had been looking for a future chronoplane, and he had succeeded. Now his laboratory was in radioactive ruins; Ishizawa and his team were all dead.

Five:

The videotapes, thought Wigner, had something of the morbid fascination of the film of the Kennedy assassination. You saw a deterministic world from which free will had been removed, where the inhabitants acted with no awareness of what was about to happen; they looked a little foolish, when they were only ignorant.

Wigner sat in his cubicle, running the videotape on his Polymath. It began with Ishizawa, in a striped golf shirt and blue jeans, seated at a control console in a large windowless lab with beige walls and fluorescent lights. Two technicians worked in the background. From the angle of the main camera, Ishizawa was on the left, with his back to it; the camera looked over his shoulder at the two-meter I-Screen generator. A digital time readout flicked on and off in the lower right corner of the computer screen.

"Okay," Ishizawa remarked conversationally into his throat mike. "This is Run 1 of Experiment 5. If all goes well, we hope to find a chronoplane somewhere in the twenty-third to twenty-fourth century. We'll turn on the generator in thirty seconds from . . . mark."

Wigner froze the scene and examined each part of it under extreme magnification from the points of view of each of the three cameras running in the lab. Everything looked fine. The technicians, a man and a woman, seemed alert and slightly excited, but not anxious or otherwise stressed. Wigner had already been over their dossiers: they were clean, with no indication of subversive or criminal backgrounds that might have induced them to commit suicide in an act of sabotage.

Another camera, mounted on the far side of the I-Screen, showed Ishizawa at the console and a small audience of hangers-on behind him: scientists, technicians, a couple of reporters, an Illinois congressman. Again, their backgrounds were so clean they were almost despicable. No one was nervous, and no one got up to leave.

Wigner skipped through the tape in three-second steps. At minus ten seconds, Ishizawa tripped a switch and leaned back. The soap-bubble film appeared in the I-Screen, its colors rich and luminous: crimson, orange, green, blue, violet.

At zero seconds, white light flared in the lab, simultaneous with a muffled bang. Voices cried out, sounding oddly distant.

The explosive decompression of the laboratory was clearly not the result of a bomb. The light, Wigner saw, had come from within the I-Screen; he even glimpsed irregular structures of some kind within the circle of glare. Closer to the camera, a mist had formed as air pressure dropped, and snakes of fog writhed toward the I-Screen. Loose objects—a clipboard, a calculator, a wall calendar, a lab coat draped over a chair, the chair itself—leaped toward the I-Screen as well.

Cutting from camera to camera, Wigner watched Ishizawa squint at the onset of the glare, then try to raise a hand to shield his eyes from the light. Behind him his watchers were doing the same. Then, in slow motion, everyone began to rise and float dreamily through the air toward the I-Screen. Ishizawa, as his feet left the floor, seemed to be groping for a switch on the console; he missed it and somersaulted toward the screen. The others were close behind him. For a few fractions of a second they blotted out much of the glare, and Wigner was able to study what was beyond the I-Screen. It seemed to be sun-baked rubble, rocks and chunks of masonry, with a little dust being stirred by the sudden gust of air from the lab.

One technician had been behind the I-Screen; Wigner turned to a camera that showed the poor woman sucked in from the other side, toward a similar terrain of rubble.

The timer on the screen indicated that the lab had been decompressed in just over three seconds. For another three, the victims could be seen twitching and convulsing before lying still. For two more seconds the I-Screen held; then it died, and a faint noise increased in volume to a scream as air blew into the lab and began to refill it.

On one wall, a radiation alarm pulsed red and a klaxon sounded.

Wigner went back to the sequence showing the deaths of the experimenters and observers. By juggling a few parameters, he was able to eliminate most of the glare and bring up details in the screen.

Now he saw a black sky whose stars were blotted out by the glare of the westering sun. The rubble was a chaotic pile of bricks, girders, and dirt, and seemed to extend to the horizon. The predominant color was a bleached yellow; the bodies of the victims were shockingly vivid in their colorful clothing and blood-splashed flesh. The congressman had evidently lived the longest and seemed to be trying to crawl back against the wind toward the I-Screen and safety. His face was a mask of blood, and most of his exposed skin was erupting with purple blisters as he finally collapsed.

The rubble was not entirely chaotic. Wigner recognized the basic structures of several familiar buildings, and even the skeletal trunk and branches of a tree, which was at that very moment growing outside the building where Ishizawa's lab had been. Wigner had no doubt that he was looking at the shattered ruins of Fermilab at a time when the Earth had somehow been deprived of an atmosphere.

He canceled the tape and ran some of the lab recordings through his Polymath. They had actually managed to identify enough stars in that sun-dazzled black sky to estimate the date: March 14, A.D. 2215.

All of Ishizawa's data were on record. Anyone could tune the field of an I-Screen to that new chronoplane, provisionally named Ulro. Wigner was aware of a project to send another robot tank through; it would learn something, but not enough. Scores of forays into that terrible place would be necessary.

The Agency already had three I-Screens in operation and three more under construction. At least one of them ought to be devoted to researching the hellworld in the future, but at the moment all were committed to exploring the past.

He sighed, hooked into the office LAN, and paged Clement to ask for an interview. Permission came at once.

Jonathan Clement's office was large and well furnished, with windows overlooking East 52nd and Lexington, and Ben Shahn prints on the walls. To Wigner it seemed bare and awkward because it lacked anything alive; Clement did not like houseplants.

He was a strikingly handsome man, Wigner admitted to himself. Six feet tall, age forty-six but looking more like thirty-six with the taut musculature and quick movements of a racquetball player. An intelligent man, within his limits, with a Columbia Ph.D. in political science to go with two degrees from Yale. All hopelessly obsolete now, of course. But his biggest weakness was not that he was too old to be Trained; it was his hostility to Trainables themselves.

That hostility radiated gently from Clement as he sat barricaded behind his desk. The two men had much in common: social class, education, family backgrounds in public service, a whole spectrum of shared attitudes and experiences. Yet they counted for little against the single difference of Trainability. Clement's nonverbal antagonism overrode the geniality in his words.

"Good morning, Eric. You've reviewed the tape."

"Yes. Sabotage is out of the question. Ishizawa just opened the wrong door."

"Poor man. May it stay shut forever."

"Oh, I don't agree, sir. If something disastrous is going to happen between now and 2215, we certainly ought to know more about it."

"Hazardous, Eric. Hazardous."

"Of course. But if we can find out what caused the disaster, perhaps we can prevent it."

"Eric, we have limited resources. We've had to shut down almost a dozen programs to pay for the I-Screens we now have. They're fully committed to exploring the downtime chronoplanes."

Downtime. At least Clement picked up quickly on the jargon.

"For the time being that's certainly sensible. Before two long, however, we should turn our attention uptime."

"No doubt," Clement said. The man, thought

Wigner, had a marvelous ability to turn you down while agreeing with you. "In any case, thank you for reviewing the tape. There was something else as well?"

"I need a recruit seconded to one of our New York proprietaries. An Alpha-18 named Gerald Pierce."

"Oh, yes. Fellow out in Wyoming?"

"Idaho. He's the T-Colonel for District 23."

"Mm. You even invited him to the briefing at Fermilab, didn't you?"

Clement was paying attention to the paperwork. "Yes, sir. I've been following Pierce's career. He's a remarkable young fellow—lots of brains, plenty of physical courage, and the common sense to know when physical courage is beside the point. I think we'll be able to use him very successfully on missions through the I-Screen."

"I realize you're biased in favor of Trainables, Eric, but surely there must be a *few* unTrainables out there who'd make good agents. After all, we got along without any Trainables for two generations and more, didn't we?"

Yes, and look at the mess we're in now, Wigner thought as he nodded soberly in answer to Clement's remark.

"I'm keeping my eyes open, sir. In the meantime, I like this fellow's looks. His dossier has been filed for your review."

"I'll look it over when I find a moment. Meanwhile, I'd like an update on the People's Action Front for this afternoon."

The poor old PAF is finished, Wigner answered silently. *Even if it had half a million armed members, it'd be irrelevant. Bloody fool.*

"Have it for you by two this afternoon, sir."

"Don't rush it, now; do a good, thorough job."

"Of course."

In a cool rage, he walked out and headed for Jasmin Jones's cubicle.

"Lunch?"

"Where?"

"Pietro's."

"Let's go."

They left the building and walked down East 52nd. At Lexington, a shabby old man stood on a kitchen chair, shouting to anyone within earshot that the end of the world was coming because of nuclear testing and a falling away from Jesus. He had a sizable crowd, large enough to attract the attention of two policemen with holstered Mallorys and nightsticks in their big fists. Wigner and Jaz skirted the crowd just as the police moved in and began prodding people.

"Best news some people ever heard," Wigner remarked.

"Including you."

"Ha!" True enough. Well, he wouldn't be interested in her if she weren't bright and observant.

Pietro's, thanks to its connections with the Agency and other government organizations, still had a considerable menu. Those connections ensured that Wigner and Jaz were given a booth in the rear. They chatted casually, ordered saltimbocca, and raised glasses of wine to each other.

"I need your opinion of the Ulro phenomenon," he said.

"Little old men on street corners?"

"Middle-aged men in corner offices."

"Hard to persuade."

"Persuasion shouldn't be required."

"We're all having trouble coping with the news. Some of us try to blank it out."

"You?"

"Ignore things and they go away," she said with a smile. "Besides, we've got two hundred years."

"Cute." Meaning her facetiousness was inappropriate.

"What's your attitude, then?"

"Making friends. Influencing people. Eliminating the middleman."

Jaz smiled. "Exciting! You sound like a take-charge guy."

"No. I just go with the flow. The flow is uphill, but papa wants to go downstream. I need more paddlers. Want to come along?"

"My heart belongs to Daddy, Eric."

"You're too charitable."

"He has his talents, we have ours. He's still in charge."

"I'll say no more."

"Neither will I."

As the saltimbocca arrived, Wigner reflected that he could have done worse. He hadn't recruited Jaz to his new network, and she had confirmed her loyalty to Clement, but she had also slipped in a nice little option clause that would let her buy in later if she wished, on condition that she not advise Clement of Wigner's activities and attitudes.

They slipped into a more public mode of conversation, gossiping about relatives and swapping rumors. The discovery of the chronoplanes had been made public only a few days before Ishizawa's death, and that could not be covered up, so the world was uncertain what to make of events. Jaz had learned of several millennarian groups springing up all across the south; some were camping out on hilltops and waiting to be raptured by Christ. Wigner had a report that several universities were pooling resources to build their own I-Screen. That seemed to be pushing free enterprise entirely too hard, and Jaz agreed. He had also heard of a Pentagon faction under a General Pendlehurst that was arguing for using I-‛ reens as weapons against the Soviets and Arabs.

"The idea is to ship nuclear weapons back to Beulah or Eden, transport them to Moscow and Baghdad, and then build a new I-Screen and toss the bombs through."

"How do you manage to ship nuclear weapons across the Atlantic and Europe in the eighteenth or twelfth centuries?" Jaz objected. "Not to mention everything you'd need for an I-Screen, including the power."

"When you care enough to send the very best, someone will come up with a vehicle. But it shows how out of control people are getting. With the bad news from the future, we can't afford clowns like Pendlehurst any more. Nationalism is dead."

"Oh, you sound so trendy," she sighed.

"The Iffers are more than a trend, my love. It's our big chance to get everything back under control." In the wake of the discovery of the chronoplanes, the International Federation Movement had sprung up; the glimpse of Ulro had strengthened it. Latest Agency estimates put its membership at over 100 million; even the Soviets and Arabs were afraid to hinder it.

"Whose big chance?"

"Yours and mine. And anyone else with enough sense to see what has to be done."

"Which is?"

"Surrender of sovereignty to a central world government, with representation on the basis of gross national product divided by population. Then we can start developing the chronoplanes in some kind of orderly way, instead of claim-jumping and trying to toss bombs at one another."

"Beautiful dreamer. I'd never have taken you for an idealist."

"Sensible of you. If we go on as we have, I get nowhere. In an international federation, I get everywhere."

"I'll watch your progress with interest."

Doria refused to spoil their last evening together by weeping or complaining. It had been a fluke, falling into an affair with a boy, really, discovering that at a certain time and place they offered each other some comfort and pleasure. She was seven years older than he, old enough to know that they could not have lasted much longer together in any case. His leaving would only put a clean end to it, she told herself. And then she could look around for a man her own age, with eyes that didn't mask secrets, whose dreams didn't make him gasp in his sleep.

Pierce came over and made dinner—poor man's spaghetti, with a vegetable sauce—and they talked cheerfully about nothing in particular: school problems, a knife-fight at Hometown Mall, the TV interview last night with George Washington. They agreed Washington had not been very articulate.

After dinner they sat by the fire drinking Spanish brandy and not saying much.

"I'm going to miss you," she said quietly.

"It's going to be lonely."

"You didn't have to take the job, did you?"

"I think I did. They can use me better back east, and I can help make sure the right decisions are made."

"And how will you do that," she said with a smile, "with a couple of tear gas grenades?"

"You guessed my secret. No, it's just a matter of being close to what's happening. Most of the I-Screens are back east, and they want me to go through a few of them."

She couldn't keep from asking: "Are you going to be back here?"

"Maybe. I hope so, but I'm not sure." He read her feelings in her closed eyes, her embarrassed smile. "I like you too much to lie to you, Doria. If I can come back to you, I will. If I can't, I can't."

"I understand. It's okay." She leaned against him, put her head on his shoulder, and enjoyed the heat of the fire, the solidity of his body. Enjoy them while they last, she thought. They don't last long.

"General Pendlehurst?"

"Speaking."

"I'm, uh, an admirer of yours, sir. I represent a consortium of firms in the defense field, and we're very impressed with your quick response to the opportunities that have recently arisen. Uh, am I making myself clear, sir?"

"Yes, I think so. How did you get this number?"

"Mutual friends, sir. Well, sir, we're aware of the controversy over your suggestion, and we can see how political pressure could put you in an awkward position. We're interested in backing you up and giving you all the help you require, including financial aid, sir."

"Well, I appreciate that, Mr.—"

"Brown, sir. Richard Brown. Uh, General, I realize how a conversation like this can be misunderstood if it's monitored. Believe me, we have no desire in complicating life for you. Would it be possible to meet with you personally to discuss matters in more detail?"

"Well, Mr. Brown, I suppose so."

"Would you be free for dinner this evening at the Washington Plaza?"

"I think so. About 8:00 P.M.?"

"Excellent! I'll be with a couple of associates in Suite 1020. I think you'll remember them from '82."

"Indeed! Well, it'll be old home week, then."

"It sure will! Well, thank you, sir. We're looking forward to this evening."

Pendlehurst was a tall, erect man with close-cropped white hair and oddly droopy eyelids. Wearing a three-piece blue suit under a camel's hair overcoat, he entered the elevator at the Washington Plaza. He pressed the button for the tenth floor. The elevator rose smoothly to the third floor and stopped. The doors slid open and Pierce walked in wearing the black suit and gold nametag of a floor manager. General Pendlehurst smiled absently at him. Pierce smiled back, pressed the button for the ninth floor, waited until the doors closed, and shot Pendlehurst in the left ear with a Mallory at Impact 5: hard enough to drive the flechette into his brain, but not hard enough to rupture the skull and make a mess.

On the ninth floor he hauled in a waiting trolley that normally carried fresh linens in a heavy canvas bag, and dumped the corpse into it. The elevator descended to the subbasement, where Pierce pushed the trolley out and down a corridor to a parking garage with a loading bay. The trolley went into the back of a black Ford van with magnetic signs on the sides:

VERSATILE CLEANING SERVICES, SILVER SPRING, MD.

Pierce took off his jacket and stowed it in the trolley. He pulled on a heavy gray cardigan sweater lying on the front seat of the van. Then he got in, started the engine, and drove out of the parking garage into the sleeting January night.

"It's certainly been lively," Wigner said. March drizzle fell steadily outside Pierce's Bleecker Street apartment.

"You're a master of understatement," Pierce said, tossing him a can of Tuborg. It was worth twenty-five dollars in the stores, if you could find it, but the Agency looked after its own.

Wigner was comfortably slumped on Pierce's couch, with his feet on the teak coffee table; Pierce settled into the armchair by the window. The apartment was furnished in Salvation Army modern, and Wigner was gratified to see five or six houseplants, including a healthy young avocado. He felt comfortable here as he did not on East 52nd, and he expressed it in a manner of speaking that Jaz Jones would have found prolix.

"Great times we live in, old son. Six downtime chronoplanes and promises of more to come. Colonists screaming to be allowed to emigrate to the wide open spaces. Chiliasts howling about the coming of the Lord. It's almost enough to let you forget the people starving in the subways and the mutiny of the 101st Airborne."

"Never would have happened in District 23."

"I'm sure. We've also managed to forestall at least one putsch, and the other factions in the Pentagon are biding their time."

"Pendlehurst was no putsch."

"No, but his disappearance was food for thought for a gentleman on the Joint Chiefs of Staff, and life has been happier since his decision to retire."

"You know Senator Cooledge has gone over to the Iffers."

"Yes, isn't that wonderful news! Brilliant woman. California is clearly ahead of the country on the International Federation issue. We will do what we can to smooth her path. But we are a long way from moving the whole country. The bureaucrats are against us; most of the politicians are against us. Two centuries of cheap jingoism are against us. The IF has an unpleasant Third World aroma to many of our fellow-citizens."

"But we have Ulro on our side."

"Ulro. The tank went through yesterday at Fermilab."

Pierce's eyebrows rose. "Did it?"

"Without incident. The chamber was evacuated, of course, and it did acquire a little residual radioactivity. Otherwise, no problem. It's programmed to travel east to the lake and then return."

"They must have learned a little more already."

"Mm. The vacuum's not quite as hard as they'd thought... What could have removed the *atmosphere*? I've done a couple of physics courses this winter, just to have a basis for speculation. Didn't matter, it's still beyond me."

"The media are full of alien invader stories."

"And they could be right. If the aliens see our tank, let's just hope they're ignorant of I-Screens."

Pierce snorted. "You're not serious."

"I give aliens a very low probability, but not zero. The public likes the idea a lot. We'll have to respect their anxiety if we're going to explore Ulro as fully as we should. It will be easier when one of the Agency I-Screens is assigned to Ulro."

"Has it been?"

"Not yet. I'm hoping the tank will tell us enough to make our ignorance all the more painful, especially to Clement." He sipped his beer. "And I want to be in charge of that I-Screen, at least part of the time."

"Why?"

"Curiosity. About a great many things."

Pierce looked at the ceiling. "How Ulro was destroyed."

"Of course."

"What happened before it was destroyed."

"Ah. Especially what happened between, say, 1990 and 2010—our present happy spot on the timeline."

"And to whom it happened, and why."

Wigner raised his beer can in silent homage. Then he asked: "Why should the Beulans be the only ones to benefit from hindsight?"

"Is it a benefit?" Pierce was thinking of poor Washington, preserving his dignity at the price of his speech while cameras stared into his florid face and confirmed that he wore wooden teeth: Washington who already knew he would become the president of his country, and who must already wonder if the task was worth it.

"Of course."

"We could also find out about ourselves, you know."

"So we could. I'd love to know how I turned out."

"I don't know. Suppose you learned that you'd married someone, had children, grandchildren. That'd all be changed, even if you knew who the woman was. It'd be like being robbed of a life."

Wigner lighted his pipe; he no longer thought it

made him look more mature, but he had grown fond of it.

"All those lives were snuffed out, Jerry. And the billions who might have followed them, for all eternity. Perhaps on Ulro Eric Wigner and Jerry Pierce were happy fellows who had good careers and beautiful wives and fine children. They're all dust now. Happiness on death row is all very well, but it doesn't postpone execution. Besides," he added, "on Ulro we may have been miserably unhappy and dead before we were thirty."

"Indeed," Pierce agreed with a smile, thinking: It could happen on Earth as well.

"In any case, we certainly won't waste time on egocentric searches for our own dossiers. I'm thinking about much more prominent people in the government, and in whatever government would have followed this one. Who won, who lost, why? Who had unpleasant sexual tastes, who took bribes, who made mistakes?"

Wigner puffed his pipe, filling the room with the aroma of Rattray's Red Rapparee, and looked out the window at rainy Bleecker Street. People hurried down the sidewalk in groups, almost never alone, while a three-man army patrol stopped some at random for ID checks.

"We're going to save the world, old son," he said with a chuckle. "You and me and a small circle of friends. But to do it we're going to have to whack some people's balls as they've never been whacked before."

Six:

When the Fermilab I-Screen came on again, the tank had been waiting. Radioactive as expected, it did not return from Ulro; instead, it launched a shielded canister of tapes and photos through the screen. Copies were soon in Wigner's possession.

In addition to containing an I-Screen, the Agency safe house, on West 45th between 10th and 11th avenues, was now a training center as well. Behind its decrepit facade the five-storey apartment building was now a complex of labs, briefing rooms, dormitories, and offices. In one office, Wigner and Pierce reviewed the tapes and the reports based on their data.

The tank had moved east from Fermilab across a flat terrain of glassy rubble, avoiding occasional hillocks of drifted debris. Approaching Chicago through the suburbs of Wheaton, Glen Ellyn and Lombard, it had found the terrain scoured bare and baked.

"It looks to me as if the western suburbs were never rebuilt after last year's riots," Pierce suggested. "At least not substantially. So the disaster just cleared everything, blew it away to the north somewhere."

"'Effects are consonant with a heat flash and blast wave moving from south to north,'" Wigner recited from one of the reports. "Trouble is, the effects should have dropped off exponentially from wherever ground zero was, but they don't."

"A line of H-bombs?" Pierce suggested.

"Seems likely," Wigner agreed.

"I wonder what New York will be like."

"Much the same, I'm afraid."

If the Agency was not yet exploring Ulro, others were. Within days of the tank's survey, five I-screens opened up on the dead chronoplane. Two were in North America, two in Europe, and one in China. All sent probes through: two American tanks carrying men, two modified French cruise missiles, and one small Chinese rocket that was launched two hundred kilometers straight up, sending televised images back through the open I-Screen for almost three minutes.

The data, as they came into the house on West 45th, were fragmentary and often enigmatic, but they formed a clear enough pattern.

On April 22, 2089, the world had been at peace. To some extent it must have been a peace of exhaustion, Pierce believed, because vast stretches of the planet's surface had been abandoned after a series of wars and upheavals early in the century. The population had fallen from six billion in 1995 to just under one billion in 2015, with most of the fatalities due to famine and biological warfare. Most nation-states had disappeared by 2020; after two decades of warlordism, a new kind of society emerged to dominate the planet.

The terms for it varied: Groups, Arrays, Collectives, Systems. Whatever the term, the new societies were highly regimented and technically advanced beyond the dreams of the late twentieth century. Many of those who survived the fall of the old order had been Trainables. They had inevitably gained power, and their new societies had reflected Trainable concerns. UnTrainables were used for menial tasks not worth automating, and otherwise allowed to amuse themselves with sports, drugs, and nonreproductive sex. They were the minority now; the Trainability gene sequence had been identified, and four out of five children of Trainables were also Trainable. (An apparently popular theme in the literature of the period was the domestic sorrow of rearing an unTrainable child.)

By 2089 the population had climbed to three billion and stabilized there. Reclamation projects were underway on the desertified Amazon basin, on halting the disintegration of the West Antarctic ice sheet, and on bringing the planet's mean temperature back down to mid-twentieth-century levels after a century of increasing greenhouse effect. A lunar base had been established, and another on Mars was having difficulties but surviving. The horrors of the first decades of the century were receding. The plagues, the revolutions, the martyrdoms, the famines, and warlords were now the stuff of entertainment for the younger generation.

That much, at least, was comprehensible. Many of the objects brought back by the manned expeditions were inexplicable scraps of a technology based on unknown principles. A few written records had been retrieved, most of them in an elliptical form of English with a substantially changed vocabulary; they were ambiguous at best, baffling at worst.

Pierce and Wigner studied photos of one object, a fist-size glossy black teardrop with a small yellow symbol embossed on it.

"They can't even tell if it's damaged or not, or how to turn it on," Wigner said. "If it can be turned on."

"Could the symbol be a logo?"

"Maybe." Wigner puffed his pipe and smiled. "Suppose an eighteenth-century spook like Fouquet was handed an electronic camera with no explanation.

Would he have any idea what it was, how to operate it, what it could do for him? That's how I feel looking at that object."

Nothing, out of all the data retreived and derived, indicated that Ulro had known anything about I-Screens and chronoplanes, or had any reason to expect catastrophe. The physicists were unhappy about that, although Ishizawa himself had suggested that "Heisenberg cascades" could work from the quantum level to influence events in different ways on different chronoplanes.

The cruise missiles and the Chinese rocket had provided a glimpse of a world as strange and dead as a Jovian moon. Only traces of water could be found on the surface, evidently frozen out of the atmosphere at night and then restored by sunlight to the thin haze of carbon dioxide and methane that served for an atmosphere. The dead sea bottoms were basins of evaporites, gray wastes of salt beds and dried ooze; the continents were predominantly pinkish-brown, evidently from rapid oxidation in the superheated atmosphere before its deoxygenated residue had been blown into space.

Only the rocket had found the worst mark of the disaster: a belt of chaotic, fused terrain about three thousand kilometers across, apparently running clear around the planet on the equator.

Wigner and Pierce, in their darkened room, studied the Chinese tapes and reports; Pierce had even taken two days off to learn Chinese, rather than risk losing something in translation.

"Something hit us," Wigner said. "Not an asteroid or comet. Looks as if we've been turned on a lathe."

"Good comparison," Pierce said. "The Chinese theory is a beam of some kind of energy. It hit us somewhere in the Pacific Ocean, just off Ecuador and moved west. The first strike vaporized the ocean under it, and then it just kept on going. Where the ocean had been, the sea bed was molten, so water coming in was also explosively vaporized. Even as far north as Batavia, the shock wave was strong enough to tear everything apart."

"Like an atmospheric tsunami."

"Of superheated steam. At least it was quick. Probably no one was left alive within twenty-four hours. But they estimate the energy beam was locked on us for seventeen days, going over more or less the same track. By that time the oceans and icecaps were gone as well as the atmosphere, just boiled away at well over escape velocity. The rocks under the beam were liquefied by then; some of the atmosphere that's there now was boiled out of the crust.

"Then the beam just quit." Pierce brought up a frame showing part of the southeast Asian coast and Hainan Island. Beyond their recognizable coastlines, the chaotic terrain extended far to the south. Even without computer enhancement, the terrain showed a distinct boundary line, running roughly north–south. "That seems to be the spot. Since then, the whole surface has undergone severe earthquakes and volcanism. The sea beds are all rebounding, and the fusing of the crust along the equator temporarily locked a number of tectonic plates. They've started breaking apart again."

"And that's the source of the atmosphere."

"The main source. Outgassing of carbon dioxide and methane."

"And the radioactivity."

"Right. Some came from space, but most was just

the scattering of naturally occurring isotopes buried in the crust."

"Do you think the bases on Mars and the moon could have survived?"

"No. The tank teams listened for signals. Nothing."

Wigner turned up the office lights. "You said you wanted to go through to Beulah. Does it alarm you that I want to use you on Ulro instead?"

Pierce shrugged. "It alarms me, sure. But it's more important than Beulah right now."

"It's more important than anything else in the world."

"You have a bee in your bonnet about Ulro," Clement said affably to Wigner. They were in the rear booth at Pietro's enjoying pene all'arabbiata.

"I know, I know. With everyone going crazy about the downtime chronoplanes, I'm really out of step. But it's a chance to sneak a look at the end of the story."

"How so?"

Wigner privately reflected that a nation that promoted its intelligence officers on the basis of their looks, taste in sports attire, and prep schools deserved whatever it got.

"Remember that old phrase, 'He's history'? To the people on Ulro, we're history."

"I'm aware of the gist of what's been found there, thank you." Clement looked pained. Wigner ignored the sarcasm.

"The downtime worlds are going to be extremely useful to our political masters," Wigner said. "But they still have to live in this world, which is unfortunately full of bad guys. We know who a lot of the bad guys are, but some of them are thoroughly unknown to us. They may be doing us a lot of damage right now, and we won't know until it's too late. Or they may be planning some very nasty moves, and we'll be caught flatfooted. The bad guys' reward will be to go into the history books of the twenty-first century. Our reward, if we find out about them first, will be to nip them in the bud." Amazing how a conversation with Clement could sink so rapidly into cliché.

Clement bought time to wrestle with the concept by spearing a bit of pasta. He nodded energetically.

"Okay, an interesting point. We could, in theory, learn some useful stuff. But how are we going to find it? It'll be like finding a needle in a haystack."

"It'll take a lot of preparation, I admit. But we know where our main repositories of information are in New York. We can assume that the Agency on Ulro maintained the same repositories until the collapse of the United States in 2011. They're deep in the bedrock of Manhattan Island, among other places, and they very likely survived the catastrophe. If we can get through the surface debris, we can find the whole script for the next decade or two. All the leaders of the People's Action Front. Who's been funding the Wabbies. Which of our own people are working for the Soviets or the Japanese."

Clement had either grasped the concept in its totality, or he had caught a red pepper between his teeth. He stared into the distance for a few seconds.

"It would certainly make our lives easier, wouldn't it?" Clement said at last.

"Much."

"Give them something to think about in Langley."

"Especially if we could hand them six or seven spies all at once, and the Wabbies' fundraisers."

Clement's eyebrows rose as he nodded again.

"Okay, I'm sold. Young Eric, you have a head on your shoulders."

Better there than up my ass, Wigner thought.

Spring was late as always in Taos, and snow had fallen on the first flowers. The Sangre de Cristo Mountains blazed white in the sunshine. Pierce and his mother Annette walked downtown to the plaza. She was a tall woman, her graying brown hair cropped short, with a long stride and a smile as dazzling as her son's.

"Not much like the old days," she said as their feet squeaked and crunched on the snow. "Hardly any skiers any more. The artists have all starved or moved away. And not many tourists."

"It'll get better soon."

"God, I hope so. I'd sure like a job again." She was living on her late husband's pension from the New Mexico State Police, and what Pierce sent her every month.

They walked past the old Piggly Wiggly supermarket, and his mother reminisced about the days, before he could remember, when you could buy anything you wanted in there and the parking lot had been clean and shaded by huge cottonwoods. Then the squatters had drifted in, and the food-stamp program had turned into rationing. Pierce remembered it when the market had become dim and shabby, patrolled by armed guards, but even after it became Federal Footstuffs Dispensary 1207, everyone still called it the Piggly Wiggly.

The plaza was almost deserted except for three or four Apaches in heavy blankets. The last effort at sprucing up the shops must have been over a decade ago, and the plaza looked sad.

"You never really explained how you got this new job," Annette said as they windowshopped past forlorn craft displays of pots and weaving and watercolors.

"Met a guy who knew about the opening. He thought I'd work out, and I did."

"He must have some clout, to get you out of the army."

"I'm not out. I'm seconded. What the army calls TDY."

"And what exactly have they got you doing TDY?"

"Reading a lot."

"C'mon, Jerry, you can tell your poor old mom."

"No, really. It's a research project for the government, and that's about all I can tell you."

"It's okay? Really okay?"

"It's okay. Actually, it's kind of interesting. And it pays better than the Idaho job."

"Man, that blew my mind. My kid running a whole district, like a state governor or something. Weren't you ever scared?"

"Sometimes. It was a lot of work."

"You should hear the rumors about *our* T-Colonel. Little sawed-off Chicano guy. He sounds like a real bastard."

"That's the best kind."

She laughed, and he enjoyed the sound of it. They went into a drugstore (the name had stuck, though all drugs were now sold only in federal pharmacies) and browsed through the magazines and paperbacks. The racks seemed quaint to Pierce. He was already used to fichemongers' shops in New York, where Trainables could pick up such materials in microfiche strips for flickreaders.

"All this stuff about the chronoplanes." Annette

was scanning the newspaper headlines. "They're talking about people emigrating to Eden, can you believe that? And those other places. Never catch me doing that."

"Why not?" Pierce was surprised.

"I like it here. No drugstores in the eighteenth century."

"It's pretty nice, actually. Clean air and water, good soil, no toxics."

"Leave it for the pioneers."

He bought her a few magazines and a big bar of chocolate.

"Remember the time we got mugged for our groceries?" she said with a laugh. "That goddam Pete Gomez and his little gang. And I'd paid three damn stamps for a chocolate bar. It was supposed to be our big treat."

"I remember." He'd been too young and weak to protect her. The memory still burned.

"I saw his mother a few weeks ago. Poor Pete joined the army and got killed in Venezuela."

"Cheaters never prosper."

"Jerry! What an unforgiving bum you are."

"It's the secret of my success. Don't you remember he mugged us again the next week, and we didn't eat for two days, and you cried?"

"Yeah, I guess so. Those were lousy times for everybody."

"Jerks like Pete helped make them that way."

"Aw, come on. He was a kid. A hungry kid."

"So was I."

"Let's go home and make some lunch, hungry kid."

Pierce regretted what he'd said, and made an effort to be cheerful and positive. He had come here, after all, to make sure he saw his mother at least this once before he went through to Ulro. No point in being unpleasant while he was here.

He was having bad dreams about Ulro.

For Jasmin Jones, lunch with Jonathan Clement was no perfunctory matter of popping down to Pietro's to eat pasta and gossip. Instead, they walked west to the Museum of Modern Art on West 53rd to tour the exhibits before adjourning to a Greek restaurant nearby.

Jasmin restrained her impatience; Clement insisted on spending up to two minutes in front of works that she understood in seconds. *Guernica* required a reverent three minutes; Jaz passed the time by reviewing everything she knew about Picasso, which was a great deal.

The current main exhibit was a holographic retrospective of the works of the old avant-garde Swiss sculptor Tinguely. He had specialized in odd little machines, running on asynchronous gears, that rolled about in unpredictable ways and attempted to destroy one another or themselves. Jaz thought they were delightful, and the holograms themselves were beautifully sharp and lifelike reconstructions of machines long vanished.

"If a machine can be lifelike," she murmured.

"Sorry?" said Clement.

"Nothing, just marveling at the machines."

"Great fun. The old modernists got more enjoyment out of their work than today's artists do."

"Too bad Tinguely never built his freeway machines."

"I hadn't heard of them."

"One was supposed to roll down a freeway, painting an abstraction on the road. Another was supposed to follow, erasing the painting."

Clement chuckled. "He didn't build it because we already had the patent."

Jaz burst out laughing. "That explains so much."

Their cheerful mood persisted through a lunch of Greek salad, satsizi, and lamb souvlaki. Clement told stories about his early days in the Agency and dropped a few juicy bits of current gossip. Jaz offered nothing in exchange except her wide-eyed and appreciative attention.

She was curious to know what Clement's agenda was: if it was sex, she was half tempted to accept because she considered him sexy, and half tempted to refuse because it would complicate her job. Come to think of it, accepting would complicate her job also.

Over coffee, he settled back and asked: "How are you enjoying your work these days?"

"I like the technical challenges, and I try not to think about the implications of the information."

"Good attitude. How about your colleagues?"

Tactful choice of words, she thought. Made her sound more professional. "I like everyone. They're good people."

"The best. I'm really lucky to have you all. But I've got one problem there."

"Eric."

His eyebrows rose. "Why do you say that?"

"Eric's a little impatient with unTrainables."

"Well, you hit the bull's eye, Jasmin. For some people Trainability is a blessing, and for some it's almost a curse. And I'm not one of these no-brow bigots, believe me—far from it. We paid too high a price for that stupidity in the riots."

Jasmin nodded. She had been just a kid during the worldwide anti-Trainable riots a few years back; she hadn't even been old enough to be tested. But she remembered the two girls who had been lynched at Santa Monica High; one of them had lived two blocks away.

"Only it's more than impatience," said Clement. "I worry about the boy because I'm afraid he's getting in over his head."

"Ulro?"

"Oh, he's probably on the right track there; we should be finding out what we can. But he's taking on more responsibility than he can handle. Hell, he recruited some T-Colonel from out west, got me to hide the guy in some proprietary, and now he wants to send the guy through a screen to Ulro. I kind of admire his ambition, but if anything goes wrong it'll reflect badly on him. Maybe even abort his career."

So, Eric was really doing something to make friends, influence people, and eliminate the middleman. "Why not yank his chain a little?"

"I *don't* want to discourage initiative. Not for a minute. Eric's aggressiveness is one of his best qualities. He even reminds me of me when I was his age, all guts and no brains. The last thing we need, especially these days, is a bunch of yes-men and timeservers. The last thing. But I also don't want something to blow up in my lap. So you could help me—and Eric—by keeping an eye on him. Find out what he's thinking, what his motives are."

Jasmin looked him straight in the eye, knowing that the impact of her big blue eyes could unsettle any normal heterosexual male. He looked straight back.

"Jonathan, are you asking me to spy on Eric?"

"Jasmin, I certainly am."

"All right."

He nodded, smiling faintly. "I'm not asking you to do a Mata Hari. Just keep in touch with him, be a sympathetic listener, encourage him to share his feelings."

She nodded and smiled. "I already do."

To his credit, he didn't try to pump her about what feelings he might already have shared. "Just keep me posted from time to time. And speaking of time, we'd better get back to the shop."

They walked back in bright spring sunshine, through sparse crowds. These days most people ate close to work, or in the office; the street beggars were more persistent all the time and often got violent. Four Black youths followed Clement and Jasmin for half a block, asking half-heartedly for change. Clement finally tossed them a five-dollar coin, just to be rid of them.

"God," he murmured, "I can't wait to move all the jigs downtime. Solve eighty percent of our problems."

Seven:

Training with a capital T was a method of
drills and drugs that enabled Trainables to absorb vi-
sually obtained information at extremely high rates,
and then to retrieve that information at once and in
perfect detail. Training with a small t, simple kines-
thetic programming, was still a matter of time-consuming practice.

Through much of the spring and early summer,
Pierce was in training. He spent several weeks in
Houston's NASA facilities, accustoming himself to
working in a Newtsuit, a rigid carbon-fiber diving suit
modified for use in near-vacuum.

"You're going to bump into too many pointy objects," his trainer told him. "A fabric suit wouldn't
give you enough protection. Besides, the Newtsuit can
carry a lot more shielding."

Armored, he plodded across dusty plains and up
rocky gulches while monitoring scores of readouts
around the inside of his helmet. Armored, he dug
through stony soil with picks and shovels, while the
inside of the suit stank of sweat and urine. Armored,
he drove a tank over rugged terrain and from within it
he operated the tank's backhoe to take apart piles of
broken concrete and dirt without triggering slides or
cave-ins.

Off duty, he socialized very little with the training

staff; instead, he retreated to his room with his flickreader and the latest information from Wigner about the chronoplanes.

Eleven of them had now been found downtime, scattered from the late eighteenth century to 73,000 years before the present. Four were in historical time: Beulah, Eden, Ahania in the late first century A.D., and Los, almost a thousand years before Christ. Albion, over 8,100 years before Christ, was in the early stages of the agricultural revolution. The rest—Orc, Luvah, Urthona, Vala, Thel, and Tharmas—were in various phases of the last ice age.

The photographs and tapes from the first exploring parties showed worlds of marvelous beauty: the glaciers on Urthona looming mistily above the Atlantic where Long Island would one day be; the wind blowing through the tall grasses and groves of the Sahara on Orc; the vast redwood forests on Los, extending from central California to Puget Sound; mammoth herds trooping across the muddy steppes of central Asia on Luvah.

Few of the first parties had contacted the natives— endochronics, they were now called—but telephotos showed small hunting parties on some chronoplanes far downtime. A band of Neanderthals had been positively identified in southern France on Thel: they were taller than anyone had expected, warmly dressed in fur and leather, and they wore their platinum-blond hair in long and elaborate braids. A Cro-Magnon tribe on Luvah was spotted hunting aurochs in Poland. The hunters were tall, brown-skinned, and handsome; their naked skins were elaborately scarred and painted, and their hair hung down their backs plaited with eagle feathers.

Contacts with endochronics on the historic chronoplanes were being made as carefully as possible. The Americans on Beulah were already deep in a political crisis because of the arrival of the first explorers from Earth. A German expedition to Eden in the twelfth century had opened negotiations with Frederick Barbarossa to allow scholars to study his government and society. For the time being, Ahania's Mediterranean region was declared off-limits to exploration: no European government wanted contact with the early church fathers of the first century A.D. for fear of political repercussions on Earth.

Doria wrote to him from Mountain Home: *Everybody's talking about going downtime, but most people want somebody else to go. They want the Wabbies and the PAF to be plunked down in the twelfth century to make life miserable for the Indians. Boy, I wouldn't want to go if those guys were my neighbors. The kids in school talk about Doomsday, about how weird things look on Ulro. A few of them get upset by what they see on TV, but most just shrug it off. I guess 2089 is a long way away to a bunch of fifth-graders.*

The emigration issue was growing. Pierce suspected Doria was right: apart from some back-to-nature types and every historian, anthropologist, and archaeologist in the world, most people preferred to stay on Earth regardless of their troubles. Many people wanted to use the downtime chronoplanes as a dumping ground, or as the ultimate survivalist hideout; others warned against the impact that colonization would have on endochronic cultures.

The Iffers, increasing in strength, were calling for no emigration except as directed by an international authority. So far, that had provided national governments with a convenient excuse to do nothing, although the Americans, Soviets, and Japanese were accusing one another of planning national emigration programs. The media were full of disinformation, and governments had put security clamps on much of the data from uptime and downtime alike. For Trainables, however, the data flow continued unimpeded.

Pierce and Wigner talked every couple of days on a secure circuit. Near the end of the Houston course, Pierce said he wanted to talk with the men who'd gone through to Ulro.

"Not available, old son. They're both psychologically upset and undergoing treatment."

"Wonderful."

"They lacked your assets. First, they had no specific program to fulfill; their job was just to go through and find whatever they could. Second, they were on Ulro much too long. You'll be there only a few hours."

"And you're going to pump me full of tranquilizers before I go."

"Maybe."

"When am I going to meet my backup?"

Wigner paused. "Ah, that's a dicey problem. You have no backup, old son."

Pierce's pause was twice as long. "That's crazy."

"I agree. We're spending well over twenty million dollars on this project, and it's all down the toilet if something goes wrong."

"I'd better pray it goes wrong on this side of the I-Screen," Pierce said dryly.

"I could tell you how bitter I am about this, Jerry, but you wouldn't believe me. Clement keeps shrugging and saying yes, what a false economy it is, ain't it awful, but that's the way Langley approved it."

"And you bought it?"

"Not for a nanosecond, old son. It means Clement is hoping we'll succeed and make him look good for endorsing the project, but he's also hoping we'll screw up and make me look bad for starting the project. Office politics, I'm afraid."

Pierce thought for a moment. His personal safety was not in extra danger because of this; he knew the specs of the tank's systems and had no reason to expect them to fail under Ulro's conditions. The danger was to Wigner's project and to his career.

"Is Clement likely to encourage a failure?" he asked at last.

"Sabotage? No, that's spy novel stuff. Anyway, Clement's smart enough to know that sheer entropy can do more harm to your enemies than active intervention."

"Well, we'll just have to do it all right the first time."

"Precisely, Jerry."

Late in July Pierce was back in New York. The summer was even worse than last year's, an endless succession of what were now called ninety-ninety days. The city sweated through the heat and humidity, welcoming the frequent thunderstorms despite the floods and blackouts they brought.

On one of the hottest days, when the sky was dirty white and air conditioners whined and failed, Pierce walked north along Broadway, following a parade.

He had known it was planned and had gone out to get a look at it out of curiosity and interest: curiosity as to how the authorities would handle it, and interest in how many people would turn out.

Within minutes of seeing the parade, he showed his

military ID card to a policeman on a motorcycle at 15th and Union Square.

"Where's the CO of march security?"

"Up around 35th, Colonel. They're trying to keep level with the middle of the march."

Pierce's eyebrows rose. "So the parade must be at least forty blocks long."

"Be longer before it's over, sir. They estimate Washington Square's still got a hundred thousand people waiting to start."

Pierce strode north on the sidewalk, sweat trickling down his bare legs and sticking his T-shirt to his chest. The marchers filled Broadway, extending north and south in ragged ranks. He paced alongside, looking at the police and soldiers lining the route. One mistake, one wrong order, and everything would go wrong.

The marchers weren't sullen hicks like the Wabbies in Mountain Home, looking for a fight they didn't have the guts to pick themselves. They were very ordinary-looking people, many of them young, dressed in shorts, T-shirts, light summer dresses. They carried few signs, but everyone seemed to be wearing a ribbon or sash of rainbow-colored cloth. Dozens carried rainbow flags, the stripes running from red at the top to violet at the bottom. This was the first major Iffer demonstration in New York City, and Pierce estimated close to two hundred thousand people must be taking part.

Despite the heat and glare, the marchers seemed cheerful, lively, a little impatient. They stepped out of ranks to buy soft drinks and ice-cream bars, or to take each other's picture. An occasional marching band filled the humid air with old tunes from Broadway musicals. The only really strange thing about the marchers was that they carried no American flags, no flags of any nation.

They scared Pierce, because he knew they must scare the government. He walked faster, until he finally found an armored personnel carrier parked at Times Square. The security CO, a round-faced major with a bristly moustache, greeted Pierce civilly.

"Heard you might be on your way, Colonel. What can I do for you?"

"Just keep things as cool as possible. Whatever you do, not a shot, not a drop of Mace, not a single violent thing," Pierce said. The major nodded.

"Know what you mean, Colonel. Funny thing, though. Five years ago, these folks'd be traitors and we'd be kicking their ass. Now I'm damned if I know what the hell they are."

Pierce walked back home, watching the marchers flow north under their rainbows and their terse signs —LET'S GO; IT'S TIME; THE WORLD NEEDS US. The bystanders on the sidewalk seemed reserved, amused, sometimes baffled, sometimes hostile. But no one shouted insults, no one threw a bottle. Looking in the eyes of the hostile ones, Pierce could see why: the size and mood of the demonstration were powerful deterrents. That would change in time, he suspected. Reaction would come, probably a violent one. No social system dies quietly.

At home he watched the TV newscasts, ignoring the announcers' bias, and when the broadcasts were over he looked out his window and rejoiced that no one had been hurt, no one had been shot.

Early the next morning, before the sun had risen too high, Wigner picked Pierce up in an Agency Ford and took him uptown. They went up Broadway, the

Ford's red license plate sticker enabling them to slip quickly through the roadblocks. The car's air conditioning wheezed.

"See the parade yesterday?" Wigner asked as they drove through Times Square.

"Some of it."

"Most impressive. Nothing like it since the days of Martin Luther King. All those Iffers marching through here to Central Park, in filthy hot weather. A hundred thousand, I heard."

"That was a low estimate."

"No doubt. Senator Cooledge made an excellent speech. We may be at a cusp."

"A cusp?" repeated Pierce, willing to play the straight man.

"A radical change in direction. At some point in the middle ages, one serf too many decided to light out for the towns, and feudalism was finished. Yesterday, we had thousands of people marching to demand a reduction in national sovereignty. Perhaps it's true, you know, that a dying culture seems most vigorous in its death throes. Chivalry was at its peak when the urban businessmen already owned the rural nobility. Nationalism was in its glory when we were kids, and now it's on its way out."

"Not a minute too soon, either."

"Indeed."

Wigner parked the Agency Ford in the basement garage of a twelve-storey apartment building at Riverside and West 84th.

"We own the building," he said. "The tenants are all Agency people. The first three floors are actually offices and storerooms. This is the upper basement. Below this is where they're building the I-Screen. And the subbasement is also the access to the repository."

They left the garage and walked out onto Riverside Drive. A squad of joggers—running together for mutual protection—was just coming out of the park a block away, but otherwise the neighborhood was deserted.

In shorts and T-shirts, Pierce and Wigner could have been joggers, too, but they only walked across the drive and into the park.

"The tunnel runs under the street and down the hill to the repository," Wigner said. Pierce, looking around at the terrain, nodded. "It's about a hundred and fifty yards west and ten feet down."

"Why here?"

"We needed someplace in the city that wouldn't be buried under too much rubble in a nuclear attack, so that meant a park. We already had this building, which turned out to be really convenient. There's an old abandoned tunnel under here, used to be part of the water system. We sealed off a thousand yards of it and put in some extra reinforcing. I'll take you down and show you the layout in a little while."

"So, I bring the tank through, move north about a hundred and fifty yards, and start digging."

"No, you'll probably have to dig first. We're assuming the screen will open onto rubble. We'll do two quick reconnaissance openings before you go through, and adjust the location of the screen if it'll do any good. But then you're on your own."

"The screen's not likely to stay stable for more than a minute or two."

"I know. Means you may have to dig yourself out a couple of good scrapes at a time while we turn the screen on and off. But we did a computer simulation," Wigner added helpfully, "and figured out where the buildings probably fell. The I-Screen's being located with that in mind, so you shouldn't have too much trouble."

They walked a little farther downhill along a cracked asphalt path, past a deserted and vandalized playground. The trees and shrubs were luxuriant in the humid warmth. Traffic on the Henry Hudson Parkway, on the western edge of the park, was sparse and mostly military, and the river was empty. Across the Hudson, the Spry sign was barely visible through the smog.

On the edge of a long, narrow lawn, Wigner stood and pointed north.

"That rocky outcrop might be your best landmark. Just to the left of it, just to the west, is about the farthest point in the tunnel where we're still storing files. The north-end wall of the tunnel is maybe two hundred yards farther north." They walked up the lawn and sat on the outcrop: black Manhattan schist.

"I reach here and I start digging," said Pierce. "I cut a trench from about there"—he pointed a few yards to the west—"into the tunnel. Then I go into the tunnel and find the Daily Executive Briefings and the Senior Personnel Files for the next ten years, and I bring out as many of them as possible. Then I hop in the tank and come back to the transition site."

"You'll have exactly four hours."

"And I'll have thirty seconds to a minute to get back through the screen."

"Yes. On foot."

"Because of radioactivity?"

"In part. A bit awkward to decontaminate a tank." Wigner looked embarrassed. "But we can't just leave it there and use it again for the next expedition. People in Washington seem to get their most reliable intelligence from the *National Enquirer.* Some of our masters appear to believe that the catastrophe was caused by an alien invasion, and that the aliens might still be there."

Pierce sprawled across the rock, laughing silently.

"It's true, Jerry. Some of them are even scared to send the tank through at all. They're afraid it'll leave tracks or be spotted. So, when you get back to the screen, you have to activate a bomb that'll blow the tank into nice little pieces no alien monster would ever notice."

Pierce stopped laughing and sat up. "Are you serious?"

"I wish I weren't." He shrugged. "Politics, old son."

"It's crazy."

"Crazy? If people find out that we're opening an I-Screen to Ulro here on the West Side, with twenty thousand people living within a few blocks, *then* you'll see crazy."

The city government knew nothing about the Agency's Riverside Drive building except that it housed federal VIPs and had suddenly acquired the need for a great deal more water and electric power. Extensive remodeling to the subbasement was also necessary. Sooner than go through municipal red tape, Wigner saw to it that several officials were placed, as the phrase had it, on retainer. Among other services, they provided detailed maps and engineering data on all underground facilities on the upper West Side. Pierce reviewed them carefully.

The computer simulation had been accurate; two quick checks showed the I-Screen, oriented to the southwest, opened very close to the local Ulro surface. A gap of about two feet showed at the top, and simply opening the screen caused convenient landslides of rubble into the transition chamber, widening the gap to five feet. Radioactivity was a nuisance, but a manageable one; the infallen debris was shipped to a nuclear waste disposal site in Vermont, and the chamber decontaminated without difficulty. Nothing leaked into the rest of the building or the neighborhood.

On the first Sunday in August, in a pouring rainstorm, a tractor-trailer rig delivered the tank. It was the same one Pierce had trained on in Texas, and he was glad to see it again.

It was, however, a tank in name only, designed to Agency specifications by a consortium of International Harvester and McDonnell Douglas. With its backhoe arm and low-slung body, it looked, thought Pierce, like a scorpion. The cabin, mounted between two eight-foot caterpillar treads, was covered by a Plexiglas canopy with its top painted over to shield the driver from the sun. Power came from an array of batteries and solar panels capable of running all the tank's systems for twenty-four hours straight, even through a night on Ulro. The tank was painted in camouflage shades of yellow and beige and rust—the better, Pierce supposed, to deceive genocidal aliens still looking for survivors on a dead planet.

Pierce himself drove the tank down the ramp to the subbasement and into the transition chamber. There it squatted with only inches on either side and ten feet between it and the ring of the I-Screen. That, said the engineers, would give Pierce enough room to dig a passage. Pierce, sitting in the tank, hoped they were right. He had unpleasant fantasies about being jammed halfway through the I-Screen when the field broke down.

* * *

The night before the mission, Pierce stayed home in his apartment on Bleecker Street. He tried to call his mother in Taos, but the phone system was down all over the southwestern United States. He called Doria, and found her grading papers. They talked happily and inconsequentially for a few minutes before he said good-bye and promised to call again soon. He did not mention what he was about to do.

Wigner was a passable cook and sometimes invited RSD people for dinner. This evening he'd had four of his colleagues, all Trainables but none in the network yet. One was Jasmin Jones, and he was pleased to see that she volunteered to stay and help clean up. The others tactfully excused themselves.

"So you're boldly going uptime tomorrow," Jaz said as she dried dishes.

"Thank God, I thought we'd never get around to talking shop. No, I'm boldly going uptown. Jerry Pierce is doing the rest."

"I'd like to meet him someday. How did you ever find him?"

"District 23 suddenly enjoyed a low crime rate, domestic tranquility, improved church attendance. My Polymath couldn't believe it, so I looked into the matter. It was all true, and Jerry Pierce was the T-Colonel."

"So you're going to throw away this paragon."

"Nonsense. He's going to Ulro because he's got guts and he's coming back because he's got brains."

"With the dossiers on the spies we haven't caught yet."

"If there's any justice in the world."

She looked solemn. "There wasn't any on Ulro."

"They died that we might live, dear. Would you like to be part of the analysis team?"

"With the Ulro data? Eric, you sweet man."

"It may be disappointing," he cautioned her.

"Never. But why ask me?"

"You're a good analyst."

"Lots of us in the woodwork, and I'm not one of your gang."

"True. I need a degree of credibility with our revered elders. A semblance of working for the greater good, not my own greedy self. You are one of my biggest nonfans, so I want you on side."

"A figurehead."

"Much more, Jaz."

"I believe you're serious."

"Yes."

"Then I accept your kind proposal, sir."

"You have made me the happiest dishwasher in the world."

The I-Screen team totaled fifteen men and women, but in the wide space of the subbasement they seemed few and scattered. Pierce came through an airlock; the ramp to the parking garage was sealed off, and so was the existing tunnel to the information cache, over on the west wall. The air had an unusual metallic smell. The transition site was on bottled air now; nothing would circulate between the subbasement and the outside until any radioactive contamination had been dealt with.

Wigner accompanied Pierce across the floor to a dressing area where a woman technician helped him into the Newtsuit. It was painted a dazzling white; the suit would be easier to keep warm at night than cool in the daytime. He spent half an hour checking out the suit, and another half an hour dealing with a small problem in the communication systems.

Six technicians and two engineers had gone over the tank in detail all night long. Pierce walked to the transition chamber, shook hands with Wigner and a few other people, and went inside. The chamber still held air, and the voice of Project Control echoed around him as well as murmuring in his headset.

"We'll begin the checklist whenever you're settled, Colonel." He had a strong Brooklyn accent; Pierce thought it made the man sound intellectual and sophisticated compared to his own New Mexico twang.

"Fine." Pierce climbed to the top of a tread and released the catches holding down the Plexiglas canopy. He lowered himself stiffly into the driver's seat and buckled himself in. Only then did he pull the canopy back down and seal it.

"I'm sealed and suit air is working fine."

"Very good," said Project Control. They ran through a long checklist of tank and suit systems before Project Control said: "Transition chamber evacuation beginning now."

A gauge on the dashboard registered rapidly dropping air pressure outside. Within the cabin it remained normal, but if Pierce left the tank the air would evacuate and he would have to refill from a small reserve.

"All right, Colonel Pierce. We'll have the field up to strength in about thirty seconds. As soon as the screen is up, be ready for a few rocks to bounce in you."

"I'm ready."

Project Control counted down the seconds, interrupted by Wigner's shouted "Good luck, old son!" At zero seconds the I-Screen swirled with soap-bubble colors. Dust whirled up as lumps of rock and concrete suddenly rolled through the circle. They were gray in the tank floodlights, but above them Pierce could see a harsher glare, and above that a chord of blackness: the sky of Ulro late in the afternoon of a spring day in 2089.

Moving the tank over the tumbled rock, he extended the backhoe and rapidly scraped rocks and masonry down into the transition chamber. In a minute and a half he had a ramp dug to the outside.

"We can sustain the screen another 45 seconds," Project Control said. "Are you ready to go, Colonel?"

Sunlight glared in his eyes through the faceplate filter. "I'm gone," Pierce answered, and steered the tank forward and upward.

Eight:

In the rearview mirror, Pierce could see the transition chamber, its floor strewn with rubble. Then it vanished, replaced by an irregular crater in the side of a mound of bricks and concrete: the ruins of the apartment building.

He guided the tank over a low ridge of broken bricks. The sun, sinking toward the west, glared in his eyes through the canopy and faceplate and made it hard to see the terrain around him. He steered right, down toward the park, and was at last able to see where he was going.

To his right, the tall rampart of the apartment buildings on Riverside Drive was gone, replaced by a long moraine of dusty debris. Beyond it he could glimpse occasional hillocks, standing out clearly in the near-vacuum: ruined highrises on West End Avenue and Broadway. The moraine had the same eroded look of the ruins of Chicago, the result of the atmospheric tsunami on Doomsday. The shock wave had struck Manhattan from the southwest, blowing over thousands of buildings like so many sand castles.

To his left the park was a smooth hillside, dotted with rocks like a Martian plain, running down to the great fragments of concrete: the shattered highway. Beyond was the bed of the Hudson River, darker and smoother than the yellow-beige of the park and ruins.

He could see far up the river, but saw nothing where the George Washington Bridge should have been. The Palisades across the riverbed were a black horizontal of shadow below sun-gleaming spikes at the top of the cliffs. The Spry sign was gone.

Pierce found himself beginning to hyperventilate. He leaned back and relaxed, and remembered to start describing what he saw and did for the tape recorder. Murmuring into his microphone, he swung the tank farther right and headed along the slope. The rocky outcrop where he and Wigner had sat was clearly visible, rising out of yellow soil and sharp-edged pebbles. The hum of the electric motor and the crunch of treads rolling over rock made the tank cabin noisy, but at least he didn't have to put up with the constant chatter of trainers as he had in Texas.

He glanced up at the black sky, unable to see any stars at first and then spotting a few to the east, away from the glare of the sun. Even after the Chicago tapes, the sky seemed unreal and made everything else look false as well. He felt for a moment as if he were simply driving across some kind of film set, that the rocky hillside and the moraines of ruins were some art designer's concept of the end of the world. He did not say so for the recorder.

Then he was positioning the tank for the dig, and concentrating on the job. The backhoe extended smoothly and struck the surface; a metallic rasp vibrated through the tank body to the cabin.

"Soil's very hard," he said, knowing that the camera would have shown that already. After three more attempts, he had done nothing but disturb some of the surface rocks and the top inch or two.

"Dryness and heat seem to have severely compacted the soil and rock," he remarked calmly. "I guess water freezing and evaporating near the surface has kept it relatively loose, but below that it's like brick. Moving twenty yards south to see if it's any better."

It wasn't. Pierce extended the tank's drill and began to punch a hole into the rocky soil. Blasting would be time-consuming, but the possible need for it had been anticipated.

After twenty minutes, the drill failed. It had reached less than a foot below the surface, and the top of the repository tunnel was ten feet down.

The air in his helmet tasted sour. The shadow of the tank was lengthening: soon the sun would be down and he would have to operate by floodlights. For a few minutes more, Pierce scraped at the surface with the backhoe and then abandoned the effort.

He sipped a little water and reviewed what he knew about the repository and the terrain. The old water tunnel had been walled off by the Agency, and the north-end wall was only a couple of hundred yards beyond the rocky outcrop where he had begun digging. If he could get into the tunnel somewhere along its length, he could blast through the wall with ease.

Perhaps even that wouldn't be necessary; the original access tunnel might still be open, concealed under a thin layer of rubble. Pierce drove back to his starting point, to the dimple in the moraine, and did some experimental clearing. At first nothing happened. Then he managed to pry out a couple of blocks of concrete, and the loose bricks below them were easy to remove. Rapidly he cleared a broad stretch running roughly north from the transition point. The access tunnel had been only a few yards from the transition chamber; he ought to be able to cut across it.

The shadow of the Palisades crept over the site as

the sun went down. Pierce swung around in his seat and saw sunset: a slight oranging of the yellow-white disk revealed the vestiges of an atmosphere, and a brief rainbow arc appeared in the black sky just as the sun went below the horizon. Evidently some water vapor was still up there, ice crystals in what remained of the stratosphere.

With the sun down, the tank's radiation counters showed a sharp drop. His trainers had told him to expect it; from the earlier expeditions, it seemed likely that the planet's magnetic field was very weak, the Van Allen belts were gone and solar radiation, from X rays to infrared, was pouring unimpeded to the surface of Ulro.

He switched on the floodlights and kept digging. Ice crystals gleamed outside the canopy, and he saw the faintest web of hoarfrost on the upper surfaces of the tank. With each load from the backhoe, a little dust fell and drifted in a thin carbon dioxide wind.

Pierce realized he had dug right through the tunnel when the backhoe scraped against its floor. Clearly the tunnel had collapsed; it would not give him entry to the repository.

Without stopping, Pierce spun the tank around and drove back down into the park. Something gleamed in the floodlights: a battered but recognizable metal toy truck. He mentioned it for the tape, but his mind was elsewhere: on the maps he had studied of the tunnels, sewers and conduits under the upper West Side. Somewhere up around 96th Street there had been a sealed-off access door to the old water tunnel. If he could find it and the tunnel was intact, he could walk back to the repository, blow the wall, and reach the records.

The tank crunched steadily along. On the dashboard, his mission clock recorded elapsed time: he had been on Ulro for almost two hours. The radio receiver, automatically scanning dozens of wavelengths, reported only silence and occasional static. The odometer recorded about half a mile from the transition site. Here the terrain was different, barer, with more recognizable landmarks: concrete shapes that had once been park benches, a short stretch of shattered brick walkway, and then, unexpectedly, a crumpled vehicle lying on its side. It had no wheels, but otherwise looked much like an ordinary compact automobile.

And there, in the floodlights, was the manhole cover. Nothing obstructed it except a couple of pebbles and a film of hoarfrost. Pierce spoke quickly and calmly into the recorder, explaining what he planned to do. Then he gathered the items he would need, put them into a chest pack, and clipped it to his suit.

"Ready to pop the canopy," he said, and did so. The air in the tank puffed out in a cloud of ice crystals, glittering against the blackness. Pierce clipped the audio recorder to his suit also and gave the holotape recorder a farewell wave. Then he stood up and climbed carefully down from the tank.

"I've got one hour and forty-five minutes," he said. With a geologist's hammer he levered the manhole cover up and away; the lamps on his helmet and belt showed the shaft clear. Without pausing, Pierce let himself down the ladder. At the bottom he was disoriented for a moment, until the helmet compass showed him which way to go: north again, about two hundred yards, to the door connecting this storm sewer to the water tunnel.

This tunnel had suffered some damage, and he stumbled over chunks of fallen masonry in the darkness. The only sounds, apart from those of the suit systems, were those he made scraping against the sides of the sewer. Pierce carefully counted his steps and wished the suit contained a pedometer. He might overshoot the doorway—

No. Here it was, sealed tightly, the handle spiky with tiny frost needles. He put his hand on it, pushed down, and it swung open effortlessly. Pierce laughed briefly; the sound inside his helmet was unpleasant.

About sixty yards more now, down a gentle slope. It looked unscathed, the light fixtures in places. Ahead was the door to the water tunnel.

"Stuck." He used the pointed end of the hammer to try to pry it open, and got nowhere. Out of the chest pack came two 150-gram discs of plastic explosive. He placed them on either side of the lock and imbedded their detonators. Then he plodded back up the tunnel and through the first door before detonating them. The tunnel flared with light. Pierce walked back down through rapidly settling dust. The door was open, but he had to pull hard on it to make enough space to get through.

"I've got an hour and thirty-two minutes."

And now he was in the water tunnel, tilting his head back to see the roof thirty feet above. The far side of the tunnel was fifty feet away, and the floor was covered with a layer of fine gray sediment.

The sediment had footprints in it.

Pierce stopped and very carefully detached his belt lamp. Holding it with both hands, he swept it back and forth, up and down the tunnel. The footsteps began right at the door to the storm sewer, and went south into the darkness. Part of his mind wanted to describe them on the tape, but he could not make his voice work.

Slowly he stepped out onto the sediment, feeling it give slightly beneath his feet. The prints he made were much sharper than the others. He walked south, holding the lamp in one hand and the hammer in the other. Inside the suit, he was sweating.

Something ahead reflected light. Pierce stopped and swung the lamp back and forth, producing more reflections: glints of color against the gray sediment and black rock of the tunnel walls. They seemed to move, but he was certain the movement was only the shadows caused by his lamp.

He moved forward. When he was fifty yards from the reflecting objects, he knew they were humans, and dead.

Six of them lay scattered in a line near the east wall of the tunnel: four adults and two children. They wore the glossy clothing Pierce had seen in some of the pictures retrieved from Ulro. Their skins were yellow-brown, drawn tautly over their bones: they had been mummified here. Strewn for yards around them were bags of leathery material, now crumbled away and revealing more clothing, some plastic containers, a piece of burst metal that might once have held water. In the shirt pocket of one corpse, a flickreader nestled.

The bodies seemed to be screaming.

Pierce knew it was only the effect of dessiccation, the muscles and skin contracting and pulling the jaws apart. Most showed signs of broken bones; all had bled from ears, nose, and mouth. They had probably died instantly and painlessly, seeking shelter where there was none and dying in the same moments as everyone else in the city. But they had found a tomb that would preserve them.

He turned away and walked quickly south. The sediment here was free of footprints, though in a few places a stone block had fallen from the roof of the tunnel.

"One hour and twenty-two minutes," he muttered.

The tunnel seemed to have no end. Then the floor showed a change of color up ahead: the pale institutional blue Pierce had come to associate with the Agency.

It was the north-end wall of the repository, and it would not have to be blasted; from somewhere farther south, air had been driven into the tunnel and forced northward like a huge piston. The wall had been torn loose and scattered in fragments for fifty yards.

So had a false ceiling fifteen feet above the tunnel floor. It was strewn across the rows of filing cabinets that filled the repository from wall to wall. The cabinets' weight and closeness had preserved them from destruction; despite the mess, the repository looked very much as it had when Pierce and Wigner had visited it.

The cabinets were locked, but Pierce had an array of master keys. Choosing a cabinet at random, he found a key that opened it. Inside, the drawer was packed with the crumbled residue of cardboard boxes and very ordinary-looking microfiches. An index tab indicated that the drawer's contents dealt with Central Asian Economic Documentation, January–April 1995.

He left it and began moving down an aisle between cabinets, flashing his light on each drawer. Within a very few minutes he had found what he was looking for: Daily Executive Briefings, the intelligence summaries prepared for the White House. They filled three cabinets, and dated back to the 1950s; Pierce found those for the early twenty-first century. They ended with the summer of 2007.

A year's briefings made a sizable handful, even on microfiche. Pierce shoved the briefings from 2007 into his chest pack, then worked backward toward the turn of the century.

His secondary goal was harder to achieve. For over twenty minutes he scanned other cabinets until he found Senior Personnel Documentation, 1980—; he opened it and took the files for 2000 to 2004.

"Forty-five minutes."

He had what he had come for. Pierce turned and strode back north, marveling at his luck. The shock wave that had blasted through the repository must also have sealed the tunnel within a second or two. Compression within the tunnel must have heated the air somewhat, but the heat pulse from the energy beam had not reached this far, saving the tunnel from the intense heating that had sterilized the surface. A heat pulse through the repository would have melted the microfiches into solid lumps.

Again he came to the six dead Ulrans. They had had enough warning to seek shelter, and their luck, too, had been good. The shock wave must have killed them instantly. Others had no doubt found deeper holes and had lived to roast alive, or to suffocate as their air reserves were used up. Perhaps a few had survived the seventeen days of cataclysm and had communicated with the lunar and Martian bases. But what could they have said to one another?

His own breathing seemed unnaturally loud in his ears, and the suit systems whirred and clicked in unpredictable rhythms. He slowed to a cautious pace, keeping his lamps trained on the east wall so that he wouldn't miss the door to the storm sewer. God, if he overshot he could go for miles through this place. What if his lamps burned out? Perhaps he'd better keep one in reserve. He turned out his belt lamp, then turned it on again at once. The tunnel was too black without it.

The LED readouts around the rim of his helmet

faceplate were reassuring glows of orange and green, telling him that this was not the only world, that living people were close, that he was not really the last man in the world even if he was the only man on this world.

"Ah. Here we are." The door! He sidled through it awkwardly, afraid of snagging himself. Imagine being caught here, unable to move forward or back. He would have to use the geologist's hammer to shatter his faceplate and end it quickly. Now he was through and the tunnel was clear. He quickened his pace.

"Thirty minutes. My God." He was pushing it. Easy: remember it was only a mile back to the transition site, a twelve-block jaunt. No problem except getting bored waiting for the screen to come on.

Up the ladder. On the surface. He stood and caught his breath for a moment, then leaned down and pulled the manhole cover back into place. *Requiescat in pace.* He remembered his stepfather's funeral, the banal finality of dirt falling on the cheap coffin. At least his sky had been blue and rich with clouds.

Pierce looked up and grunted. The sky was a blaze of stars, more than he had ever seen on even the clearest nights in New Mexico or Idaho. The tank's hoarfrost gleamed in starlight; the machine silently waited to take him back to safety and light and air.

"Twenty-six minutes and boarding for the return trip," he said. Into the cabin, down into the seat, seal the canopy, something was wrong—

The instrument panel lights were out.

The tank was dead.

Pierce reset the circuit breakers. Nothing. Something had failed for good. Maybe he could find the cause in thirty-six minutes and maybe he could even fix it, but that would do him no good at all. For all he knew, the tank's self-destruct was still in perfect running order; it was set to go off thirty minutes after the I-Screen came back on.

Grimly, he yanked the holotape and put it into a pouch at his waist. He unsealed the canopy once more, pulled himself out and jumped recklessly from the tank tread to the ground. Again a moment of disorientation: which way was south? He found it, then checked the suit compass for the first time on the trip. Its digital readout was three zeros, intermittently flashing random numbers. Not enough magnetic field on Ulro.

Pierce set out across the stony terrain. The tank had not left much of a track, but the lamps threw encouraging ellipses of light ahead of him and he could see a few landmarks. He passed the toy truck and was tempted to bring it with him. But this was no place for souvenirs; the toy would be radioactive.

"Nineteen minutes." He seemed to be making good time. Maybe he'd walk right through without breaking stride. Wigner would be amazed at the material. It would give him unheard-of leverage, undreamed-of power. The bad guys were in trouble, all right.

"Twelve minutes." He came to the futile scratches he'd put in the ground by the rocky outcrop. Less than four hours ago. It seemed like years. He could see faint tracks left by the tank, and he followed them up the slope of the hill to the crater in the side of the moraine. Eight minutes to spare.

Pierce stood and breathed deeply, shivering a little. His underwear was soaked, and his feet were getting cold. The tank had been designed to survive twenty-four hours, and it had failed in less than three. His suit would keep him alive only a couple of hours under these conditions, unless one of its systems also failed.

The thermometer registered minus 90 degrees. All

the heat absorbed during the day was being rapidly lost.

Transition time came. The I-Screen did not open.

"Come on, come on," Pierce said. He stamped his feet to try to warm them, and the bricks slid away. Staggering, he regained his balance. "Come on, come on!"

The moon, three-quarters full, rose over the moraine. Pierce saw his shadow extend across the rubble.

He was the only living thing on the planet, unless somewhere, in some pitch-black sealed cave, a few spores awaited resurrection. Above him was the sky, full of stars and a moon that looked exactly as it always had. Below was the dark land, dry and dead, silent forever. No, not forever. The volcanoes still shot their gases and stones into the emptiness, and eventually after millions of years this world would have an atmosphere again. Millions of years. This world would be born again, scarred and crippled, but he would not.

Something caught his eye. He looked up, trying to find it amid the stars. There it was, a bright spark, a little blue-white star that twinkled.

But the stars didn't twinkle here, not in near-vacuum. And the stars didn't move so quickly, nor from south to north.

A flash glinted in his helmet's rearview mirror, and Pierce spun awkwardly around to see the fading glow of the explosion that had destroyed the tank. A moment later he felt the thump under his feet.

Oh Christ it went off and they're right overhead they must have seen it they'll know I'm down here come on come on open it come on—

The I-Screen opened again four hours and thirty-two minutes after Pierce had first gone through. He lurched down the ramp of rocks and bricks toward the beckoning lights, through the screen. It must have winked out at once; he could hear the scream of air pumping back into the chamber, and then see the sudden high-pressure jets of water and detergent shoot at him from the ceiling and walls. The chamber disappeared in a frothing swirl of bubbles across his faceplate, and he could feel the jets drumming against his suit.

After a moment or two he decided he needed to sit down. He was shaking too hard to stand.

Nine:

"No, I do not consider the mission a failure," Wigner said calmly.

Eight men and one woman looked at him from around the long table in the Research Services Division meeting room. Summer rain was falling silently from a yellow-black sky beyond the windows. Jonathan Clement, chairing the meeting, sat at the far end of the table; the others, all from Langley, were clustered near him. Each had a cup of coffee and a bulky agenda. Wigner sat alone, dressed in a sober blue suit with a maroon tie. He was item four on a fifteen-item agenda.

"I can understand your point of view, Eric," said one of the Langley men. "After all, you did send your man through, and he got back alive with something."

"He got back with a great deal, considering the condition of the repository. We're working on the data now, and we think it'll be extremely helpful."

"I'm sure it will be," said the woman, smiling. "But we're not exactly getting advance warning of Pearl Harbor, from what I understand."

"That remains to be seen, Muriel," Wigner replied. "We've given the microfiches only a quick review so far. Deep analysis will tell us much more. I have no doubts about that." He kept his tone aggressively confident, just the far side of defensive.

A tall, sallow man looked pained. "I hope you're right, Eric, but frankly it just looks like in-house gossip. We didn't have to travel to the twenty-third century to find out that Phil Warden sleeps around."

The others burst into roars of laughter: a Langley in-group joke. Wigner smiled uncomfortably.

The woman spoke up again. "We think you showed a great deal of initiative and imagination in mounting this project. And luck as well. It could have been much worse, yes? Well, even so, we must consider the results. Something over twenty million dollars spent, almost half our divisional research budget, much of it on a piece of high-tech junk—excuse me, Eric, I have to say what I think—that failed miserably. A young agent who appears to be highly competent, very nearly killed. And he's now undergoing rehab up in Woodstock, I understand."

"Yes."

"Poor man. Let's hope he recovers."

"Dr. Franklin says the prognosis is excellent."

The sallow man cleared his throat. "Eric, we're not ganging up on you. You had a very good idea, and you pushed it through masterfully. Masterfully. I wish we had more young people like you. So, I recommended that your project go ahead, although I had my reservations, because we need to encourage ambitious, aggressive young guys. I know Jonathan feels the same way."

Clement grinned and nodded.

"But we haven't become the kind of organization we are by ignoring facts," the sallow man went on, his voice lilting almost musically. "The facts are that mounting an expedition to Ulro is a damn dangerous business with not much return on the investment. We're better off leaving it to the universities and the military, and picking their brains afterward. The Administration is much more concerned about the downtime chronoplanes, and with good reason. We can *do* something there. On Ulro—" He shrugged.

Wigner leaned back, elbows on the armrests of his chair, fingers steepled. He paused for a moment.

"I could argue, I suppose," he said quietly. "I'm still convinced that Ulro is a critically important area, especially for us. But you're right, Dr. Benson," he said to the sallow man. "I hope I can face facts, too. For the time being, Ulro is low priority, and I accept that. At least we took a shot at it, and I thank you all for giving me that opportunity."

The others shifted cheerfully in their places, smiling faintly at one another and at him. He smiled back, a little ruefully.

"Now the question is what to do with our Young Turk," Clement said happily. "How long will the data analysis team need, Eric?"

"Probably not more than a couple of days."

"No, I suppose not. Hard to spend more time than that over six microfiches, even if they are from the future."

"Tomorrow's *Times* would have been a lot more helpful," said a fat man who had been silent so far, and everyone chuckled.

"For the lottery numbers or the horses?" Eric asked, smiling.

"Let's not be distracted, please," Clement said. "Any suggestions, Eric? Want to go back to straight political analysis? God knows you're good at it."

Wigner studied the table. One beat. Two beats. "Actually, Jonathan, I think I need a change. I'd like a couple of weeks' vacation and then something new. How about something in economic analysis, maybe with Semiotronics?" That was the proprietary that had hired Pierce as a systems security man.

Clement's dark eyebrows rose, as if an unexpected idea had been put to him. Wigner watched him struggle to keep from smirking.

"Well, I don't know. We'd hate to lose you here, and I'm not sure you'd be entirely happy there. Lot of busy work, you know, lot of paperpushing."

"Jonathan, I'm not the fire breather you think I am. You gave me a chance for a hell of an adventure, and I learned the hard way that I'm not really cut out for it. I think I need to sit somewhere quiet for a while, someplace where I won't get into so much trouble."

He stared at the table and allowed his lips to twitch just a little: the fair-haired boy confronting his own inadequacy.

They chuckled understandingly. Clement nodded slowly, looking reluctant.

"Well, let me think about it, Eric. Is there anything else you'd like to say? No? Anyone else? Then thank you, Eric. And thank you for your constructive and positive attitude. We all appreciate it."

Wigner stood up, smiling, and excused himself. The people from Langley smiled and waved, then turned their attention to the next item on the agenda before he was out the door.

Please don't throw me in that ole briar patch, Wigner thought.

Two days later, Wigner was back in the meeting room, in the same chair. At the table were the four other members of the data analysis team. Since all were Trainables, they had no need for bulky agendas; each had only a flickreader and a plug-in keyboard linked to the office's central computer. Although they all worked on East 52nd, this was the first time they had met as a group. Rather than crowd into someone's cubicle, it had been easier to communicate by LAN.

"I've got a draft," Wigner told them, booting it up on the pop-up screens set into the table. "Take a look."

They read silently at their varying rates, their faces impassive. For about half a minute, the only movements were fingers tapping silently on keyboards. Wigner monitored the revisions they were suggesting, accepting most of them.

Jaz Jones was finished first. She rubbed her eyes and shrugged sympathetically at Wigner. Seconds later the other three were done as well.

"Good enough," said a plump young man in a loud sport shirt. "I added a couple of minor things, but you got the whole thing down right."

"Yes," said Jaz. "I just wish we'd had more material to work on."

"Me, too," said Wigner with a sour smile. "Hell, with no access to current personnel files, I already knew about three of the alcohol problems."

"Nice to know we're gonna run a successful operation in Lisbon in 2004," the plump young man said.

"Except we won't need to now," Jaz replied. "God, how could they be so dumb?"

Everyone understood her to be referring to the senior staff whom Wigner had met two days before.

"Gotta be more there," said a teenager with a curly black beard. "Odds on. Even with the repository trashed, he got this in a few minutes. Go back there for a day—wow."

"Someday," Wigner sighed. "Anyhow, thanks for your help."

"Word is you're getting a lateral arabesque," said the teenager.

"A change is as good as a rest."

"It's not fair," said Jaz quietly. He winked at her.

"Not just the six microfiches," the teenager said. "What's in 'em."

They all nodded and frowned. Wigner shrugged.

"The content wasn't that much of a surprise either," he said quietly. "We've been projecting the fall of the Emergency government for months. Admiral Bannister was the likeliest one on the Joint Chiefs to stage a coup, and he's no friend of ours, so, of course, the Agency got shaken up."

"Dismantled," said the plump young man.

"At least he doesn't seem to be thinking about a coup here on this chronoplane," Wigner observed. "Be interesting to see how the I-Screen has influenced events."

"Still," said Jaz, "it wasn't a picture the committee was happy to see."

"Would you like to see a photograph of your own corpse?" Wigner asked.

"Yes," she retorted instantly, "if it gave me a clue as to how I died. These guys just aren't thinking it through."

"Please, Jaz. You'll provoke me into saying something I'll regret later. Maybe, with a little time to think, they'll have second thoughts about Ulro."

The meeting broke up. The plump young man suggested dinner at Pietro's, but Wigner declined. He had too much work to do.

The whole business was a dangerously near thing. The power failure delayed the reopening of I-Screen, and Wigner came as close to losing control as he ever had in his life. While the techs cursed and shouted, trying to get power to the transition chamber, Wigner paced outside it, glaring at its blank steel airlock door. He was already wearing a radiation suit, and he slapped his gloved hands against the crinkly metallic fabric. Perhaps he should have worn a Newtsuit instead; it simply hadn't occurred to him that a screwup like this could have happened. If the screen opened and Pierce wasn't there, or couldn't come through, the whole point of the exercise was lost. Wigner wished again that they'd given him a backup. Stupid bastards. He'd had just the guy picked out, too, not as tough as Pierce but good enough for a quick rescue sortie.

Then the power came on. The video monitors showed the transition chamber lighted once more and the soap-bubble colors forming in the I-Screen. The screen was opened onto Ulro at night; a couple of bricks slid down into the chamber.

Then Pierce staggered into the chamber after them and lurched a few steps forward.

"Kill the screen!" Wigner shouted into his microphone. "Repressurize the chamber!" Two techs, also in radiation suits, moved forward. He waved them off.

"I'm going in alone. I'll bring him out. As soon as pressure's up, get the sprays going."

He cycled himself into the airlock; its inner door had a window showing Pierce sagging awkwardly into a seated position. Frost sparkled in the rushing air, making delicate traceries on Pierce's suit. When the green pressure lights went on, Wigner plunged into the chamber. The cold hit through to his skin.

"Jerry! Are you hurt?"

Pierce's voice was muffled inside his helmet. He looked disoriented and exhausted. Wigner squatted beside him, gripped his arms. Radiation meters were flashing digital readouts from four sites around the chamber: nothing too bad, but Pierce would need a good hosing down before he could be moved out of the chamber.

The detergent sprays gushed from the ceiling, filling the chamber with mist as well as liquid. Wigner reached into Pierce's chest pack, felt the microfiches. With detergent pouring down over his faceplate, Wigner could made out little but colors: the buff of the daily briefings, the pale green of the personnel records. He unhooked the chest pack, let the sprays wash over it.

Pierce hardly seemed to notice. When the sprays finally stopped and they could look at one another again, Pierce leaned forward until their faceplates were touching.

"They're up there, Eric. The aliens are there."

Wigner felt an odd tremor. "But not here, old son. Can you stand?"

"Yes." But he made no move to. Wigner tried to help him to his feet, but he was too heavy and inert.

"I need help!" Wigner barked. In seconds, the two techs were with him, helping Pierce to his feet. They guided Pierce to the airlock while Wigner followed behind, moving close to a radiation meter. With the chest pack right in front of it, the meter registered only a fraction of a rad. Good.

The two techs and Pierce cycled through the airlock while Wigner waited. When it was his turn, he plunged his hand into the chest pack and pulled out the microfiches. A cabinet hung on the airlock wall; he opened it, stacking the microfiches neatly atop the first-aid equipment. Everything went into the cabinet except six personnel microfiches from 2002, which he returned to the chest pack. He hoped he wasn't mentioned in them.

The techs had Pierce out of his suit by the time Wigner came out. Pierce was shivering violently.

One of the techs looked at Wigner. "We better get him to the infirmary upstairs."

"Right."

"Eric?"

"Yes, Jerry."

"Eric, did I do all right?"

"You did fine. Fine."

"Good. God, Eric, they're there. They're really up there."

"Who are?" asked one of the techs, wrapping Pierce in a blanket and easing him into a wheelchair.

"The aliens. The aliens. I saw them."

Wigner saw the techs' faces go pale. Most of the rest of the project team was in earshot, and he heard one man swear.

"Don't worry, old son. You're perfectly safe. Everything's fine. Get him upstairs quickly, please."

When Pierce was gone, Wigner gathered the rest of the team around him.

"Our man is obviously upset by his experience. I wouldn't put too much credence in what he said. In any case, it is not, repeat not to be repeated to anyone and you are not to discuss it among yourselves. I'd like to thank you for what you've accomplished today. Let's get the place closed down as quickly as we can."

"Dr. Wigner? Did he bring anything back?" asked one of the physicists.

Wigner held up the chest pack and withdrew the microfiches.

"Six messages from the future. Again, that is top

secret information, not to go outside this room and not to be discussed. Understood?"

They nodded, and he curtly nodded back. Bless their hearts, they would be talking about this within minutes. Soon the whole Agency would know Pierce had brought back six microfiches and had seen aliens on Ulro. That would cause plenty of distraction. Wigner wanted distraction.

Three hours later, when the project team had closed everything down and left, Wigner went upstairs to see how Pierce was. The medics had sedated him, and Dr. Franklin in Woodstock had been notified.

Wigner went back downstairs and let himself into the subbasement. Five minutes later he was driving out of the building with an overnight bag slung on the seat beside him, headed for Pierce's apartment on Bleecker Street. He left the bag in the back of a closet. Then he went back to his car and drove a hundred miles north up Highway 87 to Woodstock.

Wigner liked Tom Franklin. He was well over sixty, a man who could remember the day Roosevelt died, but a natural ally of the young. His aquiline features and wavy white hair typecast him as the benevolent general practitioner; very few people outside the Agency knew that he had been a major figure in the development of Training, and that he had made psychoconditioning a genuine science rather than a branch of magic. He had enlisted in the Agency back in the 1960s out of a mix of patriotism and opportunism, since his country was quite prepared to serve him as lavishly as he served it. A decade earlier, the Agency had run some clumsy experiments in Canada on the effects of LSD, the kind of effort Franklin called "Auschwitz science." He had moved far beyond that.

Wigner reached Woodstock in the evening, with light still in the sky. The town looked more decrepit and abandoned than ever, with not a decently paved road in the place except the one leading to the Woodstock Clinic. It wound off north of the old summer stock theater, through a stand of maples to a high brick wall and a steel gate. Wigner gave the password to the guards and was allowed in.

The road curved through another half mile of woods and meadows before ending in front of a three-storey colonial mansion complete with pillared portico. Off to one side were the tennis courts; to the other was a two-acre lawn where three young women were doing tai chi in the twilight.

In the foyer of the house a tall young blonde woman welcomed him and escorted him to Dr. Franklin's office suite. Franklin strode out from behind his desk to shake Wigner's hand.

"Haven't seen much of you these days, but your reputation precedes you, Eric."

"I'll have to start driving faster."

"Come and have dinner with me."

The refectory was quiet and comfortable, done in colonial style with a lot of polished wood and brass. Franklin and Wigner took a table overlooking the lawn and watched the tai chi exercise while awaiting their roast beef and Yorkshire pudding.

"I understand your man will be arriving later tonight."

"Yes. He's pretty rattled, I'm afraid."

"Given what I know about him, his experience must have been a very bad one."

"Apparently so. I feel bad about it, since it was my project and I handpicked him."

Franklin smiled. "Is that why you came up here? To apologize?"

Wigner shrugged. "I suppose. In part. Mostly I'm here to ask for special treatment for him. He's a remarkable young guy and he could have an important career, if he bounces back from this."

"I can't promise miracles, Eric."

"Of course not. I should mention something else. He's been engaged in some very sensitive assignments."

"I understand. We won't dig into that, and if anything comes out accidentally we'll maintain normal security."

"No. Extreme security. Anything having to do with his case must go through me alone."

The waiter arrived with their meal. Neither man spoke for a moment; then Dr. Franklin leaned forward a little.

"Why not through your boss?"

"Dr. Clement isn't authorized to take part in this assignment, even through passive advisement. And he's no longer my boss, even pro forma. I'm transferring to Semiotronics."

"Indeed. This smells like intrigue, Eric."

"More like perfectly done rare roast beef."

"I'll need something in writing from your superiors, whoever they may be."

"In good time. Meanwhile, just take care of my friend, and if he babbles don't tell anyone else what he says."

"Those are very, mm, awkward terms for me."

"And for me, believe me."

One of the three women on the lawn stopped doing

her tai chi and crumpled onto the grass. Curled into a fetal ball, she struck at the grass with her fist. Even through the double-glazed window, the two men could hear her shrieks. The other two women quickly picked her up and carried her out of sight.

"That one's a stubborn case," Franklin muttered. "Poor dear. We'll have her fixed up eventually. All right, Eric, we'll play it your way." He suddenly smiled again, a conspiratorial glint in his eye. "Just to see what you're up to."

"Thank you, Dr. Franklin."

Driving through Kingston on his way back to New York City later that night, Wigner heard sirens and gunshots in the heavy summer air. The radio gave no hint of trouble; it was probably just another food riot.

Nevertheless, the authorities had set up roadblocks on the approach to Highway 87, and riflemen were guarding the tollbooths. With all their windows shot out and bloodstains on their doors, a couple of pickup trucks stood empty on the edge of the toll plaza. Wigner's Agency ID was still valid, and it got him through the roadblocks and tollbooths without trouble.

The highway was deserted except for a few north-bound army trucks, and he drove fast. So far, everything was working out fairly well. The only possible problem was Dr. Franklin: he might, if Pierce revealed enough, decide to choose the wrong side in Wigner's silent war. That would be serious, however, only if both Franklin and the senior Agency people acted very quickly indeed, and they were not known for their quickness. If it did happen, however, Wigner was not worried. Not as long as he could spend some time first with the microfiches.

* * *

The northbound ambulance passed Wigner's car at New Paltz. In the rear of the ambulance, Pierce lay drowsing comfortably. He was strapped to a bed and accompanied by two male nurses. Fifty milligrams of Diaquin had put him into a mildly euphoric state. He knew he was being taken care of, but felt no curiosity about what might happen to him. He knew he had escaped something bad, but could barely recall what it was. The thought that he had been on a destroyed world in the future seemed absurd even though, in some distant way, he knew it was true. At times he could summon up the images of the silently screaming corpses in the tunnel, but they were not as bad as another image, a small twinkling blue light.

"He's getting restless again."

"Yeah, about time."

Warm, dry fingers touched his arm and applied a small square patch of fabric to the skin. Then an instant's pressure forced the second dose through to his bloodstream. A few seconds later Pierce felt fine again.

They wheeled him out of the ambulance into a courtyard, then a corridor and a small room lighted by a single lamp on a night table. Gently they put him into the bed and applied one more skin patch, a sleeping drug. Pierce yawned and curled up under the coverlet.

Dr. Franklin began the assessment the next morning. He had hoped this might be a transient condition, a mild upset that could be slept off. The bed monitors told him otherwise: blood pressure, heartbeat, cutaneous potential all showed a man in severe shock. When Pierce woke, his eyes looked dazed and unfocused.

"Good morning, Jerry. I'm Dr. Franklin."

Pierce did not respond. Franklin pulled his chair up beside Pierce's bed and performed a quick but thorough examination.

"Your pal Eric was up here last night. He thinks you're some kind of hero, you know. Worried about you."

Saying nothing, Pierce closed his eyes again.

"Can you see Ulro?" Franklin asked.

Pierce's eyes opened.

"Tell me what you see."

"Tunnel. Black."

"Good, Jerry. Very good. Are you in the tunnel?"

Pierce said nothing, but began to shiver under the coverlet.

"Jerry, I'm going to give you a little shot that'll help you feel better. Then you can talk about Ulro without feeling bad. Understood?"

"Yes."

"Good." Dr. Franklin loaded a hypodermic gun with a handful of tiny cartridges and pressed it against the skin of Pierce's arm.

Wigner felt comfortable in Pierce's apartment; it had the same utilitarian spareness of his own, and even a few houseplants. The Polymath was a little slower than the one Wigner was used to, but it would do quite nicely.

The microfiches could have been scanned with a flickreader, but Wigner was in too much of a hurry. Instead he ran them through a textreader and into the Polymath's memory.

"Boot, Polly."

The little girl on the screen looked anxious. "I'm sorry, sir, I don't recognize your voice."

Wigner chuckled and tapped out a sequence on the

keyboard. "My name is Eric, Polly. Jerry's away for a while, and he asked me to take care of you."

"Sure, Eric. Pleased to meet you. What can I do for you?"

"You've just had about three hundred microfiches added to your files. Please collate and cross-index by the following keywords: Central Intelligence Agency slash, Civil Emergency Administration slash, National Security Agency slash, Defense Intelligence Agency slash, Union of Soviet Socialist Republics slash—"

He went on through the list, which ended with various crimes such as treason, bribery, murder, conspiracy, and drug trafficking.

"Okay, Polly? Now please give me the chronological sequence on Central Intelligence Agency and treason. Flick rate ten pages per second."

"Sure, Eric."

Wigner leaned back in the chair, enjoying the faint tremble in his hands.

Ten:

"No need to be nervous," Clement said as the MATS shuttle began its descent to Andrews Air Force Base. Out the window, Jasmin Jones glimpsed the suburbs of Washington through the smog.

"I'm not," she said.

"They're very easygoing people, very good listeners. They'll certainly be interested in what you have to tell them."

"I should hope so." What government had ever been granted a glimpse of its own future?

A Navy helicopter was waiting at Andrews. It was a hot, hazy day, and from the helicopter Jaz could see little traffic beyond the military patrols. The Black neighborhoods were busy with people on foot or bikes; every other street seemed to be a marketplace. Jaz wondered what it was like to live around Blacks or Hispanics or Asians; she'd been a little kid when the Ethnic Integrity Act had been passed, and in any case her neighborhood in Santa Monica had been lily-white already. Sometimes she thought people got along better in the ghettos than the lilypads; sometimes she dismissed the idea as neolib sentimentality.

Roadblocks were set up around every government building, and each building's rooftop held a group of sharpshooters. But the soldiers seemed relaxed: many on the rooftops were sunbathing or sleeping. The smog browning the horizon came not so much from cars as from countless cooking fires; most ghetto streets were lined with tree stumps.

The helicopter settled onto the pad outside the old administration complex on the campus of George Washington University, now the headquarters of the Civil Emergency Administration. Clement got out of his seat, looking both cool and elegant in his seersucker suit and straw boater; Jaz, in a lightweight summer suit, felt sweaty and frazzled beside him. Stepping out into the blast of the slowing rotors only compounded matters, tangling her hair and speckling her skin with grit.

"Not to worry," Clement assured her. "Five minutes in the ladies' room and you'll be spectacular again."

It took somewhat longer than that, but even so she was ready before Clement was; he had actually taken a shower, the bastard, and changed his shirt.

Someone's executive assistant escorted them to the briefing room on the fourth floor. He was a harried man with thin blond hair who asked them if they could get decent produce on the New York black market.

"We don't patronize the black market," Clement said calmly.

"Boy, you're lucky. Can't get along without it here in Washin'ton."

Clement caught Jaz's eye and made a discreet face.

The briefing room was large and airy, paneled in oak and thickly carpeted. A U-shaped table faced a smaller one at the far end; on the wall behind the small table were a holoscreen and a large green chalkboard. Tall windows gave a view of the Washington Monument rising into the smog above the campus treetops.

Only after Clement and Jaz had settled themselves at the small table did their audience enter the room:

ten men, half of them in uniforms, none younger than fifty, the Executive Committee of the Civil Emergency Administration and, therefore, the rulers of the United States.

Jaz was struck by their good looks; all were evidently fit and healthy, with sensibly light tans and good teeth. Even the two or three who were not actually beautiful had a craggy masculinity she found attractive, and all dressed well. The military men, all generals or admirals, wore few decorations; the civilians were in lightweight suits.

The ten men took their seats at the U-shaped table while another twenty, assistants, filed in and seated themselves just behind their masters. Papers and folders rustled above the basso continuo of masculine conversation. The chairman, a tall civilian with curly white hair, smiled at Clement and Jaz. He had dimples when he smiled, and when he cleared his throat the assistants ceased their murmuring.

"Good morning, Jonathan, and Ms. Jones. It's a pleasure to meet you, ma'am, and I hope we'll have the pleasure of seeing you often at future briefings."

"Thank you, Mr. Chairman." Jaz gave him direct eye contact and a dazzling smile, and watched them all perk up a little. It felt a little odd to be aware of their curiosity about her when she knew so much about each of them.

They had been senior corporate executives or government administrators, or both, before the president had declared the Emergency. He had chosen these men to run what was left of the government without interference from Congress or the courts or the media. They had done so for years now, so well that the president himself was little more than a figurehead. The last elected Congress still met, but only to pass meaningless resolutions backing the Committee's actions, and to vent the resentments of a few malcontents.

"Mr. Chairman," said Clement, "the purpose of this briefing is to acquaint the Committee with the results of our mission to Ulro, but we'll try to answer any other questions that might fall within the bounds of the Research Services Division."

"Very good, Dr. Clement. We have a number of issues we'd like your advice on."

Nice, thought Jaz. Courtesy on the edge of flattery.

Clement gave the Committee some quick background on the decision to try to find the Riverside Park repository, and then came down heavily on the details of its failure: the breakdown of the tank, the temporary power failure that had kept Pierce waiting, the six microfiches that had been the only real reward of the mission.

"We performed deep analysis on that material," Clement said, "and Ms. Jones was part of the analysis team. I'd like her to acquaint you with the results."

"Please," said the chairman.

"Thank you," said Jaz. God, it was going to take forever to get it all across to these unTrainables. She would have to remember to spell it out carefully.

"The records we obtained were Agency personnel files from the year 2002, mostly for persons working out of our New York offices. Most of them were cognates of people now working for the Agency, and our own data correlate very closely with the Ulro data. For example, we had the files on an industrial analyst named Ricardo Chavez who joined the Agency on August 1, 1986; our files and the Ulro files on Chavez mesh perfectly up to now. The Ulro files indicate he'll stay on the payroll until his death in 2002."

A general interrupted: "You actually know the date of this man's death?"

"April 23. But our Ricardo Chavez isn't likely to die on that date because it's an accidental death—an apartment fire in Brooklyn."

Now for the deep analysis part. "Over twenty other Agency employees are scheduled to die in the same fire, which occurred during a battle between units of the 101st Airborne and units of the American Liberation Army. The combatants were seeking control of Verrazano Bridge, and an Agency residential block was badly damaged by fire." She paused. "I'm sorry if my verb tenses are confused."

Their jaws dropped gratifyingly.

"I have trouble grasping this," the chairman said. His dimples didn't show any more. "You're telling me that some kind of civil war will be fought in New York in the year 2002."

"That was implicit in the materials brought back by the first two tank expeditions last spring, sir."

She was uncomfortably surprised herself at their ignorance: hadn't they understood anything from the earlier briefings Clement and others had given them?

"There won't be any real winners, as far as we can tell," she went on. "From about 2010 to 2020, the country will be governed by a number of different regional factions. One source calls it the warlord period. Then a whole new kind of society is supposed to take shape."

"Run by Trainables," said a Marine general.

"Yes, sir."

"Well, now we'll have the drop on these so-called liberation people," the Marine general said with grim good cheer. "Your files should have plenty of names and dates. We just have to round up their leaders and that's it."

"Unfortunately, General Phelps, the files give us no such names. No present group is clearly related to the American Liberation Army. It could be the PAF or the Wabbies or some completely new organization.

"In any case," she went on, "this is just one example. Please remember, gentlemen, that these are only personnel records—what jobs people held, what their superiors thought of them, how much they were paid, where they traveled. The information we want is only hinted at. I'll give you an example: we know it was the 101st Airborne fighting the American Liberation Army because the commanding officer of the 360th MedEvac Hospital signed all the death certificates for the people in the Agency residence. That officer is Colonel Henry R. Dumoulin, and he's already serving with the 360th."

Which is part of the 101st Airborne?" asked an admiral.

"Yes, sir."

The chairman cleared his throat. "Ms. Jones, bear with us. We're just a bunch of hardworking administrators, and we haven't had much chance to absorb all this time-travel stuff."

Then shame on you, Jaz thought.

"Can you give us, oh, a kind of potted history of the next few years, as you read these documents?"

She gave him another big smile. "Of course, Mr. Chairman. Please understand, though, that we're occasionally making some uneducated guesses, and linking our data with the material from the first two missions to Ulro. And we've concentrated on the crises, which may give a distorted picture.

"That said, the next few years go like this: Worsening civil disorders for the next two years, partly over food shortages and general lack of consumer goods, and partly over the role of the CEA. Some serious epidemics, especially something called Milan flu. A very bad rash of riots in the summer of 2000, with several political parties demanding the end of the CEA and a return to elected government. Assassination of a number of political leaders, including Senator Cooledge, which causes a shakeup in the CEA. President Norris resigns, and so does Vice President Arnold."

"Small loss," a general muttered.

"The CEA Executive Committee assumes direct control of the government in early 2001, but a number of districts refuse to acknowledge its authority. Some military units side with the Trainable district administrators, and fighting breaks out. The CEA brings back the last troops in Europe and Korea. We think the Germans make an attempt to unify, but we're not sure. We do know that we send a lot of our people into West Germany about then, and even more into the southern USSR to encourage the separatists."

The Marine general interrupted. "Why don't the Russians try to jump us, if we're in such lousy condition?"

"We think they're caught in a leadership crisis, and, of course, their food problems are even worse than ours. One of our analysts gets a commendation in late 2001 for estimating that the Russians couldn't sustain a major military operation in central Europe for more than a week."

Nor could the U.S. Army, she reflected, and that's been the case on both sides for twenty years or more. Neither side could sustain a trillion-dollar fraud when it was flat broke.

She went on briskly, sketching the pattern hidden in

those six microfiche cards: the civil war, the epidemics and epizootics, the breakdown of transport and communications, the increasing numbers of Trainables among the various factions trying to maintain themselves.

"It confirms, in general, what the first two missions learned," she said. "We did find out a few useful bits of information, like the identities of some of the Wabbies' leaders. They're in hiding, but the FBI has their names and descriptions. We've also found one serious spy in the Agency, an operative who's been paid by the British for the last three years—"

"The British!"

"Yes, Mr. Chairman. We've already dealt with the case, and the agent has been turned. The Brits are now receiving only disinformation. But we didn't find any serious Soviet or Japanese agents."

"Just shows their security is better," grunted a civilian.

"We think so, too, sir," Jaz said. And better than the CEA's, or she would have mentioned four other spies (one French, one Japanese, two Soviet) who had also been identified and neutralized.

The chairman heaved a sigh and leaned forward against the mirrorlike table.

"You know, Ms. Jones, some of your fellow Trainables have been giving us very similar projections for the next decade. I don't know whether to be alarmed or suspicious about what you've told us."

"Sir?"

"Either the projections were right, or we're being sold a bill of goods about what was found on Ulro."

Jaz brightened, a pretty girl suddenly understanding. "You're suspicious because Trainables are involved in supplying this information."

"Frankly, I am—a little."

Very aware of Clement's presence beside her, Jaz said, "Many of us Trainables are aware of that attitude. To be as frank as yourself, Mr. Chairman, the outline of the next few years look to me like just what should happen if Trainable advice and skills are ignored until it's too late."

He smiled, his dimples flashing. "No doubt I sound a bit paranoid. But what's the old gag—just because we're paranoid doesn't mean they're not out to get us."

"Even paranoids deserve sound advice, Mr. Chairman."

The ten men who ruled the United States burst into boyish giggles, while their chairman blushed faintly.

The Marine general spoke up: "You folks seem to have pulled a hell of a lot of stuff out of six microfiches, and I for one think you're giving us the straight dope. I like to think I'm open-minded about Trainables, and we have no reason to doubt your loyalty and sincerity, little lady. But how about going back for more?"

Clement answered. "When our agent returned, he was in very poor shape psychologically, but he was able to tell the mission director that the repository was destroyed. Those microfiches were all he could find in the ruins. Considering the problems he ran into, I would be very hesitant to commit us to another mission until we know much more about conditions on Ulro. The mission director agrees with me."

Clement paused and shrugged sadly. "I hate to admit it, Mr. Chairman, but we regard this mission as a failure. Perhaps that's harsh, but I'm not here to tell you fairy tales. We feel we can serve you better by good solid intelligence work here and now, and by some careful research on the downtime chronoplanes."

"Well, perhaps so," said the chairman, "but I must say we're grateful for what you've given us. You've brought us the detailed reports? Good. We'll study them with great interest. Forewarned is forearmed, after all. If people are going to be unhappy with us, we'll be better prepared when it happens."

When it happens? Jaz repeated to herself. Didn't he realize how unhappy people were already? Then she realized that the real giveaway had been his mention of the printed reports. They would be going over those in great detail and taking action, but they would try not to betray too much interest to underlings like Clement and herself.

The meeting broke for coffee and pastries; Jaz and the chairman chatted about the weather and the difficulty of getting good coffee now that Latin America and Africa were in chaos.

"Very sad," said the chairman. "Tragic. The loss of life, the waste, the misery. Makes you grateful for what we've got here. When you're living with harsh reality, the way we do, you have to pull back and keep a balanced view. This is all really just a big economic readjustment. Tough on some people, but we'll pull through it."

Jaz struggled to keep from gaping at him. "They didn't pull through it on Ulro, sir."

"Perhaps not, but they didn't have our advantages, did they?" He dimpled at her. "Now we know what the bad guys are up to, and we're sure to learn more. This time around we'll do fine."

She smiled quickly and put down her cup. "Let's hope so."

When the briefing resumed, Clement handled it: a

detailed, well-organized account of what was going on around the country. Near the end, he raised the issue of the Iffers.

"They're a real fly in the ointment," Clement said as holograms flashed on the screen: parades in New York, Baltimore, Cleveland, San Francisco. "Not a violent movement like the Wabbies and the PAF, not yet anyway, but they could be far worse. We estimate the Iffers are growing faster than any movement in American history."

"Goddam traitors," growled an admiral.

"If treason prosper, none dare call it treason," Clement said dryly. "We're working hard on the whole phenomenon of antinationalism. You know, a society under stress normally falls back on extreme nationalism, the way the Wabbies do, or it tries to redefine the nation as the PAF does. But . . . millions of people are just saying they don't feel like Americans. They feel like something else that I for one don't understand. It's damn disquieting. We'll get a handle on it, but until we do the Iffers are a loose cannon."

"I wouldn't mind sequestering some of the high-profile Iffers," said a civilian. "Like that bitch Senator Cooledge and some of her buddies. Not surprising she's supposed to get killed. These people ought to be put away for their own good."

"Very counterproductive, I'm afraid," murmured Clement.

The chairman nodded. "At this stage, of course. And it's too bad there were no Iffers on Ulro, so we'd know what they were really up to. But we'll expect your people to keep a close eye on them, Dr. Clement."

"Certainly, Mr. Chairman."

"Ms. Jones, perhaps it's in the written report, but I

can't help asking you one more question about the Ulro data. Is this Committee mentioned anywhere in your documents?"

"Several times, sir. Various Agency members in the files were asked to supply information to this Committee. The only specific mentions, however, are to Committee members Dr. Nathan Melkin and General Andrew J. Reynolds."

"But they're not on the Committee."

"Apparently they will be by 2002."

She watched the ten men ponder the implications. Would the newcomers replace two present members, or be added? Would they be the only ones? Melkin and Reynolds, she knew, were old political opponents of several important Committee members; would their ascent signify their faction's success, or their own opportunism? Jaz wondered if the ancient Greek oracles had felt the same detached amusement at their clients' bafflement.

The chairman nodded and looked at his watch. "Fascinating. Now, I'm afraid we have no further time. Dr. Clement—Ms. Jones—thank you for a most useful session. We look forward to the next one."

Smiling, the Committee members left the room and the thin-haired executive assistant escorted them back to the helipad.

"Very successful," said Clement as they climbed aboard. "You handled them very well, especially with that paranoia line. They liked that."

"Thank you. Still, Eric should have been the one to do it."

Clement shook his head. "Eric is history now. He had his chance, and he blew it."

Jaz was buckling herself in beside Clement. She thought about something he had said during the briefing: that Pierce had told the mission director about the ruined repository. Pierce had told no one else anything; he had gone catatonic within moments of his return, yet he had managed to blurt out that crucial fact. Or Wigner had lied.

For days, Wigner left the Bleecker Street apartment only briefly, to spend a few ration stamps at the nearest food dispensary or liquor store. He slipped into a new kind of circadian rhythm: sleep for four hours, work for eighteen, sleep for four hours more. He kept the curtains drawn and knew only vaguely if they blocked out daylight or darkness.

The collating and cross-referencing grew steadily more complex as he traced a hundred criminals and a thousand crimes, scores of political careers, and dozens of corporate schemes. From what he learned in the microfiches, he could turn to current databases and find the first misdemeanors of his criminals, the first elections and stock issues. If they were hidden, he turned to the wailing-wall network. Back came passwords, files, more threads for the wonderful tapestry he was weaving. Over a hundred Trainables came to the wailing wall with news for Wigner, and went away again with new instructions.

Usually they understood little or nothing of what they were asked to find, but the smarter Trainables saw the patterns in the data and saw where the patterns should lead. Information came in trickles, then spurts, then floods.

But the apartment showed no sign of it: no printouts, no notes, only the rapid flicker of the computer screen throwing green light across Wigner's face. Pierce's Polymath was strained to its limits; Wigner copied the data to a larger computer in a rented office uptown, then cleared the Polymath's memory to make room for more.

He hardly needed to look outside: he knew what was going on, what would be going on.

He knew his own future.

He found it not in the remaining personnel records but in the briefings. The Wabbies had launched a coup attempt, spearheaded by a brilliant computer virus. A hacker out in someplace called Salmon Prairie, Montana, had devised it, and it had virtually decapitated the Civil Emergency Administration.

ExComm had fought back, but it had been a near thing. A Wabbie death squad had assassinated Senator Cooledge and most of her staff in the hours after the crash of the computer system. In retaliation, Wigner had sent Jerry Pierce to eleminate the Wabbie executive. He had succeeded, but had then been captured by the FBI, tortured, and killed. A crude but effective chemical interrogation had revealed Wigner's involvement in this and a dozen other assassinations; Wigner took careful note of his cognate's victims.

The FBI had then passed the word to Clement; Wigner had been arrested and interrogated by much more subtle methods. He read extracts from his interrogations, and thought he sounded exactly like himself. He did not like an unflattering psychological profile from an Agency psychoconditioner named Suad, but supposed it was pretty accurate. Most of the wailing-wall network was rolled up soon after his arrest, and the members jailed. Wigner had gone to a detention camp in Wyoming; early in 2003 he was reported as shot attempting to escape.

"Well," Wigner said, pausing the flickerscreen.

He stood up, stretching, and went to the bathroom. Strange to read one's own obituary, to know it had been read by the president and the CEA Executive Committee. Far from making him feel glad to be alive to read it, the account of his death (complete with postmortem photograph) made him angry with himself.

His cognate's efforts seemed pathetic, a frustrated and unimaginative lashing out at symptoms while the root causes of misery lay untouched. Even with assets like Jerry Pierce and the wailing-wall network, the Ulro Wigner had botched it. Here on Earth, he had planned nothing different until Ishizawa had changed everything. He would have blindly followed the same path to oblivion. On Ulro he had tried to save the world and could not even save himself. On Earth he had at least a fighting chance to save both.

Eleven:

Outside Pierce's room, the morning sun glowed through the leaves. The window was open, and someone was playing Bach on the guitar: *Jesu Joy of Man's Desiring*. Pierce lay on his bed under a sheet, one hand tapping in time to the music. He had lost some weight; his cheekbones stood out.

"I don't believe in reliving a trauma as a means of overcoming it," Dr. Franklin said from his chair beside the bed. "Might as well cut into a scar to see how deep it is. But sometimes we just have to do it, Jerry, so we can understand what made the scar and how deep it runs."

"I understand." But Pierce spoke absently, as if he were bored.

"You know what Dymoxyn is; it was part of what made you a Trainable."

"Memory drug."

"Exactly. We're going to give you a fairly large dose and see what turns up."

"Sure."

Simply getting Pierce to this stage had taken almost two weeks. Now he was at least conversing and seemed capable of understanding what was happening to him. The Agency did not worry much about legal subtleties, least of all since the declaration of the Emergency, but Franklin had no intention of being

155

sued over administering a potent substance like Dymoxyn: Pierce's remarks, on tape, would show he had agreed to treatment of his own free will.

A nurse attached electrodes to Pierce's scalp. The electrodes were connected to a relatively new machine, a cerebrospinal field scanner. It was a pair of black metal boxes about the size of videocassette recorders, linked by cables to a flat-screen monitor. As he spoke, Dr. Franklin could see the effect of his words on Pierce's brain.

"Remember when computers were first coming in?" Dr. Franklin said. "Everything was incompatible with everything else. You had to go through a real hassle to take information from an IBM disk and make it understandable to an Apple." The screen showed the characteristic red-blue pattern for an apple

"Well, people's brains are something like that. We're all genetically incompatible. Maybe if we weren't, we could read each other's minds." He saw more familiar patterns: *people, something, read.* "Now we're just getting to the point where we can print out cerebral functions, but we don't always know what we're actually reading. Imagine someone was writing down a series of Chinese ideograms as someone else was speaking Chinese. Maybe you couldn't understand the words or the ideograms, but after a while you'd see some repetitions. You hear the word *shan* and you see a particular ideogram." Dr. Franklin drew it on the palm of his hand so that Pierce could see: a horizontal line with three bold verticals.

"Then you see the speaker point to a mountain when he says *shan*, and you realize what it means. From that you can start making guesses about what other words might mean. That's what we're doing these days. Once we used things like word association tests. Now we look for certain kinds of patterns in response to particular stimuli. How's your mother these days?"

"Fine."

The screen swirled with a rapid cascade of color. Dr. Franklin read love, worry, protectiveness.

"What's the earliest thing you can remember?"

So it began, the methodical review of Pierce's life. Each question put a series of doorways on the screen, and Franklin chose which to open and how far to go down the hallways beyond them before he opened yet another door. Franklin pushed back beyond Pierce's earliest conscious memories; he believed he had sometimes reached prenatal memories as early as six months postconception, but nothing that drastic seemed necessary here.

The key memory turned up in the afternoon of the first day. Pierce must have been about two years old, toddling about the little apartment in Taos. A spider scuttled across the blue tiles of the kitchen floor. Pierce's mother, seeing it, recoiled. Jerry dropped his toy truck on the spider, crushing it. And his mother picked him up, hugged him, kissed him, filled his nostrils with her sweet smell: *What a good boy! Boy, you're a brave little guy, aren'cha?*"

"Were you a brave little guy, Jerry?" asked Franklin.

"Yeah. Not scared."

"So, you like to take care of people."

"Yeah. Wilbur."

"Tell me about Wilbur." The patterns on the screen flashed with pity, contempt, anger, and pride.

An afternoon in ninth grade, the sky over the Sangre de Cristos full of puffy clouds. Wilbur Swinden, the crybaby, was eating his lunch in the bleachers on the edge of the quarter-mile track. He was a gawky little guy with not much chin and watery brown eyes. As long as Pierce could remember, other kids had picked on him because he got so upset when they did. Wilbur had no friends. His big sister, Liz, in eleventh grade, walked him to school and walked him home again, but had little to do with him the rest of the time.

Pierce saw Pancho Quiroga and his little gang drift across the field toward Wilbur. Four stocky kids, trying to grow sideburns and moustaches, surrounded Wilbur and took his lunch away from him. Pancho plucked Wilbur's book from him and riffled through it before scaling it over the fence into the street.

Of course Wilbur started bawling and yelling, and Pancho's gang began to shove him from one to another, goading him to more shouts.

Jerry, jogging around the track, saw it all. He didn't like Wilbur. Nobody did. But Pancho was provoking it, and no one else was doing anything. Jerry didn't change his pace; he trotted down the track toward the bleachers where Wilbur and Pancho's gang were. As he reached them, he stopped.

"Leave him alone, Pancho."

"Fuck you, *pendejo.*"

Jerry had already checked: no teachers on the field. His fist smashed into Pancho's nose, knocking him back across a bleacher seat.

"Get out of here, Wilbur," Jerry commanded. Blubbering, Wilbur obeyed.

"Pinche cabron, te voy a matar," Pancho snarled. Pierce shoved Sixto Gonzalez down onto Pancho. The other two did nothing except to sidle off a little.

"Come on, then," Jerry said.

Pancho disentangled himself and lunged at Jerry. Jerry stepped aside, grabbed Pancho by his hair, and flung him onto the track. Pancho grunted and struggled to his feet.

Jerry stood there, hands at his sides. No one else seemed to have noticed the scuffle. Pancho glared at him, then spat and turned away. Blood dribbled from his nose, down his chin, and across his T-shirt.

Wilbur, the retard, wasn't even grateful; he never thanked Jerry or even mentioned the incident. Pancho Quiroga and his friends never mentioned it either. But that day after school, Liz Swinden stopped by Jerry's locker.

"I hear you rescued my brother today."

"Well."

"Thanks. He gets a bad time, but he can't help it."

"Sure."

Franklin nodded as he watched the scanner screen, and opened more doors. Eventually, one door opened into Donald Dwayne White's bedroom.

"I'm glad you called, Eric. Your friend has placed me in something of an ethical bind. I think we should discuss it."

"Say no more, Dr. Franklin. I'll be there this afternoon."

As it happened, Wigner reached Woodstock late in the evening. A National Guard unit, unpaid for weeks, had mutinied on the New Jersey side of the George Washington Bridge. Traffic had been blocked for several hours before troops from Fort Dix had restored order. Franklin met Wigner in his office, as before, but this time did not offer him dinner.

"Let's go for a walk."

They strolled out into the muggy night; the moon shining through thin clouds gave a little light on the grass.

"Are you wired, Eric?"

"With a recorder? No." Wigner was telling the truth. Franklin was too good at spotting the vocal qualities of a lie.

"Good. Nor am I. This is a strictly personal, off the record conversation. You're aware of our friend's past."

"In some detail, though I'm sure you understand it better than I."

"He's a killer."

"I know. That's why I hired him."

"He hasn't killed just some two-bit rapist, Eric. He shot General Pendlehurst."

"At my request, as you must know, and not a minute too soon. I expect I'll need his services again before much longer."

"Why?"

"To help me get this country into the International Federation before it's too late."

"What's in it for you, Eric?"

"A longer and happier career, I hope. The IF will need people like me. And like Jerry."

"You're making me an accessory to what amounts to treason and murder. I'm not happy at all about that."

"Neither am I, sir. But Agency people have often been faced with hard facts and hard decisions. You more than many."

Franklin's voice was cold. "You didn't ask me to get involved in this. You gave me some cock-and-bull story about security, but you're planning some kind of one-man coup. I'm not going to go along."

"Dr. Franklin, you have to. Look—we know our whole civilization is about to collapse. We know that from Ulro as well as what's going on around us.

There's no point in trying to defend a dead society, but there's a lot of point in helping a new society come to life. That's what I'm trying to do."

"I'm quite aware of what you found on Ulro. But the downtime chronoplanes change everything. We have a new lease on life, Eric."

"No." His voice was hard. "We can't afford to settle the chronoplanes on a nation-by-nation basis, not with Doomsday staring us in the face. We'll just end up fighting a whole new series of wars. Suppose the Palestinians want to move into Palestine on Beulah or Eden? Do you think the Israelis would tolerate the possibility of being invaded from the past? The Palestinians could go downtime, open up an I-Screen into the middle of modern Jerusalem, throw a nuclear bomb through it, and that'd be it. Meanwhile we'd be throwing more bombs at whoever we thought was responsible. No, it'd be impossible. We've got to have an international government with absolute authority."

"I don't agree."

"I'm prepared to have your cooperation without your agreement if necessary. You see, I have all the details of Operation Pontifex and your role in it."

Franklin chuckled. "Operation Pontifex? I never heard of it."

"I'm sorry, sir, but you're lying. You were involved from June 12, 1981, to the end of the operation on December 1, 1987. I have the confession your cognate made on Ulro in 2005, just before you were shot as a counterrevolutionary. Also statements by three of the survivors."

"There were no survivors."

"Leon Manzari, Peter Demetroff, and Barbara Kline. I have their current addresses. Leon and Barbara are living together in Argentina, and Peter's in

Dubrovnik. If the phones are working, we can call them now."

"Jesus Christ."

"I don't particularly care what you did then. It was pretty stupid, but we've all done stupid things for the Agency. Now I want you to do something intelligent. If you blow the whistle on me, you're finished. If you don't, you'll carry on here at the Clinic for as long as you like. The IF is going to need you just as much as the Agency has. Maybe more."

Wigner touched the old man's arm. "Really, Dr. Franklin, it'll be fine. Please believe me."

Dr. Franklin walked slowly across the grass, oblivious of Wigner's hand. At last he said: "You're how old, Eric? Twenty-one?"

"Yes."

"You have a great career ahead of you."

"Hello, Ryan? Is that Ryan Andrews?"

"Yes, it is."

"Eric Wigner here. We have a terrible connection."

"Afraid so. I understand you're coming to work for us soon."

"Next week. Listen, old son, I've got a tip I think Semiotronics ought to consider seriously."

"Sure."

"Get every kopeck out of Northeast Seaboard Bank. They're about to go under."

"North—holy shit, are you serious?"

"Never more so, old son. And when they go, they'll take most of their customers with them."

"Uh, can you give your source for this advice?"

"Afraid not."

"You bastards on East 52nd are always two jumps ahead of the rest of us. You're sure about this."

"Absolutely. They'll be in receivership by the end of September, so we've got a couple of weeks to make a graceful exit. By the first of September it'll be obvious."

"Christ, Eric, do you understand the implications of what you're saying?"

"If by that you mean the domino effect, I do, indeed."

"Do your sources tell you why?"

"Brazil and India are going to default on their loans."

Ryan Andrews whooped with laughter. "In that case, who cares what happens to Northeast Seaboard?"

"Semiotronics and other major depositors."

"But the implications—"

"Are not good. Still, we'll be better off if we haul our money out now, won't we?"

"Yup."

A thunderstorm was dumping rain on the streets of Queens. Wigner handed his raincoat to the hatcheck girl, who smiled ravishingly at him. She was not about to endanger her job when the New York unemployment rate was somewhere around thirty-five percent and rising.

The lunch crowd was thin today, a few clusters of businessmen muttering over their black-market hamburgers. Wigner saw the congressman in a dark booth at the back of the restaurant.

"Hello, Mr. Charles. I'm Eric Wigner. Delighted you could make it on such short notice."

The congressman, a short, small man with a hard face under curly gray hair, did not accept Wigner's extended hand.

"Sit down. I already ordered for us."

"Thank you." The order had included a beer, which Wigner raised in a toast.

"Cheers . . . Excellent."

Congressman Anthony Charles studied him with impassive distaste.

"You Trainable?"

"I have that honor, yes."

"Well, let's get this straight. I don't like you guys. You think you're smarter than you are, and you cause a lot of trouble." He pulled out a cigar and lighted it, ignoring the NO SMOKING sign on the table.

"I can't argue with that. Some of the dumbest people I know are Trainables, and we do, indeed, cause trouble. Still, politics is the art of dealing with people we don't like, isn't it?"

"When we can't avoid it. Let's get down to it, kid. What do you people want with me?"

"Mm—more a personal concern than an Agency matter. You've been stalling Bill 402 in committee for weeks now."

"Oh, you gonna lobby me about the fucking Iffers? Tell me what a sweet bunch of assholes they really are?"

"I'm not going to lobby you, Mr. Charles. I'm going to tell you straight out to move that bill out of committee by the end of the week."

Mr. Charles sat back in the booth and squinted at Wigner through cigar smoke. "I kinda admire your innocence, kid, but you got a lot to learn about this business."

Wigner grinned and drew a bulky envelope from his inside jacket pocket. He handed it to the congressman. "We Trainables learn fast, Mr. Charles. I'll bet you do, too. Take a quick look at these items."

The congressman glanced irritably at the first document, then paused. He read it carefully, looked blankly at Wigner, and began to riffle through the rest of the papers.

"Where'd you get this shit?"

"The question is, where am I going to send it?"

"You're not gonna get anywhere with this stuff, kid. Come on, get serious. What, you're a jerk who hacked his way into somebody's database and don't even know what you got. You think you can blackmail me on this? I been in this business twenty-two years, for Christ's sake. And you come along and think you can shove me around. Sheesh."

The meal arrived, an indifferent fettucini; the salad was limp and oily. Mr. Charles dug into it without saying anything else. Wigner poked distastefully at his plate.

"Mr. Charles, I'm keenly aware of your career in Congress. I know you supported the president when he declared the Emergency, and you've backed the CEA ever since. Nevertheless, if the CEA finds out what you've been dealing in for the last two years, you'll go to Leavenworth."

The congressman chewed energetically while thunder boomed overhead.

"Let me think about this a minute," he said. "You say this is a personal concern, not Agency. Let's say you're lying and the Agency does want 402 to go to a vote. What for? They got no business screwing around trying to embarrass ExComm and everybody else. They'll just get everybody pissed off at 'em again, like Cuba and Venezuela. So fuck the Agency. Now let's say you're telling the truth, you're a little prick who happens to work for the Agency and wants to throw some weight around. So you call me up for lunch, you mention East 52nd Street, but you don't want Bill 402 moved out of committee. Even if it passed, you know ExComm would never implement it. Shit, it amounts to repealing the Emergency and giving the country to the Iffers. No way the government would stand for that. So you must want something else. What, money?"

"Bill 402 and nothing else."

"People—you know, people can get hurt playing hardball."

"They certainly can. A good argument for not trying to play hardball with me, sir."

"Where I come from, that's a threat."

"I'm from the same neighborhood."

"Tell me, Mr. Wigner. Where did you get this stuff?"

Wigner smiled.

"How's your fettucini?" asked Mr. Charles.

"Awful."

"Yeah. Okay, my friend, I'll see what I can do. But I'm gonna want the originals of these, and if you think you can yank my chain twice, you're gonna wake up with your balls in your eye sockets."

"Mr. Charles, I'm going to yank your chain whenever I feel like it." Wigner stood up. "Thank you for giving me some of your time. I really appreciate it."

Peter Todman's office was on the sixteenth floor of the Empire State Building, an oddly unpretentious location for the headquarters of the gigantic Polymath Corporation. The room would have been spacious if not for the clutter of tables and benches, all supporting computers. Todman himself was a gangling young man of twenty-seven, dressed in gray jeans and a plaid shirt. He shook Wigner's hand shyly and waved him onto a couch littered with printouts.

"Just shove it on the floor. Uh, you want a Coke or something?"

"Coke is fine."

"Two Cokes, Polly."

The dispenser behind Todman's desk lit up, and on its screen was the image of the little girl.

"Coming right up, Peter."

Two cans clunked down the chute. Todman handed one to Wigner and popped the other with a nervous, practiced twitch.

"My accountant says to say thank you for that tip about Northeast Seaboard. We had a lot of dough with them."

"That's why I passed the word."

"Crazy world. Something's really gone wrong. Plenty of work to do, and nobody working. Plenty of needs, and nobody trading. Food piling up on the docks, and people starving. I'm making two million dollars a month, and most people are on ration stamps."

"Our Marxist friends would have plenty of reasons for it, if they weren't just as badly off."

"Think it was Mexico?"

"Defaulting helped. The Africans helped when they defaulted, too. Now, with Brazil and India, we're really in the soup."

"Gee. Seems like just the other day everything was going so well. I wish to heaven we could do something. Think we ought to just migrate downtime, find some piece of wilderness and forget about this?"

"That'd be like forgetting the gangrene in your leg. Actually, Peter, I think I know a way you could do some real good. Know a guy named Bruce Fujii?"

"Flatfoot Fujii, sure. Works for Hewlett-Packard. Smart guy."

"Steal him. Any way you can, any amount of money he asks for, anything he wants, give it to him."

"Gee. You his agent?"

"Wish I were. He's got an idea about computer security, a way to protect against viruses and logic bombs. But he's not going to get anywhere with it until he leaves Hewlett-Packard, and if he doesn't come to you he'll go to somebody else."

"Well, that's kind of interesting, I guess. But lots of guys are into computer security. I'm into freer access, myself."

"Sure. So am I, believe me. But the Wabbies are planning a guerrilla war against computers. They're going to try to break the government down by zapping every computer memory they can reach, and they can reach plenty."

"The Wabbies? Those creeps."

"They're going to get away with a lot of it, I'm afraid, but if Polymath can protect its computers, it'll have a fantastic competitive edge." Wigner glugged his Coke. "No point in free access to a lobotomized computer."

"Gee. Not much, I guess. Well, I'll call Flatfoot tonight, see if he wants to come over."

"Peter, it doesn't matter what he wants. You get him under your wing."

"Uh, d'you think you could tell me what this is all about? How come you're doing me these favors?"

"Sure. I'm saving the goddam world."

"Oh."

"No kidding. I really am trying to save the world, Peter."

"I believed you the first time, Eric. I just want to wish you good luck."

"In the old days, a couple of years ago," said Franklin, "we would have put in a massive memory block that was nothing more than artificial amnesia. Amputation. We're a lot more selective now. We've studied the language of your brain; we understand the way you think and remember."

"So I'll remember—what I don't remember."

"Yes. You won't remember the feelings it produced. And they won't return when you think about it."

"I'd settle for amnesia."

Franklin chuckled.

For the next six hours, Pierce relived Ulro from beginning to end, over and over, while Franklin read the screen and administered judicious quantities of drugs. In colloidal microdroplets, the drugs traveled through Pierce's brain to predetermined locations where ultrasonic signals broke the microdroplets and released the drugs directly into the neural tissue. Beta-carboline analogs intensified his memories of Ulro, enabling Franklin to pinpoint the neural anchors for Pierce's emotional response. The price was a series of convulsions; Franklin's nurses were prepared.

Next came a sequence of benzodiazepines, blotting out the limbic responses that had driven Pierce into a fugue state.

"Sort of like getting a stain out of a shirt," Franklin remarked to one of the nurses. "Just keep scrubbing and scrubbing and putting more spot remover on it."

After the first two hours, Pierce stopped screaming. When the blocking session was over, he slept.

At breakfast, Franklin saw Pierce jogging around the lawn in his pajamas, sweat pouring down his face.

Franklin tapped on the glass and Pierce waved. A few minutes later he came into the refectory, his bare feet wet and covered with bits of grass.

"It seems to be September," he said, sitting across the table from Franklin and helping himself to biscuits and honey. "I've lost a lot of time."

"Not all that much. Tell me, Jerry, what did the people in the tunnel look like?"

Pierce's eyebrows rose. "Like mummies. Dessiccated. Why? Oh, of course. Testing."

"Yes. You passed. Would you like to call Eric Wigner, or shall I?"

"I will."

Franklin, smiling faintly, looked into Pierce's eyes and looked away again, out at the green grass gleaming in the late summer morning. Someone, or something, was still down there in Pierce's eyes. Franklin wasn't sure if it was snarling or screaming, but it frightened him.

Twelve:

"New houseplants," Pierce remarked as he entered the Bleecker Street apartment. An aspidistra stood in a corner of the living room, an asparagus fern on a bookshelf.

"Wanted a welcoming look."

"It's nice. Thanks."

"Take your shoes off and relax while I get us a couple of beers. We have a lot of work ahead of us, old son."

Wigner worked hard at being jovial. Pierce was very much his old self except in the eyes. It was mildly disconcerting to talk to an intelligent, alert young fellow with the eyes of a much older man.

For hours they sat in the little living room, eating black-market potato chips and cold cuts and drinking Tsingtao beer, while Pierce's Polymath flashed away at them and Wigner occasionally interrupted with a comment or two.

"So that's what you look like dead," Pierce said when Wigner showed him the file on their Ulro cognates. "Not much different."

"At least they did me the honor of taking my picture. *You* appear to have ended up in some nameless ditch."

"Done in by the FBI. Hate to have it happen twice."

"It won't." Wigner swigged beer. "At least our cognates got rid of some prime bastards. We're going to do a lot better."

A little later, Pierce said: "I can't believe the dope dealing."

"Believe it. Tony Charles is my favorite. The son of a bitch actually got taxpayers' money to subsidize three fentanyl labs out in Queens. Local Industry Grants. The stuff is addictive with one dose. Polly, give me the Charles file—there it is—he was making about four million dollars a month when they finally nailed him in 2001. Not bad, even with the hyperinflation we're supposed to get starting next year."

They went on through a catalogue of corruption: Agency employees working for the Japanese, the British, the moribund Soviets; politicians taking bribes in return for appointments of black-market stooges to clerks' jobs in food dispensaries or military quartermaster assignments; a call girl network dealing exclusively with senators and their senior staff, and a call boy network serving the same clientele as well as Ex-Comm.

"I always thought gays were attracted to interior decorating and modern dance, not administration," Wigner said. "Shows how sheltered my youth was."

They reviewed organized crime and its connections in the CEA, the immigration scams and the draft-dodging arrangements for the sons of CEA officials, the bribery of Food and Drug inspectors to pass toxic meats and contaminated grains, the rakeoffs and skims and rigged lotteries: names, dates, amounts, favors granted, benefits received by relatives, business associates, employees, as revealed in the briefings that had gone to the top of a government rotting all the way to the bottom.

That was only a fraction of Wigner's files. More had to do with the economic upheavals of the next few years, the national defaults, the bank failures, the corporate cannibalism, the draconian laws that staved off disaster for a few weeks more by beggaring some other nation. And with the occasional amazing strokes of technological brilliance that still flashed through the gloom: new computer designs, new breakthroughs in genetic engineering, the eradication of cancer and diabetes by minor editing of the human genome.

"It's interesting, but it's a blind alley," said Wigner sometime long after midnight.

"The issue is how we avoid running into the same mess," Pierce agreed.

"That damn Wabbie plot is the key element," Wigner said. "Now that we know it's coming, I want to provoke them to a premature move."

"Why bother, if you can stop it anyway?"

"Ah, can I? We're starting to see information gaps. The database is eroding because your old T-Colonel colleagues are losing control, the governmental structure is fracturing, people aren't feeding the computers. Better to goad the Wabbies into action while we still have enough information to respond properly."

"How?"

"All will be revealed in time, old son. But we have more on our plate. Congressman Charles is moving Bill 402 out of committee, but he's dragging his feet; I want him moving faster, or replaced by someone with more motivation. Those two ExComm members spying for the Japanese—I intend to make that public."

"You should just turn them."

Wigner looked thoughtful. "Make them feed us information, in exchange for not being exposed? It's an idea, but I prefer the idea of a paralyzed ExComm staring up its own backside. Once the CEA is completely discredited, and impotent as well, the Iffers should be able to get public opinion firmly on their side."

"Are they that strong? A genuine opposition?"

"Almost. Did you notice all the American flags as we were driving down from Woodstock? Backlash against the Iffers. It's building fast, but the jerks have nothing to support but ExComm. Take ExComm out of the picture, and the hyperpatriots have nowhere to go."

"Unless they find some leader of their own."

"They tried to on Ulro, after the Wabbie coup failed. Of course, they didn't have an International Federation to be scared of, but pathological nationalism can always find enemies. On Ulro Senator Cardwell came pretty close to uniting the jingos, but we'll deal with him in the next couple of weeks."

"All right. What's my agenda, then?"

"First, a couple of days of rest. Then we slip some information to Internal Security about ExComm, and copies to the Canadian and British media. Otherwise our own media won't dare touch it."

Pierce nodded, stretching and groaning. "Let's go for a walk. I've been sitting down too long."

"At this hour?"

Pierce grinned at him, and Wigner saw the old wolfishness glinting in Pierce's eyes, obscuring the old man's thousand-yard stare. "Afraid you'll die before 2002?"

"All right."

Greenwich Village was dark, yet the streets were full of people. They sidled along the storefronts, clustered in doorways, trading in joints and crack and little boys and girls. Occasionally an army patrol roared through in an armored personnel carrier, lights blazing, and people scuttled into shadows. Somewhere to the south, a rifle cracked twice.

Pierce seemed to enjoy the coolness of the early autumn night; he strode along the sidewalk, brushing past the beggars and prostitutes while Wigner stayed close to his side. They reached Washington Square and circled the park, then sat on a bench to listen to an old man play the mandolin.

"What a mess," said Wigner. "I'm amazed we haven't collapsed already."

"Me, too. When they stop playing music at 2:00 A.M. in Washington Square, that's when we'll really be in trouble." Very lightly, Pierce touched Wigner's shoulder. "We've got somebody on our tail," he murmured. "Been following us since we left the apartment. I put him about fifty feet behind us."

"Well done, old son. What should we do?"

"Head back to Bleecker Street."

"And then?"

"Don't worry."

They stood up and drifted across the park, two dark figures among many. Occasionally they passed a cluster of people gambling at cards or chess around a Coleman lamp or a candle; then they were back in darkness.

"Next doorway," Pierce muttered as they rounded a corner. Wigner stepped to his right without a word, and Pierce joined him. A stained sign advertising some defunct graphics company filled the door. The dirty windows were plastered with American flag posters, Wabbie logos, and defaced IF rainbow stickers.

For a minute, no one passed by. Then footsteps, quick and light, pattered erratically on the broken sidewalk. Pierce reached out and hooked an arm around an almost invisible shadow.

"Talk or you're dead," Pierce said. His Mallory was jammed in the follower's ear.

"Oh jeez, oh shit, mister, don't do nothin' please." The boy spoke in a hoarse, urgent whisper.

"Who sent you?"

"Nobody, please, I din't do nothin'!"

"So long, buddy," Pierce said impatiently, and clicked the impact setting up a couple of notches.

"I'm nobody, I'm nobody. The hit team is back at your place, Bleecker Street. Oh, Jesus and Mary, don't hurt me, I'm doin' what you said ain't I, two guys, Black dudes from Queens in this little Toyota, they work for some doper lab, I'm just s'posed to keep track a you, let 'em know you comin' back, right?"

Pierce clicked the impact setting back down.

"Good boy," he said, and shot him in the shoulder. The boy slumped; Pierce lowered him gently.

"Sounds like your friend Mr. Charles," Pierce remarked as they continued their walk.

"The little bastard," Wigner hissed. He strode in silence beside Pierce for a couple of blocks. "He's just moved himself up the agenda."

Pierce paused at the corner of his block. The crowds had thinned. Brownstones loomed darkly on both sides, revealing no light. Above, the overcast reflected the scattered lights of the city.

"Across the street—there's the Toyota," said Pierce.

"What bright eyes you have, grandmother."

"Go on down to the front door and let yourself in."

"Alone?"

"Unless you can get your mother."

"Jesus."

Wigner started walking, his eyes on the orange Toyota. The street was empty now. Pierce had vanished into the darkness.

A light in the hallway glowed faintly through the windows beside the door to the apartment building. Wigner knew he would be easily visible against the orange glow, a perfect target. Tautly, he walked up to the doorway.

Across the street, Pierce walked past the Toyota. Its windows were partly down, but the men inside were only silhouettes. Mimicking the boy's hoarse New York accent, Pierce whispered: "That's the guy," and kept walking. The two men got out quickly, making little noise. Pierce shot them both at maximum impact, then went back and shot each man again. He walked across the street and up the steps.

"All done. Let's get upstairs."

"I didn't even hear anything."

"Are you complaining?"

When the sun came up a few hours later, Wigner glanced out the window at the street. The orange Toyota was partly stripped. Two dead Black men lay near it, one in the street and the other on the sidewalk. Both looked as if they had been stripped as well: neither had a jacket or shirt or shoes. An old woman walked past, ignoring them.

"This is a pain in the ass, Jerry. The son of a bitch knows I'm Agency, and he's still pulling this kind of stuff. Not to mention that he knows where you live."

"But you need him to get Bill 402 to a vote."

"Not that badly."

This morning, Pierce's first day back on the job in months, he endured a certain amount of fussing from the Semiotronics office staff. Left alone to get on with his work, he ran a quick scan of all inputs that showed no problems. The chief security threats were computer incursions, usually from the FBI or National Security Agency, although occasional probes came as well from other corporations and foreign intelligence services. Since those organizations used almost no Trainables, their efforts at incursion were pathetic by Pierce's standards.

Then he punched into the computer in Wigner's private office on West 38th, and from there linked up illegally with the congressional LAN in Washington. Wigner had already obtained Anthony Charles's office code, so it was not difficult to tap into it. A countertap could be traced back only to the private office, which Wigner had rented under a false company name.

For the rest of the morning Pierce monitored the congressman's communications—mostly a dreary routine of correspondence with constituents, with an occasional short memo to staff members or colleagues. Finally, something interesting came through: 4227 TO-NIGHT AFTER 1900.

Congressman Charles did not acknowledge the message, whose source was a public phone in Queens. But fifteen minutes later he made a reservation for a MATS flight from Andrews AFB to Old La Guardia. The plane would arrive at 1930 that night.

Commanding his terminal to continue recording Charles's transactions, Pierce went upstairs to Wigner's office on the next floor.

"News?"

"A hasty flight to Old La Guardia this evening. Does the number 4227 mean anything to you?"

Wigner frowned, then smiled. "Ah. He used rental lockers at Old La Guardia and Kennedy for his drug transactions. Maybe he's making a pickup."

"Worth a call to the narcs?"

"Some would just rip Charles off and come back for more. Try a guy in the FBI downtown, Ollie Rivera."

"And if it's not what we think it is?"

"We know where Tony Charles lives. We'll get him one way or another."

Wigner went back to work, which was playing the futures and currencies markets. He was doing so for himself, not Semiotronics, and he was not making huge amounts of money. But he never lost.

Jonathan Clement, in his office on East 52nd, was surprised and annoyed. On his terminal, the headline in the *New York Times* was prominently displayed on page one: *Congressman Charles Arrested in Major Fentanyl Raid*. The story described the arrest in some detail, including the congressman's attempt to escape and the subsequent raids on three labs. Eight other people had been arrested as well.

Clement shook his head irritably. Something like this should not be news to Research Services Division; the congressman's sideline should have been known and exploited long ago. He could expect some jovial kidding from Langley, followed by memorandums requesting firmer intelligence on potentially embarrassing conduct by politicians.

He patched into the office LAN and linked up with Jaz Jones.

REQUEST INTERVIEW HERE AT ONCE.

ON MY WAY.

She was wearing a no-nonsense tweed jacket and skirt, and no jewelry (a woman who worked down the street had lost an ear in a robbery recently). Even so, Jaz looked elegantly lovely.

"Hear about Tony Charles being arrested?" Clement poured her a cup of coffee.

"Yes. And I thought he was just an honest idiot."

"He's right in our backyard. We should have known about this instead of waiting for the damned FBI to bring it to everyone's attention. Would you please monitor the case and see if anything else is likely to turn up?"

"Jonathan—I'm sorry, but my workload's really heavy. I've been doing most of what Eric Wigner used to handle, plus my own stuff, plus trying to fill holes in the damn database."

"Drop it like a hot potato for a week, all of it. I'm going to need running reports on all federal politicians and maybe some of the senior bureaucrats. Any whiff of scandal should come straight to me."

She rolled her eyes. "I suppose I should thank you for expecting so much from me."

"Take any three junior people you need. Tell their bosses I approved your request. But I don't want us caught with our pants down again."

"Well, it'll be a change from monitoring arsenic levels in alfalfa."

While she was waiting for her new staff to wrap up their current tasks, Jaz accessed the police files on the Charles arrest. They included a report on an anonymous phone call tipping FBI agent Oliver Rivera to the likelihood of a fentanyl transaction at Old La Guardia, the arrest of a man observed to be placing a briefcase in locker number 4227, and the subsequent arrest of Congressman Charles when he opened the locker, removed the briefcase, and replaced it with his own. The first one had contained three hundred thousand dollars in cash and twenty thousand dollars' worth of meat and dairy ration stamps. The congressman's had contained nothing but a shaving kit in which was a small plastic box full of fentanyl.

According to the police report, Tony Charles had been interrogated by the feds. Jaz turned to the FBI database; the dumb-dumbs in the Bureau thought their computer security was the best in the world, and the Agency had long encouraged them in that belief, so she had no problem accessing the Charles file. The interrogation had not yet been logged in; she made a note to check back, and then met with her new team to outline what Clement wanted. The three teenagers bitched and moaned and went back to their cubicles.

Jaz spent some time going through the congressman's files, finding nothing of interest, and then went back to the FBI. The interrogation was now logged in. Tony Charles had said very little except to demand his lawyer (a touching reminder of habits ingrained before the Emergency had made them pointless), and to say: "That little bastard Winger did this."

"Who is Winger?" Rivera had asked.

"Some little creep in the CIA, but he's really working for the goddam Iffers."

Then the congressman had refused to answer any more questions, and had been placed in a cell to think things over.

Jaz grinned. Winger indeed. It had to be Eric. But what on earth was he up to?

She decided she would have to find out, but whether she would tell Clement was another question.

Morton Friedberg and Winston Walker, both GS-10s in the Agency's Internal Security Division in Langley, gaped at the screen of Friedberg's Polymath. Using a printout that had been anonymously delivered to him, Friedberg had spent the last day tracing bank accounts from the Cayman Islands to Nagasaki. Walker, the division's expert on Japanese intelligence, had been providing advice and analysis.

"I can't believe it," Friedberg said. "I just can't believe it."

"Thornton and Hardaker," Walker muttered. "Two of the toughest bastards on ExComm, feeding the goddamn Japs."

"If this is right, they've been doing it for over two years. The Japs've known every policy decision, how everybody on ExComm voted, what we were doing in Venezuela and Canada—the works."

"I'll say this much for them," said Walker. "Moriyama's paid them a lot more than he usually does."

On the screen, Friedberg's Polly waved at him. "Morty," it said, "the Canadian Broadcasting Corporation is carrying a story about this case on its current newscast. Shall I patch you in?"

"Jesus H. Christ. Yes, please."

"—Hardaker, the former president of Transmarine Corporation, is alleged to have been on the payroll of the Japanese Secret Service for almost three years. He was appointed to the Executive Committee of the Civil Emergency Administration as soon the Emergency was declared. Sources say the Japanese have paid the two men almost twenty million dollars each.

"Neither man could be reached for comment on these charges, and American intelligence sources say they have no comment on the report."

Friedberg swore and slapped the table top. "The goddamn idiot Canadians should've jumped on this story. Hell, now it'll be all over the northern U.S."

"Worse," said Walker glumly. "That's a broadcast that gets picked up by National Public Radio. It's all over the country."

Friedberg glared at him. "National . . . Public . . . Radio? They carry foreign newscasts?"

"They have for years, Morty. But not for much longer," said Walker.

"ExComm spokesperson Theresa Lewis told reporters tonight that Hardaker and Thornton had been under suspicion for some time, and that they had been given only disinformation to pass on to the Japanese. The two men are now under arrest at an undisclosed site near Washington."

Pierce popped another Tuborg and flipped channels. The story was on every news broadcast.

"They're certainly trying to make it look good," he remarked.

"Good luck to them," Wigner said with a smile.

The next morning, Pierce left Kennedy International on a commercial flight to Albuquerque, ostensibly on an emergency trip to his ill mother in Taos. In Albuquerque he changed IDs. As Jason O'Hara, a GS-8 in the Defense Department, he connected with a MATS flight from Kirtland Air Force Base to Salt Lake City; there he rented a car and joined a convoy headed north into Idaho. He drove long into the night to Mountain Home.

A direct flight to Mountain Home would have been easier, but he wanted no one at the base to know he was around; besides, it gave him a chance to see what the countryside looked like these days.

For mile after mile, through the rich farm country of northern Utah, he saw deserted farms and orchards, fields gone to quack grass and scrub. The few occupied farmhouses were the ones with barbed wire and signs warning that trespassers would be shot on sight; some had the Wabbie logo as well. The collapse of agriculture was nearly complete: generations of technological change and economic idiocy had driven American farmers back to Third World levels. Well, they would do better in the clean soils of the downtime worlds, where the pests were not evolved to thrive on poisons and the water wasn't carcinogenic.

It was after midnight when he parked in a security garage on the edge of downtown Mountain Home. The streets were silent and empty; not even army patrols were out. He walked a dozen blocks to Doria's house without being challenged, feeling annoyed at the slackness of his successor.

A light was on in the living room; he knocked softly and called her name. A moment later Doria stared at him through the peephole in the front door. "My God, Jerry, what are you doing here?"

"I was in the neighborhood and thought I'd drop in."

The locks and latches clicked and rattled and she swung the door open. Then she stepped back to let him in. He walked in, grinning a little shyly, and undid the toggles on his duffel coat.

"Let me take that. Come and sit down and I'll make a cup of tea. Do you want something to eat?"

"Just tea, please. And a bed."

Doria stood in the doorway to the kitchen, arms folded. She was wearing a bathrobe he didn't remember. "Jerry—I don't think I can put you up. I'm married now."

"Really?" Pierce felt a faint flutter of alarm. That hadn't been in the files when he'd checked them before leaving New York. "Congratulations. When did this happen?"

"August."

"Good for you. It's okay. I can sleep on the couch."

"Jerry—" She growled in frustration and went into the kitchen. He heard a clatter of kettle and cups. Heavy footsteps sounded in the hallway and a tall man, in a bathrobe just like Doria's, came into the living room. Jerry stood up and extended his hand.

"Hi. I'm Jerry Pierce."

"Oh. Doria talks about you all the time. Hi, I'm LaMar King."

"Good to meet you. Gee, I wish I'd known. I could've brought you a proper wedding present. All I've got is some canned Polish ham."

"All *right*," LaMar said. "We haven't seen ham around here in weeks."

Doria came back in with a tea tray and put it on the end table. She seemed more composed.

"Okay, what's this all about?" she asked as she handed Pierce a cup.

"I need you to deliver something to a guy named Wes McCullough. He's got a little ranch off Highway 20."

"Why can't you deliver it yourself?" LaMar asked.

"I'm shy."

"He never did like answering questions unless he felt like it," Doria told her husband.

They chatted over tea, gossiping about events in Mountain Home—a fire at the mall, the killing of a meatlegger, problems with increasing violence among Doria's pupils. LaMar, also a teacher, was worried about his students' involvement in the Wabbies.

"They've really bounced back since you were here," he said. "You see that damn bunny logo of theirs everywhere. The kids think Wabbies are some kind of modern Robin Hoods. Even some of the other teachers are leaning that way."

"Not Joe Martin," Doria said.

"Right, and he got beat up. Hell, they even have people like Senator Cardwell backing them these days. No wonder the kids think it's cool to be a thug with a shotgun."

"They'll get over it," Pierce said. "God, I'm bushed. Is it okay if I just crash here on the couch? I'll be gone in the morning."

"I'll get some sheets and blankets," Doria said.

In the morning, Doria woke at a little after six when the front door quietly closed. She slipped out of bed without waking her husband and went into the living room. The sheets and blankets were folded neatly on the couch; on the end table was a small padded envelope and a folded sheet of paper. The paper gave instructions for delivering the envelope. It sounded awfully complicated to her, but she knew she could do it. She was annoyed at the businesslike tone of the note, as if they hadn't made love on that couch and a lot of other places in the house. It confirmed something she had sensed in him last night, a change: a coldness in his eyes, a division somewhere deep in his mind. She wondered what he'd been doing back in New York that could have changed him so much. But she would do what he asked.

Doria sat drinking tea in the kitchen, watching the sky turn rosy in the east. The 6:30 news on the radio was full of stories about the ExComm spies and some New York congressman, arrested for drug peddling, who had hanged himself in his cell. The president was calling for renewed moral firmness in government.

She wondered what a ragged-ass Idaho rancher could do with a specially delivered computer disc.

Thirteen:

Two days after Pierce returned from Idaho, he was working in his office at Semiotronics when Wigner walked in looking grim and tense.

"They've found another chronoplane uptime."

"*Uptime?*"

"Somewhere in the thirty-fourth century. The Columbia team opened it up five days ago, and it took me this long to find out."

"Well? What's it like?"

"Dead. That's all I know so far. Oh, and they've named it Urizen."

That night Pierce took the evening subway to an old apartment building on Claremont Avenue, a block from the Columbia campus. The neighborhood hired its own rifle patrols; one of them stopped Pierce as he was walking past the old Juilliard School of Music, but the Jason O'Hara DoD identification got him through. The lobby guard was a little slower, but finally buzzed the apartment of the man Pierce wanted to talk to.

"It's a guy named O'Hara from the Defense Department," the guard shouted into the intercom.

"*I don't know him,*" the answer came, "*and I'm very busy.*"

"Dr. Levy—it's about Urizen," Pierce called.

The intercom was silent for a second. "*Shit. Send him up.*"

The fourth floor apartment had been carved out of a larger one: a long hallway ran from the front door to the living room. Philip Levy, in jeans and a Harvard sweatshirt, escorted Pierce down the hall and waved him into an armchair. Pierce glimpsed a harried-looking woman at work in the kitchen.

Levy sat on a couch facing him. He was a slender, hard-faced man with intelligent and suspicious eyes.

"If you know about Urizen, you ought to know better than to blab it in public. What's the story?"

"I need you to be able to keep your mouth shut, too. Deal?"

"This smells like some kind of blackmail."

"No. You're under tight security. So am I. But we may be able to help each other."

"Maybe."

"I'm the guy they sent through to Ulro."

Levy looked startled. "I heard the guy went nuts."

"I did. Nothing lasts forever."

"So. Well, I'm glad to know you. Glad to know you're okay. Why d'you want to know about Urizen?"

"I was sent to find an information repository down in Riverside Park. It was in ruins. My boss wonders if maybe the repository on Urizen is in better shape."

"So he can send you through and make you crazy again?"

Pierce smiled. "Something like that."

"He'd be wasting your time. We've done two sorties in robot tanks, and most of Manhattan, as far as we can tell, is buried in lava."

"Lava?"

"Looks like there must be a string of new volcanoes just off the coast, or on Long Island. We had to move the I-Screen up to the fourth floor of Pupin Hall to get above the lava. But I'll tell you this—Urizen's got more atmosphere than Ulro. Almost as much as Mars."

"And volcanoes would be due to—"

"The burn zone around the equator. It must've completely changed plate structure and dynamics all over the planet. We figure Ulro and Urizen won't settle down for a couple of million years. They're in tectonic convulsions."

"So Urizen had a Doomsday, too."

"Looks that way. Eventually we'll find relics and get the details, but it all looks like Ulro plus a thousand years. Too bad."

"Yes."

"Can you imagine if we'd opened up a live chronoplane, with people, a thousand years ahead of us? God, we could learn so much."

"The way the downtime civilizations are going to learn from us."

Levy's mouth twitched. "I'll ignore the sarcasm. In any case, we still seem to be at the head of the line and headed straight for our own Doomsday in less than a century."

"What's your team going to do next?"

"Send out more tanks. Study the place. And keep looking for another chronoplane uptime."

"Think you'll find more?"

Levy opened his mouth, shut it, and shrugged. "I don't know, Mr. O'Hara. We've got unbelievable data and no theory to explain it. Ishizawa and his people speculated that maybe time was folded on itself during the Big Bang, that every particle in the universe oscillated in time and somehow left ghosts of itself at different points in the timeline. Some people are digging up Everett's old many-worlds theory."

"If a particle can jump two ways, it actually jumps

both ways and the universe splits into two parallel worlds."

"Something like that. Maybe it explains Heisenberg indeterminacy, but it doesn't explain chronoplanes. If we opened up a screen on a world just like our own, only with minor differences, that would help strengthen the Everett theory. Instead, we get these worlds scattered at random over almost a hundred thousand years."

"Just as well."

"Huh?"

"Who'd want another world almost exactly like this one?"

Like most people with an emotionally important secret, Levy was glad to talk once the secret was out. He showed Pierce some photographs the tank had taken. The landscape of Morningside Heights was black curves and edges, with occasional drifts of gray ash. The Jersey Palisades were only a long, low bluff above a flat plain where the Hudson River had been. The sun shone down out of a purple sky with just a few stars shining in it.

Pierce looked at the photographs and thought of the dead people in the tunnel, buried now forever. Then he drank a cup of tea offered by Mrs. Levy, thanked them for their time, and left.

Getting the car and enough gas had been a drag, but now that they had them the freedom of movement was exhilarating. Doria and LaMar drove the little Hyundai north on Highway 20 through a glorious autumn morning. At the National Guard roadblocks they explained they were buying eggs for their teachers' association.

The ranch was a decaying A-frame set beside a couple of orthodox log barns in the middle of a meadow. Two rusted pickups, one evidently being cannibalized to keep the other one running, stood in the dusty barnyard. Chickens darted across the yard. A man stood in the near barn, wearing a brown leather jacket, jeans, and a holstered Mallory.

"Where'd he get a gun like that?" LaMar wondered quietly as the man walked out to meet them.

"Mallorys are a big deal these days. Very macho. Hi, Mr. McCullough?"

"Yes."

"Our name is King—I'm Doria, this's LaMar. We're from Mountain Home, from the teachers' association; thought you might be able to sell us ten or twelve dozen eggs."

"I might. Afraid the price is two dollars an egg plus fifty dollars' worth of meat stamps."

LaMar sighed, but Doria answered at once: "Well, it's a lot, but people are yelling for 'em in town. I guess we can afford it."

"Come on in the barn and get some cartons."

They moved into the cool, musky air of the barn. McCullough handed them each a half dozen old plastic egg cartons and nodded toward the nests. "Oughta be able to collect 'em with no trouble."

"Thank you." She kept smiling. As LaMar headed for the nests, Doria paused by McCullough's side and slipped the disc into the pocket of his leather jacket.

"That has to go to the Wabbies," she murmured.

"What is it?"

"You don't want to know."

"Who's it from? What is this?"

"Just pass it on. They'll recognize it."

"And if I don't?"

Doria looked at him and shook her head slowly.

"Here's to the domino effect," said Wigner. They were sitting in the West End, a bar across Broadway from Columbia. Pierce had walked down Claremont and met Wigner there; they had had mediocre pastrami sandwiches and a couple of black-market beers, and were listening to a jazz trio reviving Jimmy Giuffre.

"Anything you say, boss."

"Thornton and Hardaker were only the first to fall. Now ExComm's screening itself and its staff, and so far three paper-pushers have been found with unusually comfortable bank accounts outside the country. My faith in human nature is restored."

"Have the Wabbies tried anything yet with that present we sent them?"

"Not yet. They'll want to test it very carefully before they go all out. I'm just as glad. Flatfoot Fujii has his shield program completed and Polymath's been making copies day and night, but they haven't all been distributed. We've got them, of course, and most of our friends in the wailing-wall network, but that's just a fraction of what needs to be covered. By the end of the week we'll be ready for anything."

Pierce was having a good time that autumn. The days were warm and sunny, the sunsets spectacular in the smoky air. Mozart had been brought uptime (almost certainly on a heavy regimen of tranquilizers) and was touring the Germanys; his concerts were televised worldwide and, for cultural programming, gained good ratings. A new kind of TV called polychannel holovision could, for a very high price, put Mozart in one's living room. Pierce could pay the price and then some, on what Wigner was slipping him.

Over twenty Jesuit physicians and surgeons had wangled their way onto Eden, and were trying to teach medicine and hygiene from Krakow to Granada. One of them, an ebullient Paraguayan, had become a popular figure on TV talk shows: he often came uptime to appeal for funds, and his homemade videos of twelfth-century Paris and London revealed a world of gorgeous squalor that Pierce yearned to savor firsthand.

The few surviving tabloids were screaming about UFOs sighted over the North American glaciers of Ahania, and about strange new diseases. The disease part, at least, was true enough. On the wailing-wall network people were reporting cases of yellow fever in New York, Philadelphia, and Baltimore. A form of malaria from Eden was spreading across the Middle East. Mosquitoes could travel through an I-Screen as easily as a human.

Pierce monitored it all, marveling at the images of eighteenth-century America and prehistoric Europe. He thought sometimes about Ulro, but with the detachment of someone recalling a scene in a movie.

Sometimes he and Wigner went out and picked up girls; the offer of a good dinner in a black market restaurant was too good to turn down. Afterward they would go to Wigner's new apartment in SoHo, which he had bought on the proceeds of his recent investments. It was a jungle of houseplants, amid which stood a medium-quality Polymath with absolutely no questionable files in its memory. Wigner and Pierce and their pickups would drink, listen to music, and fornicate; a few girls lasted as long as a week.

"At some point," Wigner remarked after handing two of them taxi fare and a little extra, and seeing them to the door, "you want to talk to them, and they're . . . unTrainable. What is one to say?"

"Good-bye," said Pierce.

Nosuke Moriyama, cultural affairs attache in the Japanese consulate in New York, stepped into an elevator in the World Trade Center after a hurried lunch in Chelsea. He had a very busy afternoon ahead of him, and scarcely noticed when only two other persons entered the elevator with him.

As soon as the door closed, they turned to face him—a surprising breach of Western etiquette in close surroundings. One of them, a tall young man in gray flannel slacks and a blue blazer, pointed a Mallory .15 in Moriyama's face.

"Please come with us, Mr. Moriyama," the other young man said gently, in passable Japanese. "We mean you no harm, but our business is urgent."

The elevator doors opened again, and Moriyama walked out with the tall young gunman just behind him and the police companion at the attache's side. Moriyama briefly debated eliminating them both and decided against it.

They walked into a deserted lounge, a rather grimy place with torn upholstery on the armchairs and a persistent taint of old cigarette smoke. The polite young man with the big shoulders invited Moriyama to take a seat on the least battered couch, and then sat beside him. The young gunman took a chair nearby; he would have a clear shot at Moriyama as well as plenty of warning if anyone else wandered down the hall.

"I apologize deeply for this unpleasant interruption," said the polite young man. "We did not want to disturb you in a public place like the restaurant, and still less on your own premises in the consulate. The firearm is a symbol of our seriousness, not a personal threat. I sincerely hope we have not insulted you."

"Quite all right," said Moriyama genially. He was beginning to be amused. At least this was not a typical mugging or extortion attempt. The polite fellow spoke Japanese like a Trainable, fluently but bookishly. Both of the young men seemed unusually intelligent, although the tall one made Moriyama a little nervous: he was clearly a killer, but of a sophisticated kind one rarely encountered outside Japan, and never as young as this one.

"Mr. Moriyama, I wish we could introduce ourselves, but you understand that's not appropriate. We are here simply to ask you to convey a message to your superiors in Tokyo."

"I will be honored to."

"The message is this: the Japanese government must stop its colonization of the American west coast on Eden. At once."

"I don't know what you're talking about. Is this some kind of code?" But he felt almost nauseated at what the young man's demand meant.

"Sir, you are the senior director of Japanese intelligence operations in North America. I'm surprised that you didn't warn Tokyo against the project. In the present political climate, an incursion into American territory can only aggravate the most reactionary and racist groups in this country."

"The west coast on Eden is not American territory."

"The American public has not yet grasped that subtlety, sir."

"I take it your superiors have some threat to make."

"My superiors make no threat at all, sir. I believe they are still unaware of the colony, although they're bound to learn within a few weeks. But I am prepared to warn you, sir, that this colonization adventure sets a very bad precedent. No individual nation has until now tried to establish a permanent colony downtime. Settlement would be much easier if it were directed by international authorities after careful study and consultation."

"Evidently my government feels otherwise."

"Please tell them to suspend the project, sir, and to recall their colonists. Otherwise I will be obliged to roll up all your remaining agents in North America."

An obvious reference to the fools Thornton and Hardaker. Moriyama was tempted for a moment to ask, as one professional to another, how those two agents had been identified.

"Young man." Moriyama paused to gather his thoughts, and realized the young man had used the first person singular in making his threat. "You say your superiors know nothing of this project, yet you are in a position to dismantle several networks on your own."

"I can give you names, addresses, and phone numbers, sir." The young man handed Moriyama a single sheet of printout. Moriyama read it in an instant and handed it back. It would be pointless to urge the young man to destroy the list.

"I believe I should be grateful to you gentlemen. We were evidently placing ourselves in a vulnerable position. Thank you for pointing that out to us."

The young man's face was deeply earnest: "It's an honor to deal with you, sir. I assure you that your interests and ours coincide. We will be in a position soon to reward your cooperation."

"I have no doubt of that." He stood up; the two young men stood also. "Please keep in touch with me. It has been a pleasure to meet you."

"The pleasure is ours, sir."

Smiling, they escorted him to the elevators and waved him onto one. Their farewell bows lacked any hint of mockery.

Wigner turned to Pierce. "Wow. Me, giving orders to *Moriyama*. I ought to turn myself in for felonious chutzpah."

Jaz Jones and her team had gotten nowhere. Scandal after scandal had erupted in ExComm, in Congress, in the public and private bureaucracies. She had backsearched each of them, looking for something in common, some source of information. Nothing.

It had to be Eric. Somehow he had accessed a whole cesspool and punched holes in it, but she couldn't understand how. When she monitored him, he was innocently engaged in the making of incredible amounts of money. Semiotronics had turned in weeks from just another break-even proprietary to a major economic force in the stock market. Eric's advice had done it, and on his own time he was becoming richer than anyone could have imagined.

Eric understood the Agency's methods of computer monitoring, so she had to be circumspect in keeping track of him. Still, she began to notice times when he linked up with a computer somewhere outside the Semiotronics office. On a hunch, she switched to monitoring Pierce; he, too, was linking into an unknown machine.

Knowing that, Jaz went to Clement and asked for a bug to be placed at Semiotronics.

"Our own people? Our own people are behind this?"

"I didn't say that, Jonathan. I just need to know where some people are sending messages."

"Is it Eric?"

"Jonathan! I'm trying to be professional. Now, can I have the bug or not?"

"All right."

The bug enabled her to pick up leaked radiation from all the computers on Wigner's floor. Sorting through the jumble of over forty machines, she finally found the signatures of Wigner's and Pierce's. They were accessing the same machine somewhere in the West 30s, and they weren't even being very careful about it. Jaz obtained the access code from Pierce, and after a discreet pause she entered the machine herself.

—And was stymied. The computer's defenses were formidable; any approach triggered at least three kinds of alarms, and maybe more, which could be disarmed only by someone who know specific procedures that could not be monitored. After one probe she withdrew, swearing. Her attempted entry would be recorded; Pierce and Wigner, if the machine was under their control, would be alerted and the defenses would be strengthened still further.

But what were they up to, with a private machine guarded as well as anything in the Pentagon? Mere possession of such a computer made them about as innocent as two little boys with a nuclear bomb in their wagon.

She could simply pull in the Internal Affairs people, send them off to arrest Wigner and Pierce, and transport them up to Woodstock for deep interrogation.

That would certainly answer questions. But it was almost like cheating; she wanted to beat them with her brain, not Agency muscle.

"Anything come of that bug?" Clement asked after a couple of days.

"I'll let you know. By the way, have you heard that Polymath is putting out a new computer-security program? Are we getting it?"

"I don't know; I hadn't heard. We'd better get on it. Life is tough enough without being able to get into people's databases."

"God damn it to hell!" Clement shoved his chair away from his terminal and stood up. He yanked open his door and shouted for Jasmin rather than paging her on the LAN.

"Look at this, for God's sake," he demanded as she entered his office and shut the door behind her.

The terminal screen showed the front page of the New York *Post*: RATION STAMPS CANCER SCARE! Clement slammed the return key and the screen offered the story: a scientist with the National Institutes of Health was warning that a chemical in ration stamps could induce malignant melanoma. The scientist estimated that over twelve thousand cases were already attributable to the chemical, and predicted that cases would double every month for the foreseeable future.

"Come on, Jonathan, it's the *Post*. Just more sensationalism."

"It's intolerable. Is it true?"

"Certainly not. It looks like standard disinformation."

"We might run this stuff on the Russians or the

Japs, but we'd be idiots to run it on our own people. Who the hell is behind this?"

"The Russians or the Japs?"

"Find out."

"On top of everything else I'm doing?"

"I think this is part of the whole mess." Clement glowered at the terminal screen. "Someone's trying to destabilize this country, and they're doing entirely too well."

Fourteen:

Senator Cooledge's office staff included four plainclothes bodyguards who made no effort to conceal their Uzis or their suspicions of everyone who came down the hall. They scrutinized the pass that had admitted Wigner into the Senate Office Building before one of them muttered into a newfangled ring-mike. Receiving acknowledgment through his earphone, he briskly patted Wigner down, found no weapons, and unlocked the door to the Senator's office suite.

Wigner was not deceived by the normality of the reception area or the casual, no-necktie appearance of the staff. A mirror behind the receptionist was surely two-way, with at least a TV camera behind it and probably another gunman as well. Partitions (certainly bulletproof) broke the corridors into mazes, denying intruders a clear field of fire and minimizing the blast effects of a bomb or grenade.

The receptionist sat at a desk behind a clear plastic shield; she gave Wigner a thoroughly professional smile.

"Please take a seat, Dr. Wigner. The senator will be free in a few minutes."

Wigner smiled back, more pleased than he cared to admit about being called doctor; with three Ph.D.s and two more in the works, he felt entitled. Settling into an armchair, he snagged the latest issue of *Time*. It was only forty pages long, and photos filled many of them. Advertisements were almost entirely propaganda pieces about the Civil Emergency Administration: smiling nurses in camouflage tending to ailing senior citizens, a dedicated-looking hardhat repairing a phone line (sabotaged by the Popular Action Front or the Wabbies?), a cheerfully perplexed housewife with two tots wondering how to feed her family nutritious and tasty meals. ("Have a chat with your local Food Dispensary dietician!").

The news stories were mostly media fog, although an inch was given to the investigation into the suicide of Congressman Tony Charles. Wigner found nothing about the bombing of the Iffers' Los Angeles office (three dead, five injured), the police riot that broke up an Iffer parade in Chicago, or the Wabbie attack on a National Guard armory in Little Rock. All had been big news this week on the wailing-wall network, and no doubt in ExComm's briefings.

Wigner permitted himself a mild twinge of anxiety. It was all very well to know from Ulro's history that the country was still a couple of years from real breakdown, but the I-Screen had changed matters very rapidly. Daily events no longer matched the accounts Pierce had brought back from Ulro; the future was once again becoming unknowable. In playing the markets, Wigner was finding himself losing money almost as often as he was making it. It was the loss of control that worried him more.

"Dr. Wigner, the senator will see you now." A young staffer, short and rather slim, escorted him circuitously down the halls. Wigner had reviewed the dossiers of all congressional and senatorial staff, and knew this mild-looking man to be an ex-Marine who had won a Bronze Star in Venezuela. Senator Cooledge had a knack for picking highly suitable people; she could not be expected to know that even this man would not be suitable enough when the assassins came.

The senator's office was a windowless room with a rather poor quality hologram on one wall. It showed a redwood forest, and a little girl leaning against the trunk of a giant tree: the senator's daughter.

The senator herself was standing by a homey-looking maple table with four matching chairs in the corner of the office opposite her desk. The kitchen-intimate atmosphere was enhanced by a small refrigerator and stove set into the wall.

Senator Cooledge was a tall woman with straight gray hair, high cheekbones, and a quick grin. Her sober blue suit was set off by a yellow silk blouse and star sapphire earrings. Wigner was pleased by her strong handshake.

"Good to meet you, Eric. Have a seat. I can offer you something to drink as long as it doesn't have caffeine in it."

"Whatever you're having, Senator."

"Orange juice."

"Wonderful."

She opened the refrigerator and pulled out a tall glass jug. "I think they send me about twenty percent of the whole California orange crop these days. I'd feel guilty if I didn't like the stuff so much."

"They'll find a cure for the blight."

"I'm sure they will."

"Someone specific. A Chinese geneticist named Deng Yangming."

"Really. I thought I knew everyone working on the problem."

"She's new. Doing graduate work at Zhongshan

University in Guangzhou. I've sent her some money and advice."

"If you're trying to impress me, you're succeeding. You sound very different."

"She's good. But she's not why I've asked to see you."

"I thought not." She managed to look relaxed without slumping into her chair; Wigner made himself sit up straighter. Good for her: she knew how to control even a Trainable stranger.

"First, I should point out that this conversation should not be recorded," Wigner said.

"It's not."

He knew she was telling the truth. As she knew it. He had already activated a magnetic scrambler concealed in his briefcase. If any of the senator's aides were too zealous, and had slipped a bug into the office, the scrambler would deal with it. Crudely physical eavesdropping seemed unlikely.

"Semiotronics thinks I'm here to advise you on reviving the aerospace industry," he said. "Thanks to my successes in the last couple of months, the firm's given me a lot of leeway. I'm actually here to offer my services to the IF movement."

She took it in stride. "That's very kind of you. I imagine you have a job already in mind."

"Not for now. For after. For now, all I want to do is to supply you with information and advice."

"About what, Eric?"

"Who your enemies are, for one thing."

She laughed. "My enemies usually tell me that themselves. At length."

"I mean the people prepared to kill you, Senator."

"Why do you think I have all these bodyguards? It's

a dull day without a couple of death threats around here."

"The Wabbies are going to do more than that. On Ulro, they assassinated you just a few months from now, if that makes sense. They got that young ex-Marine as well, the fellow who brought me in here, and your receptionist and five other people who work for you. And a friend of mine and I ended up getting killed for avenging you."

Her face was calm and expressionless. "How do you know this?"

Wigner explained. When he finished, she sat very still.

"It's different this time because of the I-Screen," she said.

"Yes, ma'am. We're going crazy in a very different way, but eventually we're going to have face Doomsday just as they did on Ulro and Urizen."

"And no one in this damn city understands that!" Senator Cooledge exploded. "They're still trying to wangle a new set of tires on the black market, or they're off building survival cabins in Virginia."

"That's immaterial if the IF comes together."

"It already has. Eighteen countries, ten more about to join—"

"So far it's just another gang of Third World countries. If we and the Europeans and Russians and Japanese and Chinese don't go in, the IF will fall apart. If we join, the other big powers will come in for sheer self-preservation."

"I know. So you propose supplying me with information to make it easier to move us into the IF. I'm going to need more than that."

Wigner reached into his briefcase and withdrew a computer disk.

"Have this copied and installed in every computer you have. It's for Polymaths, but it can be adapted for IBMs and Apples as well."

"What is it?"

"An antivirus defense program."

"We have them."

"Not this good. A really nasty virus is going to be used against the whole government computer network—"

"What?"

"—and any machine without this program is going to be killed. The surviving computers are going to give us an edge."

"My God, Eric, are you serious? The whole governmental network? Everything would fall apart overnight."

"That's what the Wabbies are hoping. The dumb bastards aren't even planning to pick up the pieces. They just want the government off their backs so they can sit and scratch their fleas in peace. Plus blow the heads off Blacks and Jews, and a few others like you."

"Wabbies. This is . . . bizarre. Now, you appear to have some kind of plan even if they don't."

"As soon as they've crippled the government, they're going to find a lot of their enemies still have a working network. Their hit squads will walk into ambushes. When the District Commanders start pulling things together, they'll find lists of Wabbies turning up in the database. And that will be it for the Wabbies."

Wigner drew another computer disk from his briefcase. "This is a condensed version of the database I derived from the Ulro files. It has economic information, political analysis, and a detailed chronology of the next few years as Ulro experienced them. That's already going cockeyed, but it'll give you a good idea of what to expect if the IF doesn't win."

"How confidential is this?"

"That's up to you, Senator. You can keep it to yourself, or share it with your staff, or mail it to Ex-Comm."

"Don't strike poses, Eric."

He felt taken aback.

"You know perfectly well I'd do no such thing, so why even suggest it? I'll keep it strictly personal for now. After I've studied it, maybe I'll bring in some of my people for their opinion. And thank you for it. I'm sure it'll be helpful. Now, what do I owe you for these little presents?"

Wigner was uncomfortably aware of having lost the initiative to this damned intelligent woman. "Once the IF is operating," he began hoarsely, and cleared his throat. "Once it's operating, it's bound to set up an agency to supervise I-Screen use. Everything from anthropologists to colonizing expeditions. We won't have a choice; we've got to control the downtime chronoplanes in some kind of orderly fashion."

"No argument."

"Sometimes that agency will have to take direct action to achieve its goals. It'll have to police the I-Screens to ensure they're not being used to exploit the endochronics, or to enrich some people at the expense of others. I don't think you're backing the IF just so it can turn into a new kind of imperialism."

"Fair enough. And you want a job in this agency."

"I want *the* job in this agency. Call it what you want, but I want to run intelligence gathering and analysis, economic development, and political action."

She smiled, without humor. "Meaning covert operations."

Feeling more confident, Wigner shrugged. "They're going to be necessary."

"Haven't we have enough grief out of that whole attitude?"

"We'll have more grief without it, Senator. If you have a fighting chance now, it's partly thanks to the political action I've already taken."

"You set up Tony Charles—"

"He set himself up."

"And Hardaker and—"

"That's right. Not to mention a number of other operations, including stopping the Japs from colonizing California on Eden."

"My goodness, you have been busy."

"I hope to win this job on merit, Senator."

"Eric—have you thought this through? The moral implications of what you're doing?"

"Yes, ma'am. Very carefully. On Ulro I got killed for doing a lot less."

"You understand I can't promise you what you're asking for. We have the little matter of restoring constitutional government in this country, and then joining the IF. A lot of other people are going to have opinions on time-traveling spies."

"All I want is you on my side, Senator."

She studied him carefully and a little mistrustfully. Then she picked up the jug and poured the last of the orange juice into his glass.

Wigner caught a ride in a government shuttle bus out to his parents' home in Silver Spring. He saw them rarely these days, and looked forward to having a few hours with them.

Much of the suburban belt around Washington had fallen into decay, and a few neighborhoods had been abandoned to squatters willing to tolerate the lack of safe water and reliable power. Casual arson and vandalism had done relatively little damage compared to the effects of simple neglect. But enclaves of the old order still endured here and there; Silver Spring was one of them.

The house on Madison Street, like its neighbors, was solid brick. It was set back from the street behind a wrought-iron fence whose spikes had become conveniently functional. The front yard, once a smooth lawn, was now a vegetable garden. Little still grew in it this late in the season, but a roll of concertina wire gleamed around the perimeter of the garden.

His father Woodrow greeted him at the end of the driveway, unlocking the gate and then embracing him as it swung open.

"Packing a gun?" Wigner said in mock surprise. "Don't you trust the armed forces?"

"Not a hell of a lot." Woody Wigner slapped the holster on his hip. He was a tall man, pushing sixty with a tanned, bald scalp and prominent cheekbones. He wore an old-fashioned Eisenhower jacket and jeans; both seemed a little too big for him. "It's a damn nuisance, but it beats getting kicked around. How are you? You're looking kind of porky."

Wigner, two inches shorter than his father but much heavier, gave him an amiable punch in the arm. "Not as porky as I'll be when I leave. Mom got lunch ready?"

"Almost. She's been working on it since yesterday."

They ambled up the driveway, enjoying the autumn sunshine. A little Suzuki 4WD stood outside the garage.

"Where'd you put the Jag?" Wigner asked.

"In the garage, on blocks. Maybe we'll revive it

next spring. In the meantime we manage to get enough gas to take the Suzuki out a couple of times a month."

"Still making political statements, huh?"

"Of course."

Woody Wigner was Old Democratic Money; after a few years in the family's import-export business, running the European offices, he had sold the firm and gone to work for the Carter Administration as an international trade expert. He had stayed on through Reagan's first term, then gone to work for a series of policy analysis institutes and think tanks. The Emergency had ended that; the Wigners now lived on a diminished but still considerable investment income, and Woody Wigner occasionally acted as a consultant to one branch or another of CEA.

"Still, isn't it a little dangerous to be driving a Japanese car around Washington?"

"Oh, you get some snotty remarks, but that's all. I hear it's a lot worse out west. People in Toyotas being beaten up, that sort of thing."

"Any foreign car, at least in some places." Wigner could have mentioned dozens of incidents in the last few weeks: a particularly futile form of xenophobia, given the millions of foreign cars in the country.

They went up the driveway to the backyard and entered through the kitchen door. Olivia Wigner looked up from her cutting board and smiled.

"Here he is!" He enjoyed a floury hug and the familiar sweet scent of her hair. She was smaller and fairer than Woody, with the same sprinkling of freckles across her forehead that her son had.

They spent an agreeable hour before lunch sitting in the patio, drinking home-brewed beer. The yard, like Madison Street, still kept its trees; Woody's compost heap was piled high with leaves. Woody gossiped a bit

about old acquaintances, while Olivia probed deli-
cately to learn whether Eric was serious about any particular girl.

"We were concerned when you left the Agency," his
father said after the second beer.

"Well, Dad, you know Semiotronics is a proprietary."

"Indeed I do. But it's not the same as working for
RSD."

"It's better. My boss leaves me alone to do my job,
and he's not scared of Trainables."

His father chuckled. "Then he's a dummy. When
are you going to take over his job?"

"I have my eye on a couple of career prospects."

"Back with the Agency?"

"In a way."

"Some day," said Woody, "when you're well and
truly retired, I'd love to hear what they've got you
doing."

"I'll tell it all, and you'll be bored rigid."

"Not a chance. Listen, what is happening with all
this time travel? When are they going to start seriously
exploring? You going to get into that?"

"Be exciting, wouldn't it? I just hope nobody screws
it up. Can you imagine what could happen if everybody started going downtime? They'd ruin everything."

"Eric, we have to go downtime. With Doomsday
coming, we'll have to move to Beulah or Eden or—"

"Sure, Dad, but it's got to be organized. What if the
Russians decided to colonize North America on Eden
or Ahania? Or some damn cult tried to send mission-
aries to convert the natives? We've got to have some
kind of control."

"Oh, I don't argue with that. But even if it doesn't

work out that way, it doesn't matter. We'll have all those worlds to settle, time to figure out Doomsday, a whole renaissance. God, it'll be better than going into space." He coughed, wincing. "I've been telling everyone who'll listen that we need to stake our claims fast."

Wigner smiled vaguely and opened another beer.

Lunch was a thick vegetable soup and fried chicken from a neighbor's flock.

"We're not secure enough to keep our own chickens here," Olivia lamented. "If it's not people, it's dogs. The Laffertys are really set up, though, so we trade them fruit and vegetables for eggs and chickens."

"Life in the Third World," Woody sighed.

"Speaking of Third World, what do you think about the Iffers?" Eric asked. "I hear Portugal's about to join now."

"Well, we never will," said his father. "This country is pretty screwed up, but I can't believe we'd ever give up our sovereignty to some jumped-up UN. Least of all while the present government's in power."

"Bill 402's coming to a vote any day now, isn't it?"

"ExComm's friends in Congress are stalling it. And if it does come to a vote, ExComm will buy enough votes to make sure it fails."

"Aw, Dad, come on. ExComm's in enough trouble without that."

His father grinned lopsidedly at him. "After a certain point, Eric, scandal and outrage become political anesthetics. We've heard so much lately, it's stopped bothering people. And never underestimate the effrontery of the Civil Emergency Administration and ExComm. Do you seriously think they'll end the Emergency and hold real elections? Just because some leftover political hacks ask them to? If the bill did pass, ExComm would just dissolve Congress. Six months later, who'd care?"

"Your father is a bitter and twisted man." Olivia laughed. "He never got over his crush on Jimmy Carter."

"I think the bill will pass," said Wigner. "And I think ExComm will hand power over to a provisional government."

"Only with a gun to their head," his father snorted.

"Probably."

Woody's eyes flashed at him. "Are you hinting at something? A coup?"

"Dad, come on! All I mean is, the people behind Bill 402 are damn serious."

"Not as serious as they'll be when ExComm puts them in Harper's Ferry."

"The concentration camp?"

His father looked mildly surprised. "That's not exactly what I'd call it, but that's its purpose, I guess. Not many people know about it."

"I know it's been built but not occupied. There are six others as well."

"It figures."

Olivia looked alarmed. "You don't think they'd actually put elected people in there?"

Woody looked at her and shrugged. "The ones who don't just disappear."

"My God," said Olivia. "At least Eric's keeping his nose clean."

"I sure hope so," said his father. "These guys play rough, and they—" He paused. "They play for keeps."

Wigner knew what his father had intended to say: They don't like Trainables.

"My nose is immaculate," he said. "How are chances for another beer?"

The afternoon went on in casual conversation, interrupted by a few chores with Wigner helping out. Without making a fuss about it, he installed Flatfoot Fujii's defense program in his parents' computer, along with a few other software items. Around three, Wigner made his farewells and hurried to catch the shuttle bus back into the city; he did not want to be stranded in the suburbs overnight.

On the bus, looking out through the antigrenade mesh covering the windows, Wigner felt a stab of sorrow. His father was dying of lung cancer and had told no one, not even Olivia. Especially not Olivia. A casual check of his father's medical records had revealed the facts only a few days earlier.

Wigner was angry with himself for knowing so much, yet not knowing what to say.

Pierce was about to leave work for the day when his Polly waved at him and chirped: "Message for you, Jerry!"

He keyed his bulletin board.

Dear Jerry, I'm an old buddy of Eric's. He's told me a lot about you. Would you like to meet me for dinner this evening? I think we'd find we have a lot in common. My code is JJ-125E5290. Sincerely, Jaz Jones.

Fifteen:

Indian summer was gone, and a chilly wind blew down the streets of New York under a cloudy sky. Pierce, in brown wool slacks and a tan anorak, left Semiotronics and walked briskly up Lexington to 55th Street. The day was darkening, and not many street lights were on. People leaving work were hurrying to catch the afternoon subways; no more would run until late in the evening. Surprisingly few police were around because of the big Iffer rally in Central Park, reportedly the biggest yet. Pierce hoped the Iffers' enemies would stay away; a riot now, with Congress on the verge of passing Bill 402, could endanger everything.

He turned into the dark doorway of a restaurant and knocked. A speaker in the wall crackled at him; he identified himself by sliding his ID into a slot. The door opened and a smiling man in an evening jacket greeted him.

"Ms. Jones is already here, Mr. Pierce. Please follow me."

This was a privileged place, with clean carpeting and crisp linen on the table. Candles burned, throwing a pleasant glow across the wall hangings. Only a few tables were occupied, by well-dressed couples with observant eyes.

Jasmin Jones was at a table in a far corner. She

greeted him with a dazzling smile and a firm, friendly handshake.

"Jerry. Please sit down. I'm so glad you could make it."

He sat across from her, his eyes adjusting to the dimness until he could see just how beautiful she was.

"How's life on East 52nd?" he asked.

"Dull. Semiotronics?"

"Interesting."

"I'll bet. Is Eric still getting rich?"

"Very."

"That's not all he's doing, is it?"

Pierce's expression didn't change. "He's down in Washington today, doing some consulting."

"With Diane Cooledge."

"Among others, I guess."

"Do you know how suspicious that looks to us?"

"Not yet."

"Then I'll tell you: damn suspicious. My boss thinks Eric is up to no good."

"Clement has a right to his opinions."

"Jerry, we could fence around all night. You and Eric are messing with something. We don't know just what it is, but it smells. You've got a computer that's defended like Fort Knox, and that doesn't look good."

Pierce grinned. "That's just Flatfoot's new program."

"Flatfoot Fujii? It figures. But how come you've got this new program and we don't?"

"It just went into production a week or two ago. I can give you a copy tomorrow."

The waiter arrived and they ordered after a glance at the menus. Then Jasmin said: "I'm trying to decide which way to jump, and you're not making it any easier."

Pierce lifted his eyebrows.

"Clement's had me trying to track down the source of all these scandals. I'm not getting anywhere, but I'm sure you guys are involved. I don't mind that. Maybe you've got a really good idea going. Maybe I ought to be on your side. But I need to know what the hell you're doing."

"Hey," Pierce murmured. "Eric's an ex-RSD employee. I'm an ex-T-Colonel. He's twenty-two years old and I'm eighteen. As you ought to know." He was rubbing her nose in it a little: Trainable etiquette discouraged mention of what ought to be common knowledge. "The source of the scandals is a lot of incompetent jerks. How are *we* supposed to be able to start a bunch of scandals with ExComm and the CEA and God knows who else?"

Jaz smiled and gave him a direct look over the candles.

"That's exactly what Jonathan would like to know."

Pierce looked back, and she found herself glancing away. For the first time in weeks she began to think that maybe her suspicions were wrong: Pierce would have to play some kind of important role in Eric's plans, but Pierce's eyes in the candlelight looked crazy. Crazy people couldn't function, not as Pierce would have to.

"What was it like on Ulro?" she asked suddenly.

The glint in Pierce's eyes faded a little at the shift in the conversation.

"Quiet. Really quiet. Did you think the question would rattle me?"

"No," she lied. "Just curious."

"Well, I'm curious, too. Why does Clement have a thing about Eric?"

"Eric was such a bright boy. People said he'd be

running RSD when Jonathan retired, unless something even better turned up for him first. I don't know if Jonathan liked the idea or not. Eric's a big pain in the ass, but he can be fun to be around. Never know what he'll think of next."

Pierce grinned. "True."

"And then it all got screwed up by the Ulro project. Except it didn't really get screwed up, did it? You got whatever it was he sent you for. You didn't tell Eric the repository was destroyed. You probably weren't in shape to say anything. But he was there in the chamber with you, and you gave him those six microfiches. I'll bet you gave him a lot more than that."

"You're smart," said Pierce with a crooked smile. "IQ of 175, Pattern Apprehension Response of three seconds with ten percent of a Level 20 pattern. What your files don't say much about is your ability to make strong commitments. Your dad left you and your mother when you were ten, right?"

"What's this got to do with anything?" Jaz asked coldly.

"You started sleeping with men when you were thirteen, always men a lot older than you, men old enough to be your father. You even slept with the man who Tested you. You picked men with a lot of suppressed unhappiness. Men who felt they were losing their grip, getting old. And you offered them—what? A chance to feel young and manly?"

"You tell me, Jerry."

"Whatever it was, they usually fell in love with you. And then you'd cut them off. 'If you ever come near me again I'll tell the police you raped me.' Give them a taste of your father's medicine, show them what it's like to be deserted by somebody you love. The thing is, you really loved them, too. It wasn't just casual revenge.

"So you ended up with the Agency, working for an unTrainable who's a lot like your father and all the other men in your life. He's a jerk, but he's not entirely stupid, and he's got access to your files, too. He knows you fixate on guys like him. You're a lot more grown up now, you're not going to try to seduce the head of the RSD, but your habits are pretty well set. So he uses you. Exploits you. You're a Trainable, jumping through hoops for an unTrainable, and part of you is glad about it and part of you is disgusted. So you learn more than you tell Clement, and you don't know which way to jump. Intellectually you know you ought to be on Eric's side, whatever the hell he's up to. Emotionally you can't bring yourself to leave papa. But you will."

"Because I always sell out the men who love me."

"No, you always sell out the men you love. I don't think Clement gives a damn about you." Again Pierce looked straight into her eyes. "The only question is when."

Jaz stared at the candle flame. "If you're through showing off your ability to get into my files . . . You haven't denied what I said, about Eric getting something from you in the chamber."

The waiter arrived with their veal. After a moment Pierce cut a piece, ate it, and nodded.

"Good?" she asked.

"Fair. But I was agreeing with you."

The fork was trembling in her hand; she forced herself to meet his eyes. "You mean I'm right."

"Uh-huh."

"And why are you admitting it?"

"It'd be nice to have you on our side."

"And if I sell you out, the way I'm supposed to sell out Jonathan?"

"You won't, even if you want to."

"Why not?"

"No point. First of all, you don't love Eric or me; we're not your type at all. Second, you don't have time. The government's about to fall. Any minute. How's *your* veal?"

They talked quietly in the restaurant for a long time. Then he walked her back to her apartment in Wigner's old building on East 52nd and refused her offer of a nightcap. He went to the subway station and waited in the dimness for almost an hour before the train came, packed with people. Silent, he stood in the crowded car as it rumbled downtown.

He walked across the Village, whose streets seemed deserted compared to last summer. A couple of blocks from home, he saw an unfamiliar car parked under a streetlight. It was a glossy blue Plymouth with gold trim, the kind the Agency and FBI often used. Like a poisonous butterfly, it flaunted itself so that predators would keep clear. Drawing closer, Pierce recognized the license plate of an Agency car. He wondered what the Agency was doing in the Village.

The men in the car were familiar faces from some flickerscreen: Agency goons often used for stakeouts. Pierce passed the car and turned right at the next corner. Another Plymouth, parked at the end of the block, held two more men.

For a moment Pierce felt like pausing to chat with them, then realized he might compromise their operation. Better to go on home.

—Unless Jaz Jones had talked, and he was the target of their operation.

He walked up to the second car and rapped on the driver's window. The man looked at him in the uncertain lamplight.

"You guys sure look bored," Pierce said.

"I'll be damned!" said the driver with a big grin. That confirmed it: these men were unTrainables who had no reason to recognize him. "Hey, Jerry, climb in and have a drink. Yeah, it's pretty boring, all right."

The left rear door clicked open. Pierce got in, noting that the perspex barrier behind the front seat was down. The little yellow lights on the dashboard indicated the car's defenses were operational. An assault from outside would have left him retching on the street in a cloud of Mace or worse.

"God, I could use a drink. It's cold."

The driver's companion turned around, passing him a hip flask.

"There you go, my friend."

"Thanks." Pierce shot him with the Mallory at low impact, the flechette hitting just below the man's collarbone. An instant later, as the driver was reaching for the old-fashioned microphone hanging under the dash, Pierce shot him as well.

The flechettes worked instantly, inducing a moment of shock and then unconsciousness. Pierce awkwardly lugged the driver into the backseat. Then he got into the driver's seat and listened to the others in the stakeout chatting over the radio.

"We have an acquisition on Target 1," an unfamiliar voice broke in after half an hour. "We'll maintain position around Target 1; Target 2 may turn up."

"Hope so," said the stakeout man whose car had first attracted Pierce's attention. "I wanna go home. I'm tired."

"C Group," said the dispatcher's voice, "you guys still on post or what?"

Pierce thumbed the microphone. "Copy," he mumbled.

"Stay awake."

"Copy."

Target 1 was surely Wigner, and they had an acquisition. The Agency had picked up Wigner just as everything was about to fall apart.

Pierce looked at his watch. In about fifteen minutes the men would begin to revive. He spent the time thinking and watching the occasional pedestrian or bicyclist hurry past the car.

Finally, the men began to snore, and then to gasp and smack their lips. The man slumped in the seat next to Pierce opened his eyes first. He had the usual calm, detached look of someone who'd been doped, and he looked at Pierce without fear or surprise. A few seconds later the man in the backseat, the driver, woke also. Pierce slid around a little so he could face them both.

"Where are they taking Wigner?" he asked.

"Who's Wigner?" mumbled the man in the backseat. He was stocky man with a crewcut and bad skin; Pierce was annoyed at not recognizing him.

"Target 1."

"I don't know."

Pierce looked at the other man sitting close beside him. His name was Ernest Peurifoy; Pierce had seen his files.

"Ernest. I need to know where they've taken Eric Wigner. Don't play dumb with me."

"I really don't know, Jerry."

"And where were you supposed to take me, Ernest?"

"That's not part of our job. We're just stakeouts."

Pierce sighed and glanced out the windshield. "Ernest, you and your friend are pros, all right? So save me this name, rank, and serial number stuff. In about five seconds I'll kill your friend in the backseat, just to get your attention, and if you tell me after he's dead I'll be pissed off at you anyway and I might kill you, too. If you're both heroes, you'll both be dead and your wives will get nice certificates to hang over the mantel, about what brave servants of the country you were. If you guys had the drop on me, you know damn well I'd talk. So give us all a break."

"I don't know, Jerry," said Ernest. He was tall and lanky, with straight gray hair falling across his lined forehead. As the Ketaset wore off, his expression grew more alert.

"Shit," said Pierce, and shot the stocky man in the chest. The flechette made a short, sharp *crack* as it struck a rib and penetrated. The stocky man sighed wetly and slid over onto the seat.

"That was Impact 9," Pierce lied. "Talk, Ernest."

"Oh, Jesus. Oh, hell. You *killed* him. I oughta—"

"Talk."

"I—I—it's supposed to be the building up at 84th and Riverside. They're going to pump him full of shit and find out what he's been up to."

"Who gave the orders?"

"Clement, who else?"

"When?"

"Two days ago."

"Who else knows besides the stakeout team?"

"Now, now, I really do not know, Jerry. Maybe some of Clement's office people. I don't know."

"Jasmin Jones?"

"The kid? Cute one? Jesus, I don't know. I don't think she ever gets into this kind of stuff."

Pierce fired the Mallory into Ernest's stomach. Ernest gasped and asked in a quavering voice: "Jerry, did you kill me?"

"No. Not your friend either. Go back to sleep."

As soon as Ernest had slumped against the window, Pierce turned on the car ignition and made a U-turn.

After lugging Ernest into the lee of a dumpster in an alley off Sheridan Square, Pierce heard the radio paging C Group. He hurried back, mumbled a few words into the microphone, and then hauled the other man out.

He would have to work fast, against too many variables. Even in its decrepitude the Agency had more than enough power to stop him. Everything would hinge on moving faster than it could and on not running into needless trouble.

He drove quickly but carefully north, back to East 52nd. An obvious Agency car could be parked easily in the security garage under Jasmin's apartment building; from there he went to the intercom and tapped the sequence of buttons that coded for her apartment.

"Yes?"

"It's Jerry again. I'm in the garage. I need you."

"So, we're supposed to go up to Riverside Drive and rescue him?"

She sat on the couch in her tiny living room huddled in a terrycloth bathrobe, her damp hair wrapped in a towel. Pierce sat opposite her in an armchair; between them, on a cheap teak coffee table, stood a silver tea service and two bone china cups.

"They'll pump him dry, and when they learn what

he knows they'll decide to kill him right away. As soon as Eric's dead they'll go after everyone in the wailing-wall network, everyone who got Flatfoot's program. That way they'll have a fighting chance to survive the Wabbies, because we won't have an organized group ready to take over."

"But will they even believe what Eric tells them? Everything's perfectly normal, the computers are all working, so why should they do something as drastic as killing Eric and arresting a whole bunch of people?"

"He'll be telling the truth as only drugs can make him. And they're not entirely dumb. They'll know that their chances of rolling us up are fairly good as long as they still haven't been hit with the virus. Once their computer net breaks down, the advantage will go over to us."

"Because you'll have a functioning network."

"Enough to enable the Senate to pass Bill 402 and dissolve the CEA, and then run something like a provisional government long enough to get us into the IF."

"And we've got to get Eric out?"

"Two reasons. One, he knows more than anyone else. He's the manager. Two, he's my friend."

"That's really sweet."

"Dry your hair and get dressed."

They went back downstairs to the garage. Pierce backed the Plymouth out of a visitor's stall and drove slowly to the barred gate. The guard came out of his little office and manually unlocked the gate.

"Something wrong?" Pierce asked.

"Aw, the computer's down for the whole building. Pain in the ass."

"That's never happened before," said Jaz as they

turned north on Madison. "My apartment'll probably be overheated or freezing when we get back."

"Worry more about the building defenses. That guard didn't look as if he could fight off a mean little kid." Pierce clicked his tongue in annoyance; the traffic signals, all the way up the avenue for blocks, were blinking green in all directions. Traffic was already snarling up at the intersections.

Making an abrupt U-turn, Pierce drove a block south and managed a right turn onto 51st. Traffic here was a little lighter, so they made progress despite more all-green signals. As they reached Sixth Avenue all the lights went out—signals, street lamps, and the few lights burning in the buildings.

Pierce swore and punched on the car's radio. The stakeout teams downtown were barking at one another and complaining about the blackout. Someone interrupted every few seconds by calling for C Group.

"That's us," Pierce said. "For all the progress we're making, I might as well have stayed in the Village."

"Listen," said Jaz brightly, "I'm not sure I ought to be doing this. I mean, you're the soldier. I'm not much good at close combat. I never even went to Camp Peary."

"I don't need you for combat."

"Then what? Do I get to play nurse?"

"No. I'll need you for more than that. Just be patient."

He swung the Plymouth up onto the sidewalk, turned the corner, and slid into a gap in the traffic going up Sixth Avenue. Someone honked angrily behind them; Pierce changed lanes and accelerated.

The blackout evidently covered most of Manhattan, maybe the whole city; Jaz could find no local radio stations on the air, only police and agency broadcasts and a few CBers. The pilot of a police helicopter reported a demonstration breaking up at Strawberry Fields in Central Park.

"Goddam Iffers," the pilot commented. *"Burning their little candles. Looks real pretty. Wish I could strafe the bastards."*

"That's right on our way," Pierce observed. They were already in the park. "If we have to, we'll abandon the car and walk up to 84th."

"In a blackout?"

His smile was a quick flash in the darkness. "Scared of the dark?"

"Goddam right."

"This is Tango Niner," a voice rasped from the speaker. *"Can you give us a checkout on an '82 Mercury, New Jersey license RTE 456?"*

"Tango Niner, I could walk out there and take a look. Be quicker, maybe. The computer has totally crashed. Weird. All these little honeycomb shapes, then blooey."

Pierce took a hand off the steering wheel, bunched it as if about to strike a violent blow, and then lightly tapped the wheel.

"They did it. The Wabbies have finally made their move."

Sixteen:

Wigner's body was limp in the hands of the four men who lugged him onto a stretcher from the backseat of the Plymouth. He had never been drugged before; the utter helplessness was more unnerving than the fact of being a prisoner.

With an effort, he blinked against the glare of lights that swung across his field of vision. The echoes sounded familiar; he guessed he was in the parking basement of the Agency house on Riverside Drive, and moments later he saw the familiar elevator doors. Would they hold the interrogation in the subbasement? That would show a certain decorum, a return to the precise scene of the crime.

Instead the elevator rose three floors. Mostly supply rooms and offices here, Wigner recalled, well away from the residential floors. He noticed a red-faced guard in camouflage fatigues posted by the elevator, the muzzle of a Mallory Streetsweeper automatic shotgun jutting above his shoulder. What were they expecting, an invasion?

He forced himself to think: His arrest was probably the result of accumulated suspicions, not some particular slip. They would have Pierce as well. Within an hour or two they would have the names of the major people in the wailing-wall network, of the people with Flatfoot Fujii's defense program. Well, it had always been a gamble. The odds had been better for him than for his cognates on Ulro and Urizen, but they had never been good.

His bearers carried him down a narrow hall past metal doors painted with glossy white enamel. One door opened; as they carried him through, Wigner glimpsed paneled walls hung with good prints by Dali, including the kitschy *Christus Hypercubus*.

They slid him into a dentist's chair in the middle of the room, then strapped him in and tilted him upright. Wigner's peripheral vision was narrowed by the drug, but he was aware of a glossy vinyl floor, a couple of desks, the black screen of a computer terminal.

Three men sat in armchairs below the painting of Christ suspended in midair and staring into an empty black sky. In the middle was Clement, dressed uncharacteristically in jeans and blue workshirt. The other two Wigner recognized from files as interrogation experts: Whitestone from Langley, a pale man with close-cropped blond hair, and Phelan from Denver, heavyset, with a paunch and eyelids that sagged like a basset's. Both were dressed in nondescript slacks and cheap white shirts: interrogation clothes.

Wigner tried to laugh and only choked. Clement frowned.

"Get him into shape, will you?"

Phelan reached into a small black medical satchel on the floor beside him; then he stepped forward and slipped a needle into Wigner's left arm. The arm came to painful life; with every beat of his heart, Wigner felt the antidote waken nerves across his chest, his back, his limbs. The pickup team had shot him in the left shoulder; the spot felt like a ripe boil. His mouth filled with saliva and dribbled before he could make himself swallow.

"Can you talk, Eric?" asked Clement. "What was so funny just now?"

"A . . . genuine . . . case of . . . *déjà vu*."

"How so?" Clement sounded calm, almost cordial.

With an effort Wigner cleared his throat and regained full control of his voice. What he wanted to say deserved Trainable terseness, yet these men would fail to understand it unless he spelled it out. They would also use whatever methods they thought would compel him to speak, and Wigner did not want to be drugged anymore, or tortured. The game was up.

"On Ulro," he said hoarsely, "these two interrogated me after Senator Cooledge was assassinated. I have a feeling I already know what they're going to ask."

"I'm lost already," Clement replied. "Can you help us understand?"

"With pleasure. On Ulro, just like here on Earth, I recruited Jerry Pierce as a hit man. He's a Trainable who's also a natural killer. When I ran across him, I had some vague idea of developing a new organization that would take over when the government finally collapsed. On Ulro, we knocked off a few people. Then the Wabbies' computer virus nearly overthrew the government, and as part of their coup they murdered a lot of their political enemies, including Cooledge. My cognate on Ulro sent Jerry Pierce after the Wabbie executive, and he cleaned them up, but then the FBI caught him and that led to me. Of course, on Ulro the interrogation was about a year from now, and it wasn't held here. It was in Langley."

"Amazing. And how have you come to know this?"

Wigner shrugged, although it hurt to do so. "Jerry brought back a lot more than those six microfiches. Several years' worth of executive briefings and Agency personnel records. Including the transcripts of my interrogations."

"Indeed. That's very interesting. What did we do to you on Ulro?"

"Shipped me off to a camp in Wyoming and then shot me."

"I'm not surprised at that. Your actions have deeply prejudiced your relationship with the Agency."

Wigner laughed; that hurt, too. "They certainly have, Jonathan."

Whitestone cleared his throat. "Eric, can you explain your motives for us?"

"I'll be glad to, Donald. If you'd like to drug me again, you're perfectly welcome, but it's really not essential."

"Thank you," said Whitestone with a pale smile. "It's a pleasure to deal with a professional."

"For me as well. I know you won't take it personally when I tell you that your unTrainability—yours, Jonathan's, everybody's—means you're incapable of handling the problems we face today."

"Go on," said Whitestone, his gray eyes unblinking.

"In the last half century," said Wigner slowly, choosing his words, "the world's ruling classes have been outstripped by technology several times. First with nuclear weapons, then with computers, and now with Trainability. Each advance has made the rulers less able to rule, and given more power to the rulers' servants. Ruling class incompetence has been enshrined."

"I won't argue that," said Phelan dolefully, his basset eyes turned to the ceiling. Wigner rewarded him with a smile.

"The servants have found this a pretty acceptable state of affairs. First they encourage their citizens to live in a fantasy world. The citizens periodically choose a scoundrel who pretends their fantasy world is real. Once he's in office, the scoundrel turns to the servants to find out what to do. They tell him what they find convenient, and he does it, and everything moves along comfortably."

"Please, Eric." Clement sounded mildly impatient.

"Jonathan, I am telling you now what I have never told you before. Pay attention. Now, since Trainability has come in we've had servants of servants, and I guess we've done with you what you've done with our rulers. The difference is this: we've seen that we no longer have the room that you did. You could build your careers on playing games with nuclear weapons, or fooling around with Third World economies, because the only casualties were nameless people in Latin America or the Middle East. By the time we turned up, the casualties were happening right here in America. You'd screwed up the world economy, and now it was hurting us. You'd let the technological initiative pass overseas, and now it was hurting us. You thought you could go on indefinitely as lords of creation, and now you had to hurt your own people.

"Well, Trainables could see where this was leading. We were going to be killed just to keep you unTrainables in power for a couple of years, and then everything was going to go down the toilet anyway. The Ulro documents only confirm what we've been expecting for years. Even what I gave you, Jonathan, should have made you think about where we were headed, about the stupidity of going on supporting the idiots on ExComm."

"Go on," said Clement calmly.

"But you simply treated your own death certificate as an avoidable contingency. You might accept intellectually the idea that the Trainables were the only people able to take over and run things, but you and your colleagues couldn't accept it emotionally. That would mean handing over power, real power, to a bunch of pimply teenagers. That would mean accepting the fact that you'd failed. That all the reasons for maintaining yourselves as the real rulers were phony."

"So you thought you could do better," said Phelan.

"I knew we could, the way a computer can do better than an abacus. You know it, too, or you wouldn't have hired so many of us. The whole system would have crashed years ago if we hadn't propped it up for you."

"Instead of propping it up, you seem to have worked hard to knock it down," Clement said mildly. "You were behind all these scandals, weren't you?"

"Some of them."

"And you learned about them from the information Pierce brought back, the stuff you hid from us."

"In part. The microfiches showed me where to look in our own databases."

"Did it ever occur to you that the government, with the same access to your data, might have used it at least as well as you?"

"No. You'd never have gone after Tony Charles for selling fentanyl. He was too useful in Congress, helping keep the lid on for ExComm. Would you have gone to Moriyama and told him to get Tokyo to cancel their colonization plan for Eden?"

"What was that?" Whiteside demanded. Wigner told him. Clement, for the first time, looked genuinely angry but said nothing.

"You wouldn't have been discreet about it," Wigner went on. "It would've been more convenient to make a fuss, stir up some more anti-Jap feeling, distract people for a couple of weeks."

No one spoke for a moment. Wigner rubbed his head wearily.

"I expect we'll get all the details in good time," Clement said at last. He had regained his composure. "But I'd like to know why you didn't just try to take over the Agency and run things to suit yourself. Or even stage a coup. When we finally tracked down your recent income, we knew something was rotten. According to your bank balance, you could've rented a good-sized army."

Wigner was annoyed; he had tried to cover his tracks, but bank computers were too easily penetrated. He should have known better.

"Why take possession of a burning house?"

"Is that all your country means to you?"

"Jonathan, nationalism is dead. All those stupid sentimental ideas, flags, parades, the pledge of bloody allegiance, yellow ribbons—they're *dead*, they're worse than dead. They're poisoning the living. Nationalism's killed a hundred million people in the last century, and it would've killed even more if we'd gone the way of Ulro and Urizen. It's like the bonding behavior of a baboon troop, but we're not baboons anymore. Would you trust a baboon with a nuclear bomb, or an I-Screen?"

"You're being sophomoric," Clement replied.

"Excuse me, I've been more realistic than you and your Langley friends. If we'd let the Japanese colonize California on Eden, you unTrainables would've run us into a war—not just here on Earth, but on Eden as well. We'd have been like the Europeans in the sixteenth century, fighting each other for control of places they hadn't even known existed a little earlier. For the greater glory of Portugal or Holland."

Clement looked pained. "This is ridiculous. Why should *you* care if we fight a war with the Japanese or the Russians or the Malagasy Republic? *You're* going to be okay."

"Have you been paying attention, Jonathan? The Trainables know we're *not* going to be okay. I-Screen or not, the United States of America is about to fall. It fell on Ulro, it fell on Urizen, and it would've fallen here. But instead of falling into ruins, this time it has a chance of surviving. In your scenario, I'm dead whether I back you up or not. In my scenario, I have a damn good chance of not only surviving but prevailing."

"Ah! Prevailing how?" asked Whitestone.

"The International Federation will need an agency very much like this one, only more so. I'm going to run it."

"That was your plan," Phelan grunted.

"That's still my plan."

"You don't seem to understand the seriousness of your position, Eric," said Clement. "Given what you've told us so far, plus what we've learned on our own, we could put you away just the way they apparently did on Ulro. Don't you understand that you've committed treason, conspired to overthrow the government, broken dozens of laws? Don't you understand that you're a *felon*?"

"Let's go downtime and run that past George Washington and the other founding fathers," said Wigner. "What are you going to do, put me on trial?"

"We lean toward disappearing you, Eric."

"That would be stupid. You'd be foreclosing your options."

"Dismantling the United States is not an option for us, Eric. Never."

Wigner looked at Clement: a middle-aged man with tired eyes and the flesh of his thin cheeks beginning to sag into jowls. A decent enough man by his own lights, trying to save the only world he really knew, a world he thought he understood. A patriot, a loyal member of the baboon troop ready to protect the troop even if it meant all baboons, all troops including his own, were to perish.

Wigner felt a cold spike of despair. The republic would fall, but not until the baboons had ensured that nothing could rise in its place but anarchy and bandit empires.

Phelan was jotting something down on a pad of paper. His droopy eyes looked up and met Wigner's with a concentrated glare of intelligence.

"You mentioned a Wabbie attack. That's a new one on me."

"They've got some good hackers out there in the woods. On Ulro, one of 'em worked out a nasty computer virus. It damn near wrecked the whole Civil Emergency Administration, and if the Wabbies hadn't been so dumb they might've taken over right there. I decided to provoke them, make 'em move prematurely."

"How?" asked Phelan gently.

"The details of the virus are described in an appendix to one of the executive briefings from Ulro. I put them down on a disc and passed it over to the Wabbies. I knew they'd experiment with it a little, and then go right for our throats."

Phelan looked deeply surprised. "You passed the secrets of a computer virus over to the White American Brotherhood?"

"Yep."

"You son of a bitch." Phelan seemed on the edge of losing his temper: his face turned a mottled red.

"They were going to develop it anyway. This way they'll strike before they're ready, and they'll expose themselves badly."

"Do you have a timetable for them, Eric?" asked Clement softly. "Think. You can help undo the damage you've done, some of it anyway. You can show us your heart's in the right place."

"I have no idea when they'll move. Again, you're quite welcome to drug me; I'll give you the same answer."

"Perhaps." Clement stood up and stretched, then paced back and forth in front of the Dali. "Let's begin somewhere near the beginning, shall we? In as much detail as possible."

Delay was pointless, deception futile. Wigner began to talk, fully answering their occasional questions. Whitestone sometimes took notes, scribbling busily on a small pad of paper. That seemed both sad and comical to Wigner, but he did not cry or laugh.

Half an hour into the story, the room went black for a second before the standby generator kicked in. Wigner went on talking. A moment later the red-faced guard entered.

"Excuse me, sirs. East 52nd Street reports the Iffer demonstration is turning into a riot. They thought you ought to know."

"Thank you," said Clement with a warm smile. "Please keep us posted whenever anything develops."

"Uh, that might be kind of hard, sir. We got the message by a courier on a bike. Phones are out."

"Here or there?" Clement asked.

"Looks like it's the whole city, sir. Courier says it's a real zoo out there. Traffic lights aren't working, Iffers running around fighting the cops, real crazy."

Clement nodded. "Thanks again. That'll be all."

The room was quiet for a time. Clement got up and walked back and forth. "What's your opinion, Eric?"

"My opinion's not worth a damn. If you think it's

the Wabbies, turn on that computer and hook it up to the phone lines. That'll tell you quickly enough if there's a virus loose."

Clement nodded to Phelan, who rose with surprising grace for such a heavy man and went over to the terminal. It was an old-fashioned IBM that had to be switched on by hand. Phelan tapped out a couple of brief commands while Clement and Whitestone watched from a distance. Wigner watched, too, ignoring the ache in his muscles.

Phelan switched through three commercial databases without trouble; the screen glowed in the characteristic background colors of each database. Then he opened a link with the Langley computer and the screen flashed into a pattern of green hexagons.

"I can't get it to function."

"Reset it," Clement suggested quietly.

The hexagons faded, then returned. "Nothing," said Phelan.

Whitestone cleared his throat. "That means the Langley database has been destroyed. Probably the National Security Agency as well, and Defense Intelligence and CEA and the State Department. Continental Army Command. NORAD."

"Plus telephones, radar, air traffic control. We've been decapitated," Phelan said, nodding. "Boy, that's some virus you gave them, Eric."

"If the Russians realize what's happened, we're screwed," Whitestone said.

"On Ulro the virus got over there, too." Wigner told him. "Not as thoroughly, but enough to bog them down."

"You knew this was coming," Clement said, spinning away from the terminal and striding toward

Wigner. "You must have made some kind of preparation. What?"

"A program. Wherever the virus tries to access a protected computer, the program destroys the virus and traces its origin. If this really is the Wabbie attack, we'll know every virus source before sunrise."

"Who's we?"

Wigner thought for a moment. If he could stall them long enough, just a few more hours, the District T-Colonels could swoop down on the Wabbies and wipe them out. Senator Cooledge and her allies could ram Bill 402 through while the government was still prostrated. It would be a gamble, because he had based his plans on being free to coordinate the suppression of the Wabbies and the overthrow of Ex-Comm and the CEA. This way, no one would be in charge.

If he talked, he could perhaps regain control: in exchange for coordinating the suppression of the wailing-wall network and the Iffers, he might be able to regain influence with the Agency. It and the government would owe their existence to him. He could buy time to work out some new plan to deal with the chrono-planes and Doomsday.

"I want to propose a deal," he said.

Seventeen:

The road through Central Park was crowded with bicyclists and pedestrians, people walking or riding north toward Strawberry Fields. Many carried burning candles or glowing flashlights, and rainbow flags flapped in the chilly wind. Among the Iffers were clumps of young toughs in leather jackets; Pierce saw the golden glint of a Wabbie symbol on one man's baseball cap. For a few minutes the Plymouth made slow, steady progress as part of a line of cars. Then someone noticed what kind of car it was, and threw a rock. It bounced off the window on Jasmin's side, making her wince.

"I was afraid of that," Pierce muttered. Another rock struck the windshield, and in the glare of the headlights he saw pale, hostile faces turn toward the Plymouth. Something banged against the right near fender.

"They know it's an Agency car," Jasmin said. "How do we get out of this?"

"Reach under the seat. Should be two gas masks. Good. Put one on and pass me the other." Another rock thumped on the roof. "We're both getting out on my side," he went on, and then pulled the mask over his head. It was an Agency special, with a nonfogging, shatterproof faceplate. "Ready?"

"God, no, but let's get it over with."

Pierce pulled the car sharply to the right, onto the sidewalk between two clusters of marchers. Tilting his seat all the way down, he reached back and pulled down the backseat cushion. The ignition key opened a lock; in a compartment between the backseat and the trunk was an armory with an Agency book value of close to five thousand dollars. Pierce passed two grenades to Jasmin, then pulled out a couple of clips of Mallory .15 flechettes, a Streetsweeper shotgun with a twenty-round clip, and a five-cell flashlight. More stones were banging on the car, and angry faces pressed close against the windows.

Pierce pressed a button on the dash. Tear gas sprayed out thirty feet from nozzles under the sides of the Plymouth. The breeze would dissipate it quickly, but it cleared the immediate vicinity in seconds.

"Now," Pierce said, pulling Jasmin after him.

The cars behind the Plymouth had stopped suddenly as the gas reached their drivers. The marchers meanwhile, screaming and crying, were retreating into the park, trying to get away from the blinding mist.

"Keep the grenades in your pockets," Pierce shouted through the faceplate. "Take the flashlight. Hang on to my hand and don't let go."

She obeyed, feeling the gas prickle and sting on her exposed skin. Pierce dumped his extra ammunition in the chest pocket of his anorak, and casually slid the stubby-barreled shotgun up the anorak's right sleeve. The muzzle, protruding a couple of inches, he cupped in his hand.

Walking quickly, they left the road and followed the marchers into the darkness. Dead grass hissed under their feet. Soon they found a footpath along the lake and joined other people hurrying north. Pierce pulled off his mask and tossed it into the bushes; Jaz did the same.

"Now we're just another couple of marchers," he murmured.

She coughed as a wisp of tear gas caught in her throat. "Get me out of here."

"As fast as I can."

A helicopter clattered overhead, its searchlights sweeping over the lake and then locking onto the path. Over a hundred people squinted up at it and then walked on. The buildings overlooking the park were dim outlines against the black sky; a few windows showed the glow of candles or lanterns. Sirens wailed in the distance; as the helicopter moved on, the ceaseless rumble of the city again filled the darkness.

"Clement really timed it," Pierce said quietly. "Another day, and we'd have been home free. The Wabbies would've knocked off ExComm, we'd have knocked off the Wabbies, and Bill 402 would've passed in a matter of hours."

"Is Eric that important?"

"He's supposed to coordinate the whole thing. He's the only one who really knows what's going on."

They could begin to hear loudspeakers blaring in the darkness up ahead: the Iffers had wisely brought their own generator, and someone's amplified speech echoed raggedly off the dark buildings along Central Park West. Pierce remembered the Wabbie demonstration in Mountain Home.

"You're hurting my hand."

"Sorry." He loosened his grip, but didn't let go. People were thick around them now, many holding candles or flashlights. Faces floated, glowing, in the darkness. Angry voices called out far ahead, almost drowned out by the loudspeakers. Then the loudspeakers went dead with a squawk, and a pistol went off with an unmistakable crack. People started screaming.

"Damn. Turn on the flash. We'd better cut across before we get to the Iffers."

Now she guided him behind the pool of white light as they made their way through shrubs and little groves, their feet crackling through drifts of dead leaves. Off to the north, more shots sputtered low over Strawberry Fields.

"They'll probably gas everyone," Pierce said. "Let's get out of here."

She quickened her steps, grunting a little when a branch struck her in the face or a root tripped her. The weight of the grenades was obscenely heavy in the pockets of her duffel coat.

Now they crossed another path; hundreds of people were running south, away from the demonstration. The helicopter had dropped a flare, throwing yellow-orange light over the park above the coils of tear gas.

"Get him!" someone bawled, as a young man ran past Pierce and Jaz. The man was wearing an old army fatigue jacket with a rainbow armband; six teenagers, with shaved heads and wearing black turtleneck sweaters, were close behind him. They carried aluminum baseball bats.

Pierce let the shotgun slide out of his sleeve as he stepped into the path of the teenagers. The flare swung lazily down under its parachute; the boys saw Pierce bring the shotgun up to his shoulder. They stopped.

"Put the bats down."

People behind the teenagers, seeing the shotgun, scattered frantically. The teenagers obeyed, their faces shadowed by the flare behind them.

"Turn around and run like hell!" Pierce roared.

They ran. A second later Pierce grabbed Jaz's hand again and led her at a trot toward Central Park West.

People were pouring out of the park toward the west, many weeping and coughing from tear gas, some bleeding. Gunshots echoed off the Dakota and other apartment buildings facing Strawberry Fields. Pierce led Jaz through the jammed traffic and down West 86th. Within half a block they were groping their way in blackness; using the flash might invite snipers or police. As they crossed Broadway the helicopter passed overhead, and its searchlights revealed dozens of people huddled in doorways or peering from windows. They ducked back, away from the light, as Pierce broke into a run up the west side of Broadway.

"They'll shoot us," Jaz protested.

"No. Come on." He wasn't bothering to conceal the shotgun, and two Iffers, seeing it in the glare of the searchlights, turned and bolted east across Broadway.

Two blocks north, Pierce and Jaz stopped in the doorway of an abandoned delicatessen. She was panting from the run.

"Why are we going this way? The building's back on 84th."

"We'd never get in from the street. We're going a different way."

"Ah—through the repository."

"Right."

"Can we do it?"

"Yes."

"Can *you* do it?"

He turned to look at her, his face in shadow. "That's why I need you."

"Oh . . . Wait a minute, Jerry. If you're afraid of cracking up in there, I don't think I want to be around."

"I won't crack up. You're just insurance."

"Insurance my ass. If you crack up, what good am I going to be? Think I can rescue Wigner on my own, plus hold your hand?"

"Just get me through the tunnel, Jaz. I'll look after the rest."

"Christ."

At 100th Street they turned west, crossing West End Avenue in total darkness. Across the river the lights of New Jersey still burned. At Riverside Drive Pierce guided Jaz across the road to the edge of the park, and they walked quickly south.

"I had to learn the whole underground layout of this neighborhood," he explained quietly. "Good thing I did. I don't think we'll have any trouble finding the manhole."

Close to 96th Street, the manhole cover was exactly where he had found it on Ulro. Pierce turned on the flashlight and swept it quickly around them. Trees, stumps, and shrubs surrounded the site, and a couple of concrete benches stood down a little path.

"It'll look different in a couple of centuries. Come on."

The cover was heavy but manageable. Pierce lifted it and swung it aside into the dirt beside the path. He paused for a moment, listening to the occasional shots ringing out to the south. The immediate neighborhood was very quiet, and the apartment house windows showed no lights.

"I'll go first," he said, slinging the Streetsweeper over his shoulder. He used the flashlight to find the top rungs of the ladder, then passed it to Jaz. "It's not very far."

She stood in the darkness, listening to his feet rasping on the metal bars. At the bottom, his footsteps echoed slightly.

"Okay," he called softly.

The rungs were cold and slippery. After she had descended for what seemed a long time, hands gripped her waist and she almost screamed.

"You're down," Pierce said calmly. "Flashlight."

"This is crazy. I want to go back."

"God, so do I."

"Well, let's go."

"We can't. Everyone's counting on us."

"Bullshit. Nobody even knows where we are, and nobody cares."

"We've got to get Eric out of there. Come on."

She shivered in the damp darkness, listening to the drip of water from the roof of the tunnel. Pierce took her hand and led her down the tunnel, following the bright ellipse of the flashlight beam. When they reached the doorway, Pierce started shaking.

"Through here. Open it." His voice was hoarse.

She tugged at the handle, which moved silently and easily. The door swung open, and air of a different scent puffed coldly in their faces.

"Now you have to take the flashlight. Hold my hand. You have to guide me."

"Why?"

"I'm scared. I don't want to look."

"Jerry, it's okay. It's just a tunnel, nothing's wrong with it."

"Do what I said."

In the reflected light of the flash, she saw he had closed his eyes. He did not look frightened, Jaz thought; more like someone grief-stricken. She took his hand.

"Okay, let's go. It'll be fine."

They walked slowly down the tunnel, side by side. Jaz remembered going on a blind walk in some junior high class, and felt the same awkward solicitude. This time, though, it was mixed with fear. She thought of quitting, going back, and decided Pierce would be more dangerous then than he would be if he cracked up in the tunnel.

"Almost there. Almost to the door." Her voice echoed in the metallic silence.

"I had to blow it open on Ulro," Pierce whispered.

"God. Is that why we brought the grenades?"

"Best I could do."

"Okay, stop." She tried to release her hand from his, but he clung to it. "Jerry, I need to use both hands now, okay? I'm just going to try to open the door. Here, you hold the flashlight. Right there. Right. Good."

The door opened with a scratching noise on the concrete floor. Beyond it was more blackness, colder still, and a musty smell.

"Left." Pierce's voice was barely audible. Obediently Jaz guided him through the doorway and turned to the left. The floor underfoot was covered in fine silt, dotted with tiny craters where water droplets had fallen from the overarching roof.

Something living made a noise: a quick, scratchy noise. Pierce gasped.

"Hey, come on, Jerry, it's just a rat or a mouse. God, you're scaring me more than anything else down here. Come on."

They shuffled across the silted floor, staying on the edge of the ellipse of illumination. Occasionally Jaz lifted the beam and saw only more silt, more damp stone walls, the arching vault of the roof. Pierce said nothing.

Something glinted up ahead: the north wall of the repository.

"What's that noise?" Pierce demanded.

She listened. "Sounds like an air conditioner."

"Must be. Good."

A minute later they stood by a plain cement-block wall. Protruding from it at shoulder height was an air conditioner, its top covered with caked dust. The silt below it was wet from condensation.

"Isn't there a door or something?"

"No. Put me next to the air conditioner."

She guided him to it and he put out his hands, gripping its sides. Then he heaved himself away from it, and its supports squeaked from the strain. Twice more, and on the fourth heave the whirring metal box suddenly broke away from the wall and crashed into the mud below it. Light stabbed out from the rectangular hole.

"Okay?" Pierce asked. "Can you see inside?"

"Wait till my eyes get used to the light. Yes. Is anyone going to be in there?"

"Just us. I'm going to boost you in. Then help me get in."

She scrambled through the hole, supporting herself on the top of a filing cabinet as her feet found the floor. The light seemed less intense now, just a scattering of fluorescent panels in the false ceiling. The ordinariness of the place, with its neutral lighting and pastel cabinets, seemed stranger to her than the tunnels.

Jaz turned and took Pierce's hand as he hoisted himself in. His eyes were still tightly shut, and he was breathing fast.

"Take a deep breath," Jaz commanded, but he ignored her. As he wriggled through the hole, his weight put her off balance and she stepped back. Pierce fell to the floor, hands out to stop his fall. Then he moaned.

"Jerry, are you hurt?" Jaz gripped his shoulders and helped him rise. He was shuddering, and his eyes were open but blank, with nothing in them but terror: *That* was what she had seen, she thought detachedly as she held him tightly. Deep in those calm eyes, simple terror. He shut his eyes but his expression did not change.

She picked up his shotgun and began pulling him along an aisle between two endless rows of filing cabinets. The repository looked natural and welcoming after the tunnels. Their footsteps clattered on the plastic-honeycomb flooring, and the hum of the fluorescents seemed loud. If anyone did show up—she did not know what she would do. The thought of using the shotgun seemed insane.

At a gap in the rows of filing cabinets, she turned left into a wider aisle that led straight to a broad door painted orange.

"We're here," she panted. Pierce seemed to be shivering with cold inside his tan anorak. "I'm going to open this door and then you've got to open your eyes, Jerry. You've got to open your eyes."

"No. Please."

"You bastard! I'll *leave* you down here if you don't open your eyes when we go through this door!"

She leaned on the handle and shoved. The door swung open on the access tunnel. It was just another corridor, with worn carpeting and cinder-block walls. It sloped up at a gently grade to another orange door almost a hundred yards away.

Pulling Pierce into the tunnel, Jaz shut the door firmly behind them.

"Here's your shotgun. I've still got the grenades."

He opened his eyes, blinked, and silently took the

Streetsweeper. For a moment he stood still, breathing deeply and looking at nothing in particular.

"Thanks. It was worse than I thought it'd be. I'm okay now."

"Sure," she said quickly, with an anxious grin. "Now let's go find Eric and get out of here, please."

He led the way up the corridor. Beyond the door, he knew, was a small storeroom and then the subbasement where the I-Screen had been. An elevator was located on the north side of the subbasement, and beside it was a stairwell. The building's emergency generator was one flight up, in a corner of the parking basement.

They reached the door; Pierce turned to her. "We're going to have to look for him floor by floor. He's probably not in the apartments, so that leaves the first three floors. If we're lucky we'll find someone who knows where he is, but more likely we'll just have to check each floor and see how it goes."

"What if we get in a fight?"

"We'll worry about that when it happens."

"No, you dope!" she hissed. "If we get in a fight, the whole building will know about it. We could get shot by some idiot while they're moving Eric down a flight of stairs somewhere."

He thought for a moment, and she saw the terror in his eyes recede but not disappear. Then he smiled slightly.

"Chances are no one in the building knows about this except the guys who took him. If we're very relaxed, everything will be fine. Do you know anyone who lives here?"

"A couple of people, I guess. East 52nd doesn't have much to do with these guys."

"Okay, if anyone asks questions we're looking for

one of your friends. Just knowing the name should be enough."

"God, I hope so."

"Let's go."

The storeroom was a silent cube of metal shelving modules; beyond it was the subbasement. Pierce went first, and found no one. The I-Screen was still in place, but the room looked deserted. As he and Jaz crossed it, he ran his fingers over a control console: dust.

The stairs were equally quiet. Pierce tucked his shotgun up his sleeve again and looked out into the parking basement. A few cars stood there, but no guards. He could see that the gate was in place at the exit to Riverside Drive. They would assume that any assault or infiltration would come through the gate or through the main floor entrance; otherwise they would have locked the door to the repository as well.

On the main floor the lobby was in darkness, but someone called out as Pierce opened the door without showing himself.

"Who's there?"

Pierce pulled Jaz forward. "Jasmin Jones, for God's sake. Who's that?"

"Mike Tordahl, Ms. Jones." The voice came from a corner of the main floor lobby where, Pierce recalled, a waist-high wall provided cover against an armed assault through the front door.

"Go talk to him," Pierce murmured. She nodded, smiled faintly, and walked out into the dark lobby.

"I'm looking for the interrogation," she said.

"Uh, you want to step out of the light, Ms. Jones? I recognize you all right. If anybody's out there, we don't want to give 'em a target."

She stepped into the darkness. "Mike—the interrogation?"

"Afraid I can't help you, ma'am. They dragged me down here to keep an eye on the door, with all this shit going on outside. Uh, how'd you get in here, anyway? I didn't see the gate show an opening."

"Are you kidding? It opened like a charm. You must have a bum circuit."

"Wouldn't be the first time. We go on emergency power, everything goes all to hell. What's it like outside?"

"Just like here, gone all to hell. Listen, are you sure you don't know where the interrogation is? It's really important. Jonathan Clement's involved, I think."

"Oh, sure. Third floor. I know they went up there, but I thought it was just a meeting, not an interrogation. Who they interrogating?"

"You don't want to know, Mike. See you later." She turned back to the stairwell door.

"Yeah, I guess not. Hey, why don't you take the elevator?"

"I'm scared it'll stall if the generator conks out."

"Yeah, I guess so. Well, it's third floor for Dr. Clement."

Back in the stairwell, she grinned nervously at Pierce. "I feel like Mata Hari or somebody."

"You did beautifully. Now I want you to stay behind for a while."

"What? Where, here on the stairs? What if someone comes?"

"Don't worry. It'll just be for a minute. I'll call you when the coast is clear."

"And if you don't?"

"Get out of the building. Mike'll let you go."

"I'm supposed to go out in a blackout, with everything going crazy?"

"It'll be safer than being caught in here with no good alibi."

"My God. A couple of hours ago I was washing my hair."

He smiled at her. "See you in a minute."

Pierce went upstairs slowly, the Streetsweeper slung over his shoulder and his Mallory .15 in his hand. The stairwell was silent; when he looked down the shaft he could see Jaz's hand resting on the railing. He reached the second floor landing, then the third. Even as he opened the door, he was unsure what he would do.

The door opened into a hallway. Pierce came through the door casually, saw the guard thirty feet down the hall, and raised his empty left hand in a friendly wave. The guard, a red-faced young man in camouflage fatigues, brought his shotgun up to present arms.

"I'm late for the interrogation," Pierce called. "This the right floor?"

"Identify yourself," the guard said.

"T-Colonel Gerald Pierce." He was closing the distance, casually shifting the Mallory to his left hand. In an undertone he added: "Come to attention when I address you, son."

The guard snapped to attention, lowered the butt of his shotgun to his left heel, and swept his right hand across his waist to touch the shotgun's barrel. Pierce raised the muzzle of the Mallory .15, set at low impact, and shot the guard in the solar plexus. The young man's face went pale; his eyes rolled up and he slumped against the wall. Pierce caught the shotgun before it fell, then eased the guard's slump to the floor.

The doors along the corridor revealed nothing. Pierce tried one and found it locked. So was the next. The third was not.

Feeling a little foolish with two shotguns and a pistol, Pierce opened the door.

The first thing he saw was the Dali print, then Wigner in the dentist's chair and the three men facing him. Pierce recognized Jonathan Clement and the two interrogators. Wigner looked up, startled.

"My God—Jerry!" Wigner glanced at the three men, then back at Pierce. Pierce saw the surprise in Wigner's eyes, and a moment of what seemed like inward calculation. Then Wigner nodded contemptuously at the men. "Kill them!"

Phelan was already reaching for his black bag. Pierce brought up the Streetsweeper he had taken from the guard, and fired.

It sounded like a door slamming three times. The paneling and the print of *Christus Hypercubus* were shredded and streaked with blood. The impact of the shots flung the men back into their chairs and then bounced them onto the floor.

"Get me out of this," Wigner said. His voice was shaky. "Are they dead, old son? Are you sure?"

"They're dead." Pierce's voice was flat. He undid the straps holding Wigner to the dentist's chair, his eyes scanning the room and the doorway. He noticed the computer monitor and its green hexagons. "So it was the virus."

"Yes. Yes. My God. Messy business." Wigner looked away from the dead men. "We've got to get out of here. Back to the office."

"I know. Come on." He guided Wigner through the doorway and into the corridor. The guard lay sprawled against the wall.

"Are you sure they're dead?" Wigner insisted.

"Yes."

"Good."

The door to the stairwell suddenly opened, and Jaz looked through it. Pierce lowered his shotgun.

"You scared hell out of—"

"*Behind you!*"

Pierce dropped, spinning, and saw the two guards in camouflage fatigues entering the hallway through a door at the far end. He fired and saw them double over before falling. The sound of the shot echoed down the stairwell. An alarm went off with an insistent, repetitive buzz.

Wigner had also flung himself flat. Pierce pulled him upright and shoved him into the doorway. Jaz was still standing there, looking down the hallway. The two men lay writhing in their blood. One of them gasped, hands pressed to his face as blood ran between his fingers.

"Come on," Pierce commanded. Shuddering, Jaz obeyed.

Eighteen:

Near the main floor landing, Pierce stopped and reached into one of the pockets of Jaz's duffel coat. She looked at him with huge, frightened eyes; he smiled at her and went down to the landing. The grenade was small, with a pop-off cap. Pierce pushed the door open, tossed the grenade out into the lobby, and stepped back as the door swung shut. He smiled again at Wigner and Jaz, who stood a couple of steps farther up. The detonation was a sharp crack; air shrieked briefly around the edges of the door.

"Stay put," said Pierce, and went through the door in a sudden roll. Nothing happened for almost thirty seconds; the only sound in the stairwell was the distant ringing of the alarm. "Now," Pierce called, and Jaz pulled Wigner after her.

The darkened lobby was full of smoke; shards of glass glittered faintly on the floor. The front doors had been blown open, and the lights of New Jersey were just visible through the trees across Riverside Drive. Someone groaned in the darkness. Jaz hoped it was Mike Tordahl, that he wasn't seriously hurt. Somehow she was certain that others were around her in the darkness, dead men who had been alive seconds before.

"Fast," said Pierce, guiding them over the debris. Glass broke musically under their feet.

On the sidewalk, four or five people stood with shopping bags full of loot and watched them leave the building. They said nothing, did nothing but watch. Inside, the alarm was still ringing faintly. Pierce and Wigner looked up and saw that a few windows on the residential floors were still lit, though most had black-out curtains drawn.

"What do we do now?" Jaz asked.

"Walk. How are you feeling, Eric?"

"All right. Feeling better all the time. We've got to get to the office, old son."

"What office?" said Jaz.

"A little place on West 38th," Pierce answered. "It's got most of our records and a computer link."

"I know that place." Jaz giggled. "That's where I ran into that damn defense program."

"I know," said Wigner.

"What do you mean?"

"Fujii's program locks onto probes and follows them home. That's how we're going to catch a lot of Wabbies tonight." He glanced at his wrist. "Hell, they took my watch. What time is it?"

"A quarter past one," said Pierce.

"We've got a long walk."

"Probably a useless one," Pierce said quietly. "The office on 38th doesn't have a backup generator, and our computers don't have batteries. Even if the power comes back on, if the phone lines are out we won't be able to link up with the wailing wall or anyone else."

"Good God." Wigner looked horrified. "It never even crossed my mind. Good *God*."

"Does this mean we've killed people for no reason?" Jaz asked quietly.

"Not necessarily," Pierce answered. "The power grid's out because the computers are dead. If they can uncouple the computers, the power will be back. Same for the phones. But no one may figure that out for a while."

Wigner drew a deep breath and let it out. He put a hand on Pierce's shoulder, as if seeking support or offering comfort, and then shivered.

"Damn cold, and me with no jacket. Well, let's get on with it."

They were soon on Broadway, which was jammed with abandoned cars. Off to the east, toward Central Park, gunfire was still popping away; but here the sidewalks were empty except for an occasional looter rummaging through a shattered storefront window. At 80th and Broadway a teenaged boy in a ragged blue sweater lay dead in the street, his knees pulled up under his chest. Jaz swept the flashlight beam over him and then clicked it off.

"Don't use it again," Pierce told her. "Someone might squeeze off a round at you just for fun."

They walked steadily south down Broadway, Pierce carrying his shotguns openly slung over his shoulder. A couple of National Guardsmen, nervously guarding the stairs to the subway, watched them pass but did not challenge them.

The city in darkness was still but not silent. Gunfire still sounded, and now and then a siren hooted. Music, both live and from battery-powered radios, drifted out of lightless windows: Chuck Berry, Monteverdi, a cello improvisation. On some front stoops on the side streets, people sat drinking and smoking, laughing now and then.

"Is this supposed to be a revolution?" Jaz asked. "No barricades, no one making speeches. Just smoking dope and listening to music. And dying in the middle of the street."

"The revolutions are always in the brain cells," said Wigner. "You could be brain dead for years and your liver wouldn't know the difference."

"Do brain cells use shotguns?"

"Jerry's did and a good thing, too."

Pierce said nothing. Neither did Jaz.

Lights came on suddenly as they crossed Columbus Circle. Signs flashed: street lights glowed orange-pink. In the apartment buildings facing Central Park, lights glowed and then went out again: it was late, and people wanted to go back to sleep.

"That's the best stroke of luck we've had all night," said Pierce.

Wigner was too cold and miserable to answer. Pierce passed him his anorak. He wore a striped shirt under it, and the Mallory .15 in a shoulder holster.

"Between that and your shotguns, you look damn suspicious, old son."

"I *am* damn suspicious."

"Just the same, take off the holster and Jasmin can put it under her coat."

The midtown streets were more populated. Fires burned on street corners, squatters in the old automobile showrooms were cooking whatever they'd looted, and hookers were working Times Square. Someone seemed to be huddled in every doorway. National Guard patrols were out on foot, jumpy young men in flak jackets and carrying ancient M-16s. They looked at Pierce's shotgun but kept their distance.

The office building on West 38th was dark and locked, but Pierce had a key. They let themselves into the lobby and then walked up two flights of stairs to the office.

"This is it?" asked Jaz.

"This is it," Wigner said.

It was a two-room suite whose plastered walls were cracked and yellowed. The lighting fixtures dated from the sixties and the furniture consisted of a couple of Sally Ann couches, some filing cabinets, a photocopier, and two small desks. On each stood a Polymath XCB hooked to a modem. A hot plate stood on a card table in the second room of the suite.

"Let's start with a nice cup of tea," Wigner said. "God, I'm cold after that walk. Then we'll get to work."

"Boot, Polly," Pierce commanded. The screens of the two computers came to life, with the cartoon figures of identical little girls in the lower right corners.

"Booted, Jerry," the little girls chorused.

"Polly One," said Pierce. "Link with wailing wall."

"Sure, Jerry."

Jaz sank onto one of the couches and watched Pierce's flickerscreen. "My God, you run it fast."

"Lots to do."

Irrelevantly, she said: "No houseplants. Eric always has houseplants."

"We aren't here often enough to look after them. But he tried."

By the time Wigner had brought in mugs of tea, the wailing-wall network was alerted. The screen flickered with demands: *Where have you guys been? What's happening? Can we go after the Wabbies?*

Wigner sipped his tea as he settled before the computer.

"Here we go."

Blackouts still covered many parts of the United States and Canada, but all through the night the power came back and more members of the wailing wall reported in. Wigner kept information flowing in both directions while Pierce handled the Wabbies' computer net.

"Every time the power comes on, somebody else checks in," Pierce said to Jaz. "The Wabbies figured on the blackouts. Very organized. Now they think their computers are the only ones still working. They aren't even bothering with codes."

"Why doesn't the virus knock out their own computers?" Jaz asked.

"The virus program has an immune system, so it can't take over their own machines."

"What they don't know," said Wigner, "is that we built a couple of little flaws into that immune system, so we can eavesdrop on them."

"Wait a minute," said Jaz. "When I tried to probe this machine, I could tell I was up against a first-rate shield. Won't the Wabbies realize something's up?"

"If they're looking for it," said Pierce. "But they're not. They're just probing enough of the government net to make sure it's completely crashed. If they did probe one of our machines by accident, they'd figure it was a glitch of some kind. Besides, they're too busy talking to each other now."

Jaz and Pierce skipped from one Wabbie computer to another, monitoring dozens of communications. Some were pure logistics: moving cars or people or fuel from one place to another. Pierce saw that his old informant Wes McCullough had been ordered to bring a gasoline reserve from his ranch to a rendezvous just outside Mountain Home. Others were marching orders, sending teams of gunmen or technicians to specific targets: bureaucrats' homes, radio and TV stations, highway interchanges, airports, and railyards.

Before long they slipped into a routine, with Jaz

watching the flickerscreen while Pierce notified T-Colonels, police forces, and army units about the Wabbie plans she monitored. Despite the lack of immediate warning, the wailing wall and its allies had moved quickly. In many cases they were already the local arms of government, so the paralysis in Washington was unimportant. In other cases they moved into the vacuum left by the virus attack, with the support of local authorities grateful to have any kind of computer net.

"Hit team identified heading for Washington," Pierce said from his keyboard as he transferred the data to a window on Wigner's screen. "Three men in an '86 Cherokee with Kentucky plates, just passed through a roadblock in Arlington."

Wigner nodded and murmured into his Polymath's microphone, alerting Senator Cooledge's staff and then a riot-control unit stationed in Georgetown.

"The Wabbies are *slow*," Wigner gloated. "The dumb bastards didn't realize how successful they were going to be. They should've had their teams in place before they made their move."

"Congress is convening," Pierce reported a little later. "Cooledge kept her quorum." He patched the *Congressional Record* into windows on both computers, and occasionally glanced at the words that formed painfully slowly as the House of Representatives and the Senate debated Bill 402. Wigner alerted the T-Colonel of District 11, Pennsylvania, about an assassination team in Harrisburg.

By four in the morning, the Wabbie computers were beginning to fall silent. Link after link was broken without warning. Not until almost 4:30 did a Wabbie hacker manage to send a Mayday before going off. Wigner noted six computers that suddenly jacked out of the net, and alerted the nearest T-Colonels; all six hackers were captured without incident before 5:00.

By then the interrogations were coming in, too many of them to be simultaneously monitored. First tens, then scores of prisoners were undergoing deep questioning. The whole Wabbie underground was revealed, vaster than anyone but Wigner and Pierce had imagined.

By sunrise the casualty reports were on the screens: fifteen dead and eight wounded in a raid outside Memphis; one dead, three wounded in Truckee; twelve dead, forty-one wounded or incapacitated in St. Louis. A group in Los Angeles, besieged in a house full of munitions, had blown themselves up. Two city blocks were demolished and in flames, with hundreds believed dead.

Wigner stood up and stretched.

"My lord, what a morning." He grinned wearily at Pierce. "Jerry, I do believe the worst is over."

"Let's get the Emergency repealed."

"By noon. The president will sign it by two this afternoon, or he'll wish he had. This time tomorrow we'll be in the IF."

Jaz was drinking instant coffee on the couch. Her beautiful face was pale.

"What's the matter?" Pierce asked.

"You killed Jonathan, didn't you?"

"Yes."

"Did you have to? Did you really have to?"

"He did," Wigner said quietly. "Jerry saved my life. They would have killed me by now, Jaz. I had no way out. Jonathan was...crazy. He kept telling Phelan to hurry up and finish me off. I couldn't make him see reason, couldn't talk to him. And this was the man who brought me into the Agency, the man I looked up to."

"Don't lie."

"I did look up to him once. I really did. But he couldn't learn, couldn't grow, couldn't change."

Jaz put her hands over her face and began to cry. Pierce squatted beside her and patted her shoulder.

"We had to, Jaz. To protect all those people out there, all those people who'd suffer and die if we didn't take care of them."

"I'm scared," she sobbed. "Oh God, I'm so scared. I didn't want to kill anybody."

"You didn't, Jaz. You didn't." Pierce's voice was gentle. "Don't blame yourself,"

"Why not? I could've left you in the tunnels. I could've stayed home and left you to go rescue Eric on your own. But I had to come and help kill him."

"Jaz, it's all right," Wigner said. "You know what you did? You saved the world, that's all. Good Lord, the Wabbies would have won if you hadn't helped. It's as simple as that."

"It's never as simple as that."

Sunlight, reflecting from some office window across the street, threw yellow diamonds on the spotted carpeting.

Bill 402 passed in the House and was sent at once to the Senate, where it was ratified in fifteen minutes. Half an hour later the president signed it into law.

"This marks the end of over three years of emergency," he said for the cameras. "I am confident that it means we have turned the corner into a new era of peace and hope and unprecedented opportunity. The next step will be to take our rightful place in the International Federation, and then to work for the peaceful and orderly development of the downtime chrono-planes. At the same time we will bend every effort to ascertain the nature of the tragedy that struck the worlds of the future, and we will ensure that our own world escapes that fate."

Wigner put down his can of Heineken and laughed.

"The old bastard would rather have chewed broken glass than make that speech," he said.

Pierce smiled. He had napped for a time and had just wakened. "Where's Jaz?"

"Gone home. She says she's going back to L.A. to visit her family."

"Too bad. I liked having her around."

"She has served her purpose."

Early that evening in Mountain Home, Doria was washing dishes and LaMar went to answer a knock at the front door.

"Who's there?"

"Friend of your old buddy Wes McCullough."

She heard the latch click, the chain rattle, and then a thump as the door slammed against the wall. The stranger's voice was deep and loud.

"You the son of a bitch gave Wes that program."

"What are you talking about?"

"The virus, the fucking virus. The trap."

"What are you talking about?' LaMar repeated.

Doria crept to the doorway into the living room.

"Dumb bastard. We got hold of Wes today and he told us everything. Soon as he told us you was drivin' a gook car, we knew you wasn't no Brother. Fuckin' Hyundai, pretending to be loyal Americans. Well, by order of the White American Brotherhood, you are hereby executed, asshole."

The crash of the gun was horribly loud, louder than

LaMar's cry of surprise. Doria burst into the living room, seeing LaMar sprawled on the floor with blood gushing from his chest and back, seeing a man in a pea jacket with a watch cap pulled down low over his eyes, seeing the .45 swing toward her and not caring, just running straight for the man with her hands outstretched like futile claws, straight for him, straight for

Nineteen:

"This is absurd," said Wigner. "Here we've overthrown the government, changed the course of history, and if we so much as go back to our apartments for a change of clothes and a beer, some stray Agency goon is likely to take a shot at us. Let's hope the government restores law and order before we starve to death here."

West 38th was deserted all day, except for an occasional National Guard patrol and a few furtive pedestrians. Pierce and Wigner napped, woke, drank tea, and heated some canned soup. In the evening, music drifted up from the street, echoing from the buildings. Pierce stood at the window and looked down. Three men playing accordions came casually down the sidewalk: their breaths fluttered white in the chill light of the street lamps.

"Look," he said quietly to Wigner.

As if the music had been a signal, people began to emerge from the buildings. Many, in wrinkled clothes, looked as if they had been holed up for a couple of days. But they walked easily, naturally, and sometimes they even laughed together. A gang of teenagers ran down the street toward Broadway, each in a jacket with a rainbow on the back. Car horns began to sound in the distance, the eager braying of celebration.

"The end of an era," Wigner observed. "The fall of the old republic. By God, it was a near thing."

Most of the T-Colonel District Commanders had gone over solidly to the new government, and had brought their Civil Emergency staff with them; they would form caretaker governments until elections could be held. A couple of unTrainable generals had seized Fort Sam Houston and barricaded themselves inside; no one cared. The president had appointed Senator Cooledge as special ambassador to the International Federation.

A message from the senator came over Wigner's Polymath: *I'll be in New York tomorrow on my way to Lisbon. Want to come along? D.C.*

"I certainly do," Wigner said. "If I can get out of the country in one piece, that is. How about you, Jerry? You can be in at the very beginning."

"No. Once we've got the agency sorted out, I think I'll go see my mother in Taos. I need a rest."

Wigner looked at him with sympathy. "You've earned it, old son. And what then, when you're ready to go again?"

"I want to go downtime. Do something constructive for a change. Maybe help the endos learn how to cope with us."

"They'll learn on their own, and very quickly. But if you want to be useful downtime, how about doing some recruiting?"

"Of whom?"

"Endos. One in eight of their adolescents should be Trainables, and we ought to get our hands on every one of them. Bring them uptime, Train them, and put them to work on the Doomsday problem."

"It sounds good."

"The biggest windfall we could hope for. Never

mind the oil fields, the gold mines, all that—it's the people we need to exploit. Thousands, millions of Trainables, running things and making sure Doomsday doesn't happen again."

"Like Ulro and Urizen?"

"No comparison, old son. The uptime societies were convalescent wards. They lost huge numbers of Trainables in the civil wars and famines; the best they could manage with the survivors was high-tech concentration camps. We've got all those people that they lost, plus the downtime endos. Give us a few years and we'll have Utopia."

"What about the unTrainables?"

Wigner waved a hand dismissively. "We'll find uses for them. Move a lot of them downtime, get them mining and farming. Give them a chance to get out of the slums, pull themselves together. The old frontier mystique. Your own ranch, with a cave bear rug in front of the fireplace and a saber-tooth tiger's head stuffed on the mantel."

Pierce smiled, a little absently. "What if they want shopping malls?"

"Anything their empty little hearts desire, old son. As long as we can get on with stopping Doomsday and running the world properly."

Wigner got up to go to the bathroom. Pierce turned back to the screen of his Polymath.

"Update Wabbie arrests, Polly."

"Sure, Jerry."

The mop-up was almost complete. A few prominent Wabbies were still unaccounted for, and a few others were besieged, but most of the leadership and many of the rank and file were now safely jailed. Curious to see what had happened to Wes McCullough, Pierce focused on Mountain Home.

"Status of Social Security Number 3423-890-4555," he said.

The screen gave him three pages in a fifth of a second: the report of a National Guard lieutenant whose men had found the McCullough family tortured and killed in their ranch house; a photograph of Wes McCullough's headless corpse, sprawled in his barnyard; a list of next of kin.

Pierce felt himself shiver. "Status of Social Security Number 6779-300-2187," he whispered.

Doria's autopsy report was the first document in the file. Death had been attributable to a single .45 bullet fired at close range into her head. Photographs followed of her and of her husband.

For what seemed like a long time, Pierce sat motionless. He shut down the screen and looked out the window at the lighted windows opposite. Darkness had fallen without his noticing.

The toilet flushed and Wigner strode back into the office.

"Problem?"

"I have to go to Mountain Home."

"Why?"

"They got Doria and LaMar and the McCullough family."

"Good Christ. How *could* they have—"

"Once they saw us roll up their people, they must have realized they'd been had."

"Vicious bastards. Well, old son, I'm not sure you need to concern yourself. Leave it to the people on the ground."

"They were my responsibility. I'm going."

Wigner put a hand on Pierce's shoulder. "Stop a moment, Jerry. Think. Thousands of people have been killed in the last day. It's been a crazy time, but we're out of it now. We've got to get back to a more civilized way of dealing with these problems. Are you listening? We can't just go on knocking off people. Try it and you'll be nailed. And I can't afford to lose you. Leave this to the local authorities. Are you listening?"

Pierce's blank, unresponsive face seemed to annoy Wigner. "For God's sake, old son! On Ulro and Urizen we tried to knock off the Wabbies to avenge Senator Cooledge, and it got us killed. Here we're going to have something like normality within a couple of weeks, and people won't stand for casual murders any more. Are you listening?"

"I'm going, Eric."

"If you get picked up, they'll trace you straight back to me and the Agency. It could screw up the whole plan."

"They won't pick me up. But I'm going."

"Think, old son!"

Pierce's eyes met Wigner's, and Wigner looked away. Pierce stood up and walked away from Wigner's restraining hand.

Air travel was hopeless: most airline computers were dead, fuel was scarce, and the new civilian government had reserved the few remaining flights for high-priority passengers. Pierce was not surprised.

He walked across town, stopping on the way to buy some cheap work clothes in a store on Eighth Avenue where the clerks wore sidearms. Prices had almost doubled since the day before, an indication that the owner did not share the general delight in the new government, and Pierce found himself with little remaining cash. After changing into his new khaki trousers, steel-toed workboots, checked flannel shirt, and quilted jacket, he headed for a Citibank branch at Ninth Avenue and 45th.

The bank's computers had been equipped with the defense program, and it was still in business. As a result, the automatic tellers had long lineups; Pierce waited patiently, then cleared out an account under a false name.

At the bus station, hundreds of people were trying to get out of town. This could be a little dicey, Pierce thought: if Clement's Agency people were at all organized, they might just be keeping an eye on bus and train stations. More likely they were trying to find their feet in a wildly changed world.

The huge waiting room was crowded with people, many of them standing in lines in front of closed wickets. A crude sign had been put up on a long strip of computer paper: ALL SEATS BOOKED UNTIL SATURDAY; it was now Wednesday. Pierce was not surprised.

A couple of casual scans of the waiting room showed no Agency faces he knew, but he recognized several petty criminals whose files he'd scanned among thousands of others. One, sitting alone on a bench, was a fat young man with a bad complexion and a walrus moustache. Pierce sat down next to him.

"Stan, my man, how are ya?"

"I don't know you, pal."

"Sure, I bought a little this and that off you, just after you got outa Attica. Hey, West 104th street, right? Yeah. Good to see you."

"Oh, yeah, well, I guess I do remember you now. You headed outa town?"

"Stan, I *gotta* get outa town. I got certain employees of law enforcement agencies urgently interested in kicking my balls. And here they are, not sellin' tickets."

"Yeah, well, maybe I can help you. Happen to have a ticket to Chicago I'm not gonna need after all."

"Hey, my guardian angel. When's it for?"

"Greyhound convoy leaving tonight at 10."

"What's your price, Stan?"

"Yeah, well, since we're old buddies, let's say five hundred?"

"Sheesh. Five hundred." Pierce slapped his thighs. "Well, screw me for showing how bad I gotta have that ticket. Okay, here." He pulled some bills from a zipped inside pocket of his jacket. Behind a flap of his jacket he counted out five hundred dollars. Stan's plump hand reached casually in, leaving the ticket in place of the money.

"You did me a favor, Stan. Thanks, old buddy."

"You got twenty minutes before they stop loading, pal."

"I'm gone. Say hi to Katy for me."

Stan frowned. "I never told you about Katy."

Pierce grinned, waved, and disappeared into the crowd.

The bus convoy left at 10:00 in the evening, five big Greyhounds escorted by two small armored jeeps. Pierce was in the third bus. The other pasengers were quiet, anxious-looking people who peered through the wire mesh over the windows at the approaches to the tunnel. No one talked much, least of all the old man in the seat next to him, and Pierce gratefully went to sleep before they reached New Jersey.

He was in Chicago at noon next day, bought another ticket from a scalper, and that night was in Omaha. The convoy, now just three buses, rolled on across the autumn plains. Snow whirled out of a white sky, melting as it touched the ground. National Guardsmen at roadblocks looked cold and unhappy, though many wore rainbow badges pinned to their jackets.

At bus stop cafes where they were the only customers, new and old passengers traded rumors: the president had been arrested, the president had been impeached, the International Federation had rejected the American application for membership, Congress had asked George Washington to come uptime and take over.

"You sure read that fast," one of his seatmates observed as they ate doughnuts at a station cafe in Cheyenne.

Pierce handed the four-page tabloid to the man. "Nothing much to read. Care to see it?"

As the buses moved west, the look of the towns grew harsher, more like Mountain Home—strip developments whose development had stopped, empty supermarkets, burned-out gas stations, farm machinery dealerships with no farm machinery, and gaunt, angry men standing aimlessly in every public warm place. The republic had fallen, but the millennium had not yet arrived.

At last he reached Mountain Home, late on a cold afternoon. Fresh snow crunched and squeaked under his boots as he walked from the station to the old house where he and Doria had made love, where Doria and LaMar had lived and died. Lights were on, just visible through the heavy curtains. Pierce walked to the door and faintly heard the sounds of a family getting ready for dinner: plates clattering on a table, a woman calling in Spanish to a child. He turned away and walked back downtown.

The old Hometown Mall was still busy, and outside it stood still more RVs and campers. Between two of them hung a professional-looking sign: *Beds for Over-nighters*. Pierce knocked on the door of a rusty Winnebago.

"Yo." The door opened a little; a flashlight glared in Pierce's eyes.

"Got a bed?"

"What you got in trade?"

"Nothing. Fifty dollars?"

"Hold 'em up. Okay. You from out of town?"

"Yes."

"I don't stand any crap. Any crap, you're out on your ass. It's the second camper behind you. Here's the key. Checkout time is eight o'clock in the morning."

"Fine. Any chance of getting a meal around here?"

"Try in the mall."

"Thanks."

The rotunda of the mall was a little shabbier than it had been when the Jack Mormons had tried to move in. Coleman lanterns burned here and there; in one storefront, a scrawny boy pumped a bicycle generator, keeping a few feeble lights aglow. The air was cold and smoky.

Halfway down the mall, Pierce found a middle-aged couple sitting beside a hibachi, cooking skewers of meat over charcoal. Pierce recognized their faces from the files and controlled a sudden desire to kill them. He bought a couple of skewers and sat companionably beside the couple while he ate. They chatted for a few minutes: about the weather, the price of black market meat, the end of the Emergency.

"Just the start of the Emergency, you ask me," said the man. "Eastern bastards selling us out."

"DeWayne—" his wife said warningly.

"I don't care. Still a free country, isn't it? Long as a man can say what he thinks?"

"That's right, sir," Pierce agreed. "They pulled a real fast one on us."

"Passing that bill, you mean?"

"No, sir, before that. With that computer trap."

"I don't know nothin' about that."

"Lots of good folks got hurt by it. Salt of the earth folks." He saw the man and wife exchange quick looks. "Take 'em a long time to get it back together unless their friends lend a hand."

"Well, maybe. Listen," DeWayne said suddenly, "you like another shish kebab? On the house."

"I won't say no," Pierce said with a smile. DeWayne and his wife smiled back.

He spent the rest of the evening drinking homebrew in a smoky, candlelit bar, talking casually to people. Then he went back outside to his camper and went to bed.

Before dawn, someone tapped lightly at his door.

"Hello?"

"Salt of the earth folks," a man whispered hoarsely.

In the darkness of the camper, lying fully dressed under a filthy sleeping bag, Pierce grinned.

"Enter, brother," he said, reaching for the knob and unlocking the door. A shadowy figure, smelling of armpits and homebrew, stepped grunting into the camper.

"Hear you met up with Brother DeWayne last night."

"I sure did." Pierce found a match and lighted a stump of candle in an old saucer. The battered interior of the camper became visible. Standing by the bed was a small, wiry man in a heavy overcoat and a cowboy hat. His eyes glinted in the candlelight, above whiskers as red and stubbly as Pierce's.

"Where you from?"

"Taos."

"Is that right. Good folks down there. We heard they all got picked up."

"Not quite. Pretty close, though."

"Same here. Say, brother, you got anything to drink here?"

"No, afraid not. You the only brother here besides DeWayne?"

"Shit no. We got a complete cell operatin' here."

"Operating? Really operating?"

"Taking care of business. We're pulling together a list for the Better Dead Club."

"Shit. I mean, excuse me, brother, but I been making those lists all the way up here, and it hasn't done a bit of good."

"Young fella, when we operate, people join the club. We already bagged us a bunch of traitors."

"What do you mean, traitors? You getting rid of your own people, when there's all those Iffer pricks out there?"

"We'll get around to them. But first we got the people who set us up. You know they did it right here? Passed us a computer program, looked like real good stuff, what they call a virus. Damn near worked, too."

"I know about the damn virus," Pierce muttered. "We got a copy."

"Well, it came from right here in Mountain Home. Son, you sure you ain't got a bottle of somethin'?"

"Come on, brother, who's gonna live in Mountain Home and build a program like that?"

"A coupla goddam schoolteachers. Don't it make

you sick, think of those people in charge of little kids?"

"And schoolteachers came up with this program that got us busted? Brother, excuse me, but I kinda doubt that."

"Think I know a little more about it than you do."

"That's all in the past. What are you doin' now?" Pierce demanded.

The man in the cowboy hat seemed not to have heard. "Got 'em cold. Bastards was so smug they didn't have security or nothin'. Figured we was all dog meat."

Pierce crossed his legs on the bed and leaned forward a little. "No security at all? Brother"—he chuckled—"you're the best bullshit artist I met in a long time. How'd they join the club?"

"Our top man done 'em. Done 'em all, not just the schoolteachers."

"Brother." Pierce was solemn. "That's the man I got to talk to. I didn't know if I could trust you all the way until you got onto this, but now I know you're straight and white."

"Hope to tell you."

"I have an urgent message for your man. Brother, this is an ears-only message from Brother LeRoy Krebbs."

"LeRoy—he's been jail for a long time."

"Not as long as they'd like you to think. Our people in Leavenworth got him out over six months ago."

"Holy shit!" The man grinned and giggled. "Woo! Brother, that's mighty good news. Amen!"

"I can't tell you much, understand. But he's doin' a lot of crucial work in the southwest, and we're really lucky we got him. Now, can you get me to your man?"

"I guess so. Shit, this sure calls for a drink. Sure you haven't got something?"

After the man left, Pierce handed in his key and shuffled into the mall. DeWayne and his wife were there again, selling hard-boiled eggs; Pierce bought two. He chatted affably with the couple for a while, then wandered off to join a blackjack game where the chips were mostly paid for in grain and canned goods and cigarettes. The other players were silent men who sat in for a few hands and then moved on. Pierce recognized most of them from their old files: hard-working loggers and ranchers and construction men, still trying to figure out why their world had fallen apart. They showed no sign of recognizing him, though he had been well known here. In civilian clothes, with four days' whiskers, he did not look like a T-Colonel.

Near noon, the man in the cowboy hat sauntered across the rotunda without coming too close to the blackjack game. Pierce played two more hands, lost, and threw his cards down in disgust. He stood up and walked out of the rotunda, past the campers and RVs. Snow was falling again, turning almost to rain. The man in the cowboy hat was across the parking lot, heading downtown through the slush.

Near Lincoln and Eighth the man turned into an alley. He was gone when Pierce turned the corner, but the footprints were clear: they led to a door in the side of a boarded-up furniture store. The door opened easily when Pierce tried it.

"Come on in, brother."

"Only where two or three of us are gathered together in Christ's name," Pierce answered. Like "salt of the earth," it was a recent password, extracted from the Wabbies picked up last week.

"Through the eye of a needle," another voice said.

Pierce stepped into the dusty smelling darkness and shut the door behind him.

A battery lantern clicked on, throwing enough light to hint at the size of the room—a storage area behind the showroom, now empty except for a few battered tables and chairs and some slabs of foam rubber on the concrete floor. Behind one of the tables sat a man in a pea coat, with a watch cap pulled low over his eyes. The man in the cowboy hat sat off to the man's left, with the battery lantern in his lap.

"Welcome, brother," said the man in the watch cap. "Have a seat." He extended a hand, palm up, toward an old-fashioned chrome-tube chair. Pierce sat down and crossed his legs.

"We're glad to see you," the man went on. "Every man saved is worth an army to us now. Tell us how you got here, what you've seen."

Pierce drew breath in a deep sigh and slumped into the chair. "Bus. Hitchhiking. Saw a lot of roadblocks, lot of National Guards. Lot of scared people. All I knew was they got us in Taos, and maybe there'd be somebody up north. Checked in a couple places in Denver, couple of little towns, but couldn't find anybody, not anybody until here. I understand from the brother there that this is where it all started, where they poisoned us."

"That's right," said the man softly. "But we're, we're in the eye of the storm. We're the saving remnant. They got a lot of us, but they stored up misery for the future. We'll come back, stronger than ever, purified."

"Amen," said the man in the cowboy hat.

"And someone here struck the blow at the traitors," Pierce said with a grim half smile.

"They paid."

"I wish I'd been there. How I wish I'd been there, to see their faces."

The man in the watch cap grinned. "The man didn't know what hit him. I suspect it was the woman behind it all. She was the one gave the program to one of our people. I killed her cleaner than she deserved."

"You were the one, brother?"

"It was my duty." The man in the watch cap looked down modestly, then looked up at a soft, spitting noise. The man in the cowboy hat was toppling from his chair, and the lantern in his lap rolled to the floor. In the swinging shadows and streaks of moving light, Pierce was a specter with a bone in his fist, the sleek white plastic of a Mallory aimed right at the man in the watch cap.

"I gave her the program, brother. She was one of mine."

The man heaved his table straight out as he threw himself backward in his chair and rolled to his right, toward the saving darkness. Pierce fired once, at maximum impact, and heard the wet sound of exploding flesh.

"Ah, ah, ah!" the man gasped. His left thigh was a mangled, twitching mass of destroyed tissue, spurting blood across the cold concrete. The man tried to drag himself by his fingers while his shoulders swayed back and forth. In the poor light of the lantern, his eyes gleamed with a million thoughts. Pierce walked over and squatted beside him.

"My name is Jerry Pierce," he said. "I take care of my people."

He put the muzzle of the Mallory in the man's gaping mouth and forced the man's face up toward his own. Their eyes met.

"I take care of my own," Pierce repeated, and pulled the trigger.

Twenty:

After his father's funeral, Wigner drove his mother and uncle back to the house in Silver Spring. The December sky over Washington was a pale gray, with the sun a blurred glow in the southwest. It felt odd to be driving the old Suzuki, and in something like normal weekday traffic.

"At least Woody got to see it," Olivia said. "Everything coming back again, everything getting back to normal."

Uncle Henry, who was as compact and muscular as his nephew, chuckled in the backseat.

"Normal. People time traveling, commercials on TV about Doomsday, weird new money, no more U.S. army. Really normal."

"You know what I mean, Henry. Food in the stores, for God's sake. Electricity that doesn't go out three times a day. Gasoline. Being able to go for a walk without beggars coming up to you, or muggers. At least Woody saw that much."

"Well," said Uncle Henry, "I'm a loyal Iffer like everybody else, but I draw the line at calling things normal."

"Tell us that a year from now, Uncle Henry," said Wigner with a smile. "When you get back from your holiday on Beulah or Eden."

"Holiday on Eden. Sounds like the old Club Med.

Is that what your new job's all about, Eric? Kind of a time-travel agent, buying people's tickets for them?"

Wigner laughed. "Pretty much, Uncle Henry. Moving people up and down. Lots of people downtime, a few people uptime. A time-travel agent."

"I do wish they'd come up with a better name for your organization," said Olivia. "Agency for Intertemporal Development—AID sounds like that awful disease."

"That awful disease, Mother, is about to go the way of smallpox and polio. It'll be forgotten. And five years from now, when people hear AID mentioned, they'll stand up with tears in their eyes and salute."

Uncle Henry guffawed, and Wigner joined in.

"No, really," Wigner went on. "Millions of people will be downtime, building new cities, new industries, and making room here on Earth so the rest of us can live decently. And we'll be bringing a lot of endos uptime for Training, get them working on every problem we've ever faced. Especially Doomsday. So when it comes on this chronoplane, we'll be ready."

"You get a real gleam in your eye when you talk about it," his mother said.

"AID is my baby. It's going to be responsible for—for everything. Moving people through I-Screens. Intertemporal trade. Research. Economic planning. Education. We're going to run the greatest renaissance in history."

"God, Eric, is that all?" Uncle Henry protested. "I wish you'd show a little ambition."

Wigner turned into the driveway and braked. "You're right, Uncle Henry. I'll try to think bigger."

The house was full of old family friends that afternoon: retired civil servants, some ex-military, a former secretary of state from the ancient days before the

Emergency. Most of them looked thin and shabby; one or two would doubtless soon be dead also. Yet they talked and ate with animation, arguing about the new political order, the prospects for the reviving economy. Wigner circulated among them, accepting their sympathetic handshakes and quavering reminiscences about Woody and Olivia and himself as a small boy. Most tried to get him to talk about AID; he smiled and shrugged and repeated what he had said to his mother and uncle.

After a while Wigner slipped upstairs to the computer and checked in with his new office in New York. A dozen calls had come in, demands from bureaucrats in Geneva and anthropologists in Mexico City, plus one he had been hoping for: from Jerry Pierce's mother in Taos.

He's not well. He needs help.

"Indeed you must," Wigner muttered.

"Pardon me, Eric?" asked the computer.

"Never mind, Polly. Connect me with Dr. Franklin in Woodstock."

"Sure thing, Eric."

The old Agency was being rapidly folded into AID, so Jasmin Jones wasn't surprised to find that her flight to Taos was aboard an Agency Lear. The plane waited discreetly on the edge of L.A. International, and an equally discreet young man from the Agency's Los Angeles office drove her through a series of gates right onto the tarmac. He handed her over to the pilot and copilot, a man and wife team with Oklahoma accents and big smiles.

"Take any seat you like, honey," the wife said. "We'll be on our way in just a couple of minutes."

Takeoff was at sunset; the Lear climbed through the

darkening sky above a carpet of lights. It looked like the L.A. of the old days, Jaz thought, before the breakdown and the Emergency and everything else. Everyone was so happy now, so eager for the future. Old high-school friends in Santa Monica were making plans to emigrate, poring over holographs of Southern California on Orc or Luvah, dreaming of cattle ranches and oil wells and clean water.

Her mother and stepfather worried about her: why was she home and not with the Agency, why wasn't she looking for a new job, why didn't she have a boy friend, why did she only sit and watch the ghostly flicker of her computer as a passive observer?

"I'm giving myself a holiday," she had told them, and told them nothing else. Their knowledge of the Agency had been sketchy at best, and she had not expanded it. Sometimes she would sit with them to watch videotapes of old movies, though they were painful for a Trainable to watch: each frame was distinct, and movement from one frame to the next was obvious and jerky. But her company seemed to give her parents some pleasure, and she gained a strange sense of security from them.

The phone call from Eric had changed all that. She could have rejected him, told him to get lost, and perhaps for any other assignment she would have. But Jerry Pierce needed help, Eric had said, and Jerry was a continuing responsibility of hers. He was a friend— not that she liked him very much, but they had been through too much together, they owned important parts of each other's lives. Friends were like family, Jaz thought as the Lear slipped over the darkening plains and ranges of the Mojave Desert: you couldn't really choose them.

When she stepped from the Lear at the little airstrip

in Taos, she felt exhausted, a little headachy. Altitude: the air was thin here, and sharply cold. Panting, she let herself be guided to a rented Jeep Cherokee. A taciturn young Hispanic drove her into town past darkened motels, abandoned supermarkets (one had the strange name of Piggly Wiggly), and finally to a neighborhood of narrow streets where adobe houses stood crowded close together. A light burned outside the doorway of one; snowflakes gleamed as they fell out of the darkness.

"This is the place," the Hispano said. Jaz knocked. A tall woman who looked a lot like Jerry answered the door, and the Hispano walked away. The woman welcomed Jaz inside.

"I'm Annette," she said. "Eric Wigner said you'd be coming."

She put away Jaz's coat and led her into a small living room: a tiled floor, plastered walls, a small fireplace tucked into one corner. Jaz gratefully sank into a rocking chair by the fire while Annette poured tea.

"He got here over a week ago. For a day or two he seemed fine, quiet but fine. Then one morning he just wouldn't get up. He just sleeps all the time, hardly eats anything, doesn't talk to me."

"Had he told you where he'd been?"

"He said he'd been traveling around, seeing friends."

"You didn't believe him?"

"Jerry doesn't have friends, except maybe you and Eric Wigner. He was always kind of a quiet, shy kid, but even more after he got Trained." Annette sat very upright on an old couch, her mug of tea beside her. Her gaze stayed on the fire. "Maybe getting him into Training wasn't such a good idea."

"He helped to save the country, Annette. He really did."

Annette looked at him, her eyes full of angry intelligence. "His country doesn't seem aware of that. Neither does he."

"He'll get better. I'm taking him east in the morning. He'll get the best care in the world."

"I wish he didn't need it."

"May I see him now?"

"Sure."

Pierce lay on his side in a narrow bed, a comforter pulled up under his chin. The only light in the room came from the hallway, but Jaz could see he was awake. She sat down at a desk beside the bed, close enough to smell him and remember the tunnel under Riverside Park.

"Hi, Jerry. It's Jaz."

He said nothing.

"Kind of like being in the tunnel?"

Pierce grunted faintly.

"Well, I was there. And I'm here. I'm going to take care of you."

"Take care," Pierce mumbled. "Care of you."

"Would you like that?"

"Take care of *you*."

"You did. You did a good job. I need you to take care of us some more. Take care of your mother and me and Eric and everybody else."

For a long time Pierce said nothing. Then he whispered: "I can't."

"Yes, you can. We can help you to. Dr. Franklin can help you."

"No."

"Yes. You'll see. We'll go in the morning. Soon you'll be fine."

She leaned forward in the dimness and patted his shoulder, felt him shivering.

"Good night; sleep tight. Don't let the bedbugs bite."

"But if they do," he whispered, "take your shoe, and beat them till they're black and blue."

Back in the living room, Jaz saw her own expression mirrored in Annette's: a kind of helpless anguish. What must the inside of his mind be like now? Jaz wondered. What has he been doing since the night of the tunnel?

In New York City, wet snow was falling out of a white sky. Wigner's temporary office in the old UN buildings overlooked the East River; Brooklyn was lost in the snow. He turned away from his computer to watch the clustered snowflakes waver past his window. Each flake was a unique variation on a single hexagonal theme, a marvelous expression of natural beauty, a universe obedient to natural law, yet free to obey in its own way. When conditions allowed, each tiny flake might cling to another and another, until some new form emerged, less regular but more capable of resisting the pull of gravity, of rising again on the wind for a few more moments of independence before sinking at last into the dark waters of the harbor.

"Where are the snows of yesteryear? Right through the nearest I-Screen," he murmured to himself. Then he turned to the flickerscreen, which had frozen to display a single page.

—*deaths of Agency personnel appear to be linked to a forcible entry made via the Riverside Park Information Repository sometime not long before. The purpose of the killings is unclear. It may have been linked to the unexplained presence of Jonathan Clement and two trained interrogators in the Riverside Center. A number of local assets appear to have been engaged in an operation that night, yet none are at present available for questioning.*

Given the repository break-in and the failure of Riverside Center to report any breach of security, it seems likely that the person or persons responsible for the killings were known Agency members, aware of the center's layout and purposes, and with an unknown motive for killing senior Agency personnel. Any other hypothesis strains credulity.

While this tragic event occurred before the foundation of AID, recruitment of many Agency personnel could mean that a person or persons connected with the killings is employed by AID or will be in future. If so, the consequences could be incalculable. It would be wise for AID to arrange deep interrogation of all former Agency personnel known to have been in the New York area at the time of the killings.

Wise indeed. Wigner had quickly traced the eight goons Clement had hired to pick up him and Pierce. Jerry had foolishly allowed two of them to live when he'd taken their car. Two had been killed in the lobby of the Riverside building when Pierce had tossed that grenade from the stairwell. The rest had been arrested and transported to Woodstock; Dr. Franklin had confused their memories of the night and of much else as well. They had then been sent to mental hospitals around the country, and there they would remain for the rest of their lives.

The industrious and thoughtful young fellow who'd written this memorandum was too prominent for such treatment. He could use some seasoning on one of the downtime worlds. Eden, in the twelfth century, was a fascinating place: crowded cities, violent natives, virulent diseases to which modern people were highly vulnerable. Inoculations did not always take. He would soon have more immediate concerns than some trivial episode from the unhappy last hours of the republic.

Wigner ordered the Polymath to produce Dr. Franklin's latest report on Pierce. It was highly optimistic; Pierce was responding well to treatment. A new approach to memory blocks was working better than that used in Pierce's first stay at Woodstock. In theory, Pierce could undergo any number of psychological traumas and be restored to cheerful functioning each time. Long-term consequences would, of course, be carefully monitored

"Of course," murmured Wigner. The snow was falling faster now. Pierce would have to be put in the shadows for a time, somewhere away from attention. He'd said he wanted a downtime assignment; he would have it, but in a safer place than some medieval cesspool. Back farther than that, on some world thinly peopled yet as large as any other, a world where a man could safely lose himself for a while. He owed Jerry that much, and more.

Luvah: 22,249 B.C. High summer in the Caucasus, and the streams ran milky with rock flour from the rotting glaciers that mantled the mountains to the south. Insects buzzed over the dwarfed wildflowers and mossy stones, and towering cumulus reared into the sky. Off to the north a thunderstorm shadowed the hills, stabbing its own darkness with blades of lightning. But here in this clearing, palisaded by scrubby pines, the sun shone warmly.

Not far from a noisy creek stood a shelter of skins stretched over mammoth bones. Smoke rose from a fire just outside it; tending the fire was a lean boy with the first fuzz of adolescence on his cheeks. He wore a leather smock, elaborately decorated with discs of bone and antler, and his forehead had been ritually scarred in three parallel rows. No one else was in sight; the two older men in the family group had gone hunting and the women and younger children were off foraging for roots and herbs. On the boy's right leg was a poorly healed scar running from thigh to calf; he needed a staff to pull himself to his feet.

"Very good," murmured Pierce. He sat behind a clump of trees, watching the boy through binoculars. Beside him lay a backpack and a long-barrelled Mallory rifle.

"You ready for Testing?" a voice whispered in his ear. Pierce lifted his ringmike.

"All set. You can begin moving up."

Pierce picked up the Mallory, checking to ensure that its impact setting was low. In the scope, the boy's face was even closer than it had been in the binoculars: calm, dreamy, at peace. Pierce put the scope's crosshairs on the boy's belly and squeezed the trigger.

The boy jerked, almost losing his balance, and an instant later his yelp of surprise drifted across the clearing.

"Mamaa! Mamaa!" he called. Pierce found it still wonderful that the name of mother had endured for so many millennia, had survived the glaciers themselves. The boy sat down awkwardly, plucking away the flechette and then slumping onto his side.

"He's down and ready for Testing," Pierce reported.

"Copy. Be right there."

Pierce stood up, slipped his backpack strap over one shoulder, and walked slowly across the clearing. The boy lay sprawled awkwardly alongside the shelter; Pierce pulled him into a more comfortable position. A good-looking kid. If he was Trainable, he would be uptime within a couple of days; they would probably have to operate on the leg to repair the damage. Then he'd undergo Training, and lend his talents to the saving of the human race from Doomsday and its own foolish habits. It would be rough on him for a while, adjusting to an utterly different world, and he would probably miss his family. That would pass. And if he was not Trainable, this would become only a strange memory, a visit from mysterious gods.

Drugged, the boy groaned. Pierce squatted beside him and brushed the boy's dark hair away from his forehead, waved away the flies.

"It's okay," Pierce murmured, hearing the approaching footsteps of the Testing team. "It's okay. We'll take care of you, old son."

As the team went to work with its electrodes and dials, Pierce walked off down the bank of the creek. The water rolled and roared, cold and clean and loud enough to compete with the thunder in the north, and gleaming in the high summer sun.

Pierce drew a deep breath. The air was sweet. He had never been happier in his life.

About the Author

Crawford Kilian was born in New York City in 1941 and grew up in California and Mexico. After graduating from Columbia University in 1962 he returned to California, served in the U.S. Army, and worked as a technical writer-editor at the Lawrence Berkeley Laboratory.

In 1967 he and his wife Alice moved to Vancouver, British Columbia, where he has taught English at Capilano College since 1968. In 1983 the Kilians taught English at the Guangzhou Institute of Foreign Languages in the People's Republic of China.

Crawford Kilian's writing includes several science-fiction novels, among them *The Empire of Time, Icequake, Eyas,* and *Lifter.* In addition he has published children's books, an elementary social-studies text, and two nonfiction books—*School Wars: The Assault on B.C. Education* and *Go Do Some Great Thing: The Black Pioneers of British Columbia.* He is the regular education columnist for the Vancouver *Province* newspaper.

The Kilians live in North Vancouver with their daughters, Anna and Margaret.

From the author of the dazzling Sector General Series...

JAMES WHITE

Available at your bookstore or use this coupon.

____THE ALIENS AMONG US	29171	2.25
____AMBULANCE SHIP	28513	1.95
____DEADLY LITTER	29640	2.25
____MAJOR OPERATION	33673	2.95
____STAR SURGEON	29169	1.95
____TOMORROW IS TOO FAR	30152	2.25

 BALLANTINE MAIL SALES
Dept. TA, 201 E. 50th St., New York, N.Y. 10022

Please send me the BALLANTINE or DEL REY BOOKS I have checked above. I am enclosing $_____ (add 50¢ per copy to cover postage and handling). Send check or money order — no cash or C.O.D.'s please. Prices and numbers are subject to change without notice.

Name_____

Address_____

City_____ State_____ Zip Code_____

08   Allow at least 4 weeks for delivery.   TA-35